I0675989

REVENGE SPIRAL

REVENGE SPIRAL

A BLACK GHOST THRILLER

FREDDIE VILLACCI, JR.

REVENGE SPIRAL

Copyright © 2023 by Freddie Villacci, JR.
Invincible Beauty Publishing

First Edition

ISBN: 979-8-9877886-1-5 Paperback
      979-8-9877886-2-2 Hardcover
      979-8-9877886-0-8 Ebook

No part of this book may be reproduced in any form or by any electronic or mechanical means, including information storage and retrieval systems, without written permission from the author, except for the use of brief quotations in a book review.

This is a work of fiction. Names, characters, businesses, places, events and incidents are either the products of the author's imagination or used in a fictitious manner. Any resemblance to actual persons, living or dead, or actual events is purely coincidental.

Cover design: ebooklaunch.com
Interior design: Erik Gevers

Step into the gritty and heart-pumping world of "Revenge Spiral," the fourth installment of the Black Ghost Thriller series.

When fifteen-year-old Nathaniel Braddick discovers a cold storage wallet with over two billion dollars of Bitcoin, he embarks on a path of revenge against the Black Ghost, who killed his parents when he was a child. His deadly plot sets off a turbulent spiral of mayhem, threatening to destroy all caught in its path.

Bic Green, a man with a dark past that he is trying to walk away from, finds himself at the center of this intricate Revenge Spiral between the young boy and the bloodlust of his lifelong friend, Anthony Parelli, after his wife is killed.

As the body count rapidly rises and points of no return are crossed, Bic fights for resolution both physically and morally. But it may be too late as the circles of death set in motion all around him must be closed.

Experience thrilling action, high-stakes suspense, and a cast of unforgettable characters in "Revenge Spiral," a must read for fans of the Black Ghost Thriller series and anyone who craves a gripping tale of retribution and redemption.

**To all the great achievers,
thank you for your perseverance.**

V

OUR GREATEST

WEAKNESS LIES IN

GIVING UP. THE MOST

CERTAIN WAY TO

SUCCEED IS ALWAYS

TO TRY JUST ONE

MORE TIME.

-Thomas Edison

"BEFORE YOU EMBARK ON A
JOURNEY OF REVENGE,
DIG TWO GRAVES."

- Confucius

1

One month earlier...

Five years ago, a nightmare walked into his garage on a sunny Sunday morning and broke everything. Not today, Nathaniel Braddick promised himself as he stared at his arm. He wasn't going to let that monster get the best of him on his dad's birthday. But the itch on his arm kept growing feverishly like a fresh new bug bite, telling him it was time to cut again. His heart raced when he picked up the razor, so much so that his fingers were trembling. What if he cut too deeply, or accidentally slipped and nicked a major artery? Maybe that would make the pain that never seemed to go away, go away for good.

Nathaniel never considered himself luckier than other fifteen-year-olds. True, not every fifteen-year-old was the majority shareholder of the largest social media company in the world. And on his eighteenth birthday, with total control of that wealth, he would be able to buy anything imaginable with no chance of ever running out of money. But there was just one thing he could never have that made him the unluckiest kid in the world. He'd lost his parents. His mom, who loved him more than anything and his father who till this day he still considered his best friend. He didn't just lose them. They were murdered.

The deed was done. He was good with the blade. Just a tiny little papercut, that's all. What was a papercut doing on his upper forearm? To the outside world, the answer was mind your own business. But he always felt guilt afterwards, wondering if his dad was watching from above. That he cared deeply about and after every time he would promise he'd never do it again.

The slit grew redder, redder. He gave it a squeeze. The itch was gone, replaced by a more tangible itch right on the surface. The elation followed--pain was leaking out in beads of blood. He brought his arm to his mouth and gave it a suck. More elation. This was where his pain was. No one understood. And whenever he thought about the fact that no one understood, he grew weary and depressed. But he pushed it away. He was free of it for now.

He dabbed dry and covered the cut with a black unbranded wristband. He hated brands and the kids who wore them, all those preppy sheep deserved a beatdown using their very own Gucci belts.

Now he could focus on his favorite activity.

He hopped on his computer and logged on to Stigma, the Tor browser he downloaded for access to the dark web. He kept the icon in a folder within a phony date planner app. He didn't need this kind of secrecy, not from his uncle who really didn't care about what he was up to, just as long as he stayed an arm's length away from trouble. But he enjoyed the act of closing his bedroom door and pulling the curtains closed--the crazy cleaning lady thought sunlight was good for him and would tear them open the minute she came into his room. It wasn't healthy for a boy to be in the dark, dress in black and paint his fingernails black, he'd overheard her tell his uncle. But Nathaniel picked that look for one simple reason, it said leave me alone. The message was simple, don't come too close or I might bite. He loved the idea of secrecy and enjoyed having to go hunting for one's exclusive access--like getting a password on the sly for a Prohibition-era speakeasy.

The room was black as night. He'd even cranked up the AC a notch just to enhance his isolation. And Nathaniel Braddick surfed with purpose tonight.

The site was called Degen Fight Club. The first thing to see were the classifieds, which ranged from services to have people roughed up for a modest sum to paying strangers to come to a specified location and beat *you* up. In and amongst these were folders upon folders full of mostly photos. But the real prizes were videos. And even rarer were full fights, not just a punch or two, but the full scrap.

The fights were arranged in four different categories according to their level of gore, from strongest to weakest: To the Death, ICU, Cat

Fight, and Clown Show. Nathaniel had been through all of them at different times depending on his mood.

In short, everything in life sucked and the *best* anyone could hope for was a good beatdown to make them feel alive again. Otherwise society was just a bunch of zombie sheep getting herded around.

Within the folder was an array of subfolders sorted with semi-helpful tags. He got to the subfolder labeled "Prison Fights". He found out from his latest intel there was a six on one fight in New Orleans Parish prison yesterday. The footage was going to be uploaded tonight – it was touted as such a bad ass fight, it was a pay per view event – $29.99 to watch it. Usually these were free, but the greedy promoters sold it as a once in a millennium six on one fight to the death. The main character supposedly violently throws up a gallon of blood, not from injury, but from what they're calling a glowing eyed devil possession scene that rivals "The Exorcist."

That in itself would have had Nathaniel all in, but one of the inmate combatants was rumored to be an FBI's Most Wanted declared back from the dead. A man called the Black Ghost.

2

B*lack Ghost.*
     That name in itself made the hairs on the back of his neck stand up.

Could it really be him?

Through years of snooping in and out of the corners of the dark web researching his parents' murderer, Nathaniel was able to access the FBI's files on Bic Green.

Bic was a notorious unknown assassin wanted for twenty-two cold-blooded murders all linked by a pork chop left at the scene. Only later his identity was discovered when he went on a killing spree over twenty days and assassinated eleven people from the nine wealthiest families in America for some death tax revenue scheme to pass a crooked bill in Congress. So read the report written by FBI Agent Mack Maddox, who just tallied his parents in a single sentence with the other dead billionaires.

The report wrapped everything up in a nice tight bow with the infamous Black Ghost being confirmed dead.

Case closed.

But something deep down in the depths of Nathaniel Braddick's soul knew it was bull. He may have been just a kid in the eyes of the world, but the world didn't know jack. Kids like him were to be feared for their ability to access information. Data was the gold of the digital era. And he could see through bull like it was made of cellophane.

One comment in the report sounded off alarm bells.

Wake up, you deluded morons, they burned all those bodies before the FBI actually confirmed anyone's identity. They claimed they had to do it immediately due to one of the men testing positive for the Marburg virus! Bic Green's dead body was never confirmed! Just a pile of ashes was given to the FBI claiming to be the notorious assassin and they bought it.

How could they fall for the biggest hoax since Pizzagate. Bic Green is obviously alive.

Nathaniel gritted his teeth as the countdown to the video stream release hit single digits.

He was ready to see Bic Green beaten to death. Witness what he'd played out in his mind thousands of times.

Nathaniel leaned in to his computer screen trying to get a better look. The camera was in a far corner of the kitchen as six stood against one. The large Black man fit the profile of Bic for sure, but he wanted absolute confirmation. He needed to see the man's face. The fight broke out, it was insane – everything it was hyped up to be. These fights almost never go over a minute, most twenty seconds and it's over. After over three violent minutes Nathaniel watched in awe. It truly was the fight of a millennium. To his dismay, two things hadn't happened. The man alleged as Bic hadn't been beaten to death and he never got his close up for confirmation. But suddenly that all changed as the alleged Bic held a man over his head, turned, and walked right up to the surveillance camera and screamed at it, "Clarence Green I'm coming for you!"

Nathaniel nervously gasped, as if Bic was talking to him. He captured a screenshot of the close up.

It was him. It was Bic Green. It had to be.

He observed the large African American man with crazy, milky white eyes, the right one of which was squinting due to a bulging bruise over it. The rest of it was a bloody mess, the nose twisted, the lips split in two places.

A tingle like he'd never felt before ran down his spine.

But for all its battered disguise, that face, that vicious, evil face, could never be erased from Nathaniel's memory.

His breath came in angry hitches as he studied it. His mouth watered. He imagined himself delivering the blows that formed those cuts and contusions. He imagined that this was only the beginning of it. He had Bic in a cell underground--deep underground, where no one could hear his cries of pain. Nathaniel went to town on him with all kinds of items--a rubber pipe, an electrical cord. He had some machine like the AMP suit from "Avatar", one that could give him the strength to lift Bic up and slam him into the concrete floor of the cell over and over. All while he, Nathaniel, recited the litany of charges against him.

This is for my parents, you monster. This is for locking me and Lucy up in our home theater and cranking up "Beauty and the Beast." You ruined Disney, you scumbag. You ruined my taste for popcorn and sweets by piling it up next to us so that we could stuff our faces while you murdered our mother and father. And let's not even talk about Lucy. You think I'm a mess, Bic? My little sister is ten kinds of effed up because of you.

How does it feel, Bic? I want you to tell me how it feels.

Bic would complain and cry and beg him to stop. And Nathaniel would pour rubbing alcohol into his open wounds while he described how he and his Lucy eventually got out of the home theater by shoving a metal plate from one of the many sound strips into the door jamb and prying it open. Resourceful for a child, he would tell him. Nathaniel Braddick was a genius. Bic Green was a moron.

And he'd tell him about how he found his parents in a pool of thick, sticky blood.

Over the years, Nathaniel had to fill in the blanks in these memories. In truth, all he really remembered was the look of horror on his parents' faces when Bic ambushed them in their garage. He remembered the sound of panic that they tried to hide from their children as they told them it's okay to wait for them in the theater. You can have popcorn and candy and watch Beauty and the Beast, your favorite.

And he remembered suddenly feeling like he needed to help his parents. He remembered Lucy crying, himself screaming as he pounded on the door. And he just remembered opening the movie room door and nothing after that. He had to imagine the rest. His mind just wouldn't allow him to remember it. He knew it was there, but as some kind of primal survival mechanism his brain wouldn't allow him to remember. His therapist told him it was the shock that erased it from his memory and told him that was a good thing.

But a year and a half ago he came across the picture of it when he finally cracked into the FBI files on the dark web. He clicked off it immediately, but all it took was that one second to lock his parents murder scene in his mind as his primary memory of them. Every detail that had been locked away had suddenly been released, as if a Pandora's box of pain was just opened. Two lifeless bodies on a white couch… blood everywhere… his father's eyes wide open with a bullet wound between them … his mother's head slouched over, maybe she's just hurt and is going to be okay he thought as he raised up his mom's head. No, he should have known from her ice-cold skin she wasn't okay, but he lifted her head up anyway to get a look… He ran into his closet and locked himself in the dark. Listening to his breath coming in sharp wheezes as he tried to put those images back in his mind where they came from, but after an hour the details stayed as vivid as if it was the day it happened. He was left with a flood of new painful memories and an uncontrollable itch on his leg presenting itself as the answer to his new problem. He cut into himself for the first time that day.

He steadied his breath, trying to stop his heart from almost beating out of his chest as he stared at Bic Green's evil face. The synapses in his brain fired out of control as he formed a plan for revenge. It was no longer fantasy. This one was real.

Bic Green would die, and die horribly. And Nathaniel would be the one to commit the act and purify the world.

Nathaniel grabbed his monitor with both hands, feeling the pressure building in his skull, he shook it violently as he yelled at Bic, "You're going to pay for what you did!"

3

"A little testy there, aren't you?"

Nathaniel jumped in his seat and turned to see Uncle Seth glaring down on him, a twisted grimace on his face.

He often ignored his uncle and his features, as they reminded him of Dad. But where Dad had a smile, Uncle Seth had a scowl. Where Dad's eyes were bright and full of promise, Uncle Seth's were narrow and full of cynicism. Where his Dad was clean cut and the picture of straight-laced, corporate America, Uncle Seth had his hair slicked back into a short pony tail and dressed like a hipster college professor who knew it all.

How long was he standing there? "I was just…"

"Just what, torturing yourself again?" His face softened, and he put a hand on the boy's shoulder while glaring at the screen. "You know you're free to do whatever you want in my house, as long as you keep it confined within the limits of human decency, that is." He let out an oily gasp. "I thought you agreed with your therapist, it was best to leave him in the past."

Nathaniel felt a hotness in his collarbone. "This man's alive!"

"I'm so sorry Nathaniel, I can't imagine the wound this is opening, seeing him alive," his uncle said.

"It's been five years of hell since that man did what he did, justice needs to be served."

"He's in prison and from the looks of that beaten face, getting punished pretty good."

"Trust me, the other guys got the worst of it."

"Nathaniel, I try to give you your space, but you can't keep destroying yourself like this. In a couple years we," Uncle Seth paused here as Nathaniel glared up at him, "You will be running the company in a couple of years. Your mind needs to be right, my boy."

Nathaniel glanced over at a picture of him and his father on his desk. "Sometimes you feel obligated to make things right."

"You were twelve, there was nothing you could do!" He motioned to the monitor. "That man's a monster."

"I just—"

"I miss your father too."

"I doubt it," Nathaniel snapped back with sarcasm.

"You don't mean that."

"I want that man dead!" Nathaniel said.

Uncle Seth's eyes widened. "That kind of talk scares me, Nathaniel. You want to talk about it… with me… or your therapist?"

"There's nothing to talk about. He killed my parents and he's gotta pay for it."

"I want him to pay for what he did too, but there's nothing we can do except let the law handle it."

Nathaniel fumed. His uncle was such an idiot. "I can find someone right here that'll help me do it." He jabbed a thumb in the direction of his screen. "All it takes is money."

Uncle Seth let out his righteous, oily scoff, "I am your guardian. And I would never lie to help you get access to your money for something like this."

Nathaniel hated that scoff. "If you love him as much as I did, you'd help me figure this out."

"Your father and I had our differences, but he was my little brother and I did love him." He patted Nathaniel's shoulder. "That's why, even though I want revenge too, I know he'd want me to protect you and your future instead of getting revenge."

Nathaniel swiveled his chair around removing his uncle's hand from his shoulder and heard his uncle scoff.

"I'm not going to reach you, am I?" his uncle said. "It's a good thing you can't touch your money until you're 18 without your trustee at your dad's bank's approval. Paying people to commit murder." He scoffed again, extra oily. "Maybe I need to go back to the courts and suggest they make you wait to get your inheritance. Like, say, 25? 30?" Nathaniel spun his chair around to face his uncle, he felt the fire in his eyes.

"You'd love that wouldn't you! If you wanted control of my dad's company you shouldn't have sold him out when you were part of it."

He scoffed throwing his chin in the air. "That was a mistake and the exact reason I care so much now. No matter how much you try to push me away, you're not going to get rid of me."

"Can I get back to my work?"

Uncle Seth grinned his ugly grin. "Alright, I know this is tough on you."

His uncle left the room without closing the door, which ticked Nathaniel off to no end. With a huff, he hopped over to the door and was about to give it a slam shut when he caught sight of Lucy coming toward him. His little sister was holding a paint brush and palate in one arm and motioning to him with the other. Nathaniel had never gotten used to the gruff squeak that served as her sole means of oral communication. Left speechless due to her trauma that one, horrible day, Lucy was a broken thing, a half-child, half-cipher, with pretty blue eyes that pleaded for understanding.

"What is it?" he asked, his frustration with his uncle quickly usurped by pity for her. As he approached, he noticed the fresh splotches on her painting smock.

She made an excited noise in her throat, and a smile appeared on her face.

"You finished your painting," Nathaniel guessed.

She nodded her head excitedly. Her shiny blonde curls shook like springs.

"I guess I have to go and look at it now, right?" he said.

The girl nodded again and turned excitedly to go to her room.

Feeling the burden of caring for her--she was only two years younger than him--Nathaniel had to fight the urge to allow his impatience to be known.

"Okay," he said, "I'm coming. But I'm busy. I can only look for a minute."

He entered her room knowing full well the pain she was about to evoke on him not even realizing what she was doing. There would be yet another picture of their family. Mom and Dad would be alive again--albeit in two dimensions. The walls were papered with them. Lucy was a gifted artist with an eye for vivid colors. It just sucked that she was so obsessed.

He looked at her latest work on the easel. She'd been staring at it, head tilted, when he entered. This painting was of their family standing in a void of purple and pink. Lucy had rendered Nathaniel and herself perfectly. There they stood, smiling. And between them, there was Mom and Dad. Nathaniel felt a tug in his face.

Don't cry.

"That's great," he said softly. He then squinted at the image of their mother. "Mom's wearing her pendant."

Lucy nodded quickly, lifting the pendant she wore around her own neck. It was meant to be the same one. It was a gold pineapple. It was an ugly thing, in Nathaniel's estimation. God knows why Mom had worn it. He knew moms and dads gave each other weird gifts that supposedly meant something to them but didn't mean anything to the rest of the world. All he knew was that they'd once gone away to Costa Rica and Mom came back wearing that. And she never took it off.

And here, in the pink and purple reality of the painting, Mom had never been killed, and therefore, still wore the pendant around her own neck instead of unwittingly bequeathing it to her daughter.

"You know," Nathaniel said, angry at his own creeping sadness, "maybe if you went and painted something else besides Mom and Dad, you'd be able to talk again."

Her eyes grew wide, her face livid, as she shook her head back and forth. He remembered this fire in her, this stubborn unwillingness to budge. In the past, it had been the cause of many a fight between them.

"Lucy…" he pleaded.

Clenching her fists and thrusting them downward with a simultaneous stamp of her foot, she emitted her gruff squeak that meant the topic was no longer up for discussion.

"Okay, okay, relax," he said, trying to mollify her. "Jeez, I was just making a suggestion. You don't have to go all cavegirl on me."

He returned to his room, saddened and full of angry pity for Lucy. He wanted to punch the wall. But instead an itch on his arm caught his attention. His breath quickened.

4

Nathaniel never cut himself two times in a day, but today had been a really crap day, and the growing itch reminded him of that more and more by the second.

He hid the razor inside the credit card slot of an old Velcro Captain America wallet he'd kept deep in a drawer full of junk in the nightstand next to his bed. Inside, among various baubles he'd collected over the years--including a petrified mouse carcass he found on the playground--lay his faded blue wallet.

Reaching for it, his hand grazed a Nano S Ledger storage device. The cold stainless-steel case caught his attention, he had forgotten about it for years. He stared at the device his father had given him for his seventh birthday, now with a few more scratches and a couple of other signs of careless storage.

To the non-tech person, the Nano S looked like any other USB thumb drive for extra computer storage. But he remembered the excitement in his dad's eyes when he had given it to him. It was a prototype called the Nano S. It had just been developed to store digital assets offline, making it impossible for hackers to steal. He was one of the early investors of the technology. But the device wasn't what he was most excited about, he had stored some digital coin worth twenty cents each. He had read some paper by a guy named Satoshi about decentralized currency. He recalled him going on and on about money printing and this would be a hedge against it. Suddenly dots that should have connected long ago started to connect.

"Dad, did you give me Bitcoin?" he said as if he was looking at Zeus's lightning bolt in his hand.

He walked over to his desk, staring at the cold metal stick in his hand the whole time. Two questions needed answers. *One, was there really Bitcoin stored on this wallet or something worthless? Two, if it was Bitcoin, how much?*

It took a few minutes of Google research and luckily still having the old USB connector cable in his drawer, but the wallet was now connected. All that was left between him and the answers was the password.

He typed in the eight-digit password his dad had him memorize that was for everything electronic that was his – it worked.

He gasped as he looked at a balance of thirty-three thousand Bitcoin.

He quickly looked up the price of Bitcoin-$60,926!

He grabbed his phone to calculate, but he received an error. The number was two big. He turned it sideways to the scientific version and tried again.

Nathaniel Braddick stared at the number. The itch on his arm was gone. Replaced by the mission of revenge. This was no coincidence, this was a gift from his dad that gave him two billion reasons why the Black Ghost was going to die.

He thrust his glance in the direction of Lucy's room.

Correction: two billion and *one.*

5

The Dogs of Hell clubhouse was an aluminum structure on a flat patch of weeds in South Central Los Angeles. From a distance, it was often mistaken for an abandoned storage building no one cared about. A simple drive closer would have revealed the Dogs' logo--a snarling, red eyed beast with smoke coming out of its nostrils holding a flaming bone in its jaws, and the legend "DOH" emblazoned on its forehead.

Around back, hidden from the street view the desolate structure came to life with an impressive row of blacked-out, club-style Dyna and FXR motorcycles with different quarter fairing windshields, tall T-bars or moto bars on 10-inch or 12-inch risers, with a variety of chrome exhaust and raised rear suspensions. The men who rode these bikes didn't care what anyone thought about anything, except for their bikes, which were the most important expression of who they were. And from one quick look at this row of machines, it was clear: they were outlaws.

The main space of the building resembled a bar in need of renovation. It was built for lounging, with lots of places to sit and hang out. If someone had an old couch or chair they were throwing away, it came to the clubhouse. Over the years, the place had slowly transformed into a museum of unwanted—but comfortable—furniture. A couple of members played pool as others sat around belching the fumes of off-brand beer, but the room was void of its officers.

The boardroom was one of a handful of rooms built after the DOH purchased the storage building in the nineties. The other rooms were for members to use—usually with a woman—but the boardroom was officers-only. If a patch member stepped into this room without request from one of the officers, he'd wind up in a cage match with one of the Rottweilers out back. If a prospect made that kind of mistake, he would earn himself a chain-whipping, followed by a douse of bleach.

All five officers were present in the hot, cramped boardroom, its smoke-filled air a throwback to the eighties. Most of the room's real estate was occupied by an old wooden round table. Nicknamed reaper, the table had earned this name after the DOH officers's habit of carving notches in it for every personal kill. Instead of knights of the round table, they considered themselves knights of the death table. The spot with the most tallies—twelve—belonged to the President of the LA chapter and founder of the DOH, Roman Dog.

In his mid-fifties, Roman Dog bore every mark a veteran of life's battles could bear. With his pockmarked face, leathery and prematurely aged, and partially covered with a salty beard that grew like a fungus, he looked like a storybook pirate. One that would cut your mother's face, record her screams, and play it back to you— something he'd done more than a few times.

Roman was known never to mince words or open with a joke. His opening line consisted of a peculiar stutter in the form of an *ah* or two to get him started. *"Ah-ah…"* he began, "we have a chance to turn DOH into a West to East Coast empire, take our seventeen chapters to a hundred and seventeen." He paused for dramatic effect. "Boys, we've been offered a hit for a billion dollars."

Murmurs rose like the buzzing of a hive amongst a couple of the officers.

Ugly Jesus, the Sergeant at Arms, held up his right hand, showing the rust-red puncture in his palm, regularly updated with fresh stabbings and meant as a perverted form of Christ's wounds. "Did you say billion with a B?" he asked.

"Ah, ah… yes, billion with a B."

Ugly Jesus ran his fingers through long, greasy hair then played with the bushy tangle of beard down the front of his neck as he undoubtedly thought about how many women he could put up in an apartment and stop by and bang whenever he wanted. His cut was a nice, fat load of baby mama money.

"Ah, ah… the stain on the wall that needs cleaning is Bic Green."

Ugly Jesus twisted the curls of his beard even harder, then took a drag from his Marlboro. Exhaling, he said, "So… one guy. That's it?

Not a whole cartel or crime family?"

To Roman's right, his VP, Darius Dog, obviously wasn't sharing in their excitement. Roman had noticed the look of consternation.

"*Ah, ah…* you got somethin' to say, son? Speak it."

Darius, who had been kicked out of law school for selling pills, always thought before he spoke. "A billion dollars… does anyone else see this as a bit suspicious?" He looked to his father for permission to continue. "I'd say this is some type of set up. This amount of capital, if it's real… I don't know, there's got to be more moving parts than just a simple hit of one man."

Axl, name not by birth but for his looks resembling the lead singer from Guns N' Roses, held up his hand. The combination secretary and treasurer of the organization licked his lips, "It sounds like a set up to finally get our dues caught up." He paused, holding up four fingers then changing his fingers to the letter L as he said, "For life, baby."

Several of the officers agreed with Axl's notion.

Darius stared for a moment. "With all due respect, the stench of weed in this place cuts through the air like the odor of a dead skunk, and I think it's clouding our judgment. I know we're good at what we do, but doesn't it seem weird they came to us on the biggest contract in history?"

Milo, the road captain, slammed his fist right next to his six tally marks on the table, "Me and your daddy have been puttin' people in the ground since you were just a little sperm swimmin' in his nut sac. Our reputation's what's earned this job."

"I'm just trying to make sure none of us wind up in the dirt ourselves."

"I think you're just afraid," Milo said, glaring down at Darius's spot on the table where his kill notches would be marked. There were none.

"I'll stick those six little notches right up your ass," Darius said.

Milo smothered his cigarette in the ash tray filled with butts and gray dust. "Bring it on, boy."

"*Ah, ah…* alright, enough. This job came from Clyde. We've worked with him before and I trust him." Roman unfolded an 8"x10" photograph from the inner part of his leather jacket. "Now, *ah, ah…* this here is Bic Green,"

Ugly Jesus took a look.

"He's a big chunk of dark meat."

"*Ah, ah...* they call him the Black Ghost. The legend goes bullets seem to pass right through this demon." Roman continued as Ugly Jesus handed the photo to Milo. "He spent the first half of the seventies killing gooks in 'Nam." He looked at Ugly Jesus. "*Ah, ah...* he's a fellow Marine. He's responsible for thirty-three murders, including all those billionaires. And probably fifty to hundred more that no one knows about. He singlehandedly took on a major cartel operating out of Louisiana and Texas. I could go on and on but we'd be wasting time. We're going to kill Bic Green."

"Did Clyde tell you he thinks one man is worth a billion dollars to kill?" Darius asked.

Roman became visibly frustrated. "*Ah, ah, ah, ah...* you know damn well that's not how this works. And for one billion, any of us should be happy to poke out our eyes when he walks by."

"I don't like it."

"*Ah, ah...* dammit, Darius, I've already given my word. We're killing this man."

Darius stared at the rising smoke of his cigarette. "Did they advance you anything?"

Roman bowed out his chest as he pulled up a Metamask app on his phone, then showed it. "Ten million in Bitcoin money, and it's keeps growing. It'll be worth five hundred more in just a couple of days."

"Give me that," said Darius, snatching the phone in order to begin working intently on it.

"Son, what are you doing?"

"This stuff is volatile as hell. You might have two million in here in a week. I'm selling it into cash."

Darius handed the phone back. "Here, now you really have ten million USD."

"Me and Milo," Ugly Jesus said, "we'll start planning our road trip."

"I've got a better idea," Darius said.

"Of course, you do," Milo interjected.

"We have a little over ten million. Why don't we offer it to one of our chapters to do the hit. That way, if there's something we're not aware of, we can flush it out. If they're successful, then we pay them handsomely and we collect the rest."

"Is that what those spineless turds taught you in college, how not to get your hands dirty?"

Roman put his hand up for Milo to stop talking. "*Ah, ah… ah*-like this idea. We offer ten million to hunt this animal down. Sharing this kind of windfall with the chapter that takes him out will build the bond of trust. It will lead to growth of the DOH to the Midwest!" Roman grabbed his gavel. "*Ah, ah…* all in favor?"

"Aye," Darius said.

"Aye," Axl said.

"Aye," Ugly Jesus said.

"Aye," Milo mumbled.

The gavel smacked the table in the same worn spot that had taken the hit a hundred times. "*Ah, Ah…* things are about to change around here, boys. It's time to celebrate."

"Don't have to say that twice." Ugly Jesus said, pulling out a joint and sparking it up.

Roman accepted the massive joint from his friend and took a toke that would have dropped a frat boy.

6

PRESENT DAY, END OF BOOK 3
Presidio Heights Neighborhood,
San Francisco

"Honey," Anthony Parelli called out from the top of the stairs, his grip tight on the handgun hidden under his Armani jacket, "make sure that dog of ours isn't tearing up the furniture in the study."

No doubt his wife recognized the code phrase and hopefully was headed toward the safe room accessible through the kitchen pantry.

Moments before, Barbara Parelli had called out to her husband that FedEx was at the door, insisting only he sign for a package. This made Parelli extra cautious, for he had just received a broadcasted, encoded fax with a contract offer to take out Bic Green. He'd grabbed his gun and called out the safety code, just in case the delivery man was there to kill him before he could warn Bic.

What he didn't know was that Barbara would not be quick enough in responding to it.

Before he got down his stairs, two shots rang out, and a body thumped against the hardwood floor.

"Barbara," Parelli yelled as he flipped the coat off his 1911 pistol.

Coming down the stairs, he fired four scattered shots into the drywall before making the ninety-degree turn at the landing. He'd imagined hundreds of times where a man might stand to shoot him if he was waiting for him as he turned the corner.

His instinct was proven right as the man yelled in pain, having caught one in the knee.

Parelli came down the final flight of stairs while finishing him with another to the head. Without spending another moment on the man beyond killing him, he then turned his attention to getting his fortified front door closed.

Parelli fired his last few rounds through the open door to keep the swarming men outside at bay, then he kicked it shut avoiding their incoming fire. Immediately he went to the three light switches next to the door and started the house lockdown code sequence. Up down three times on the middle switch, switch one, then switch three, then the middle switch three times.

Parelli heard the steel storm shutters rolling down to lock down his house. The men coming for him would have the resources to get into his house, so this didn't buy him too much time. He turned to see Barbara lying face down in a pool of blood.

He ran into the hall.

He called her name and he went to his knees, took his wife's body in his arms, and turned her to face him. Parelli begged for it not to be so, but being no stranger to death, he knew when a person was dead. And Barbara was dead.

"*Cuore mio*," he cried, as tears filled his hardened eyes.

The first massive bang rang out as the battering ram struck the door. All he wanted to do was to sit there and mourn his wife of forty-one years, just hold her in his arms, let the men come in and kill him so he could join her. But his instincts told him it was time to survive. He wasn't going to leave her on the floor like this. No, not like this. He lifted her up and quickly carried her lifeless body to a couch in the living room.

While adjusting the pillow to make sure her head was comfortable, he said, "I'll be back, my love, I promise. I just gotta take care of a little business."

When he reached the second floor, a violent explosion shook the foundations of the house. Plastics on the door, he surmised.

Footsteps fell like lead weights through his front door. Here, in his office, Parelli acted. He headed toward the bookcase, to a volume that blended in with the books surrounding it. On its spine was the simple title: *To Kill A Mockingbird*. He pinched the top of the spine and peeled it down, revealing a key. Under his desk, hidden, was a switch. He stuck the key into the slot, turned it, then flipped the switch.

The house fell to the total darkness of a moonless night. With all the windows locked down by steel curtains, the only light to be found in the entire house was from the missing front door.

An astute observer of interior design would have noticed that, throughout the house, some of the decor didn't quite match its surroundings. Like the spine of the fake book in the bookcase, some were meant to stick out to those who had a little more on the ball--like Parelli and his wife, for example, and unlike the paid mercenaries who were now rampaging his home in the dark looking for him.

These unique areas of decor, and the spaces they delineated throughout the house, were to be avoided at all costs.

One such space was now being traversed by a soldier with an AR-15. Washington, as he was known in the group, could not have known that, by activating the switch with the key from the spine of that fake book, Parelli had armed his house from top to bottom.

The soldier passed by a painting on the wall, a high-end oil copy of Vincent van Gogh's *Self-Portrait with Bandaged Ear*, paying it no mind. He also paid no mind to the tiny squib of clay on the floor, one that was hidden underneath the area rug. This particular squib had two wires stuck into it. As Washington stepped on it, the wires came together.

A hydraulic sound ensued. A spray of a hundred needles shot out from behind the painting, covering a widespread area like a shotgun shot, at about twenty miles an hour, hitting the soldier everywhere at once.

The AR-15 dropped to the ground as the man put his hands to his face, blinded, bleeding, and howling in pain.

Parelli listened carefully for the location of his other hunters. He crept out of the office, having upgraded his 1911 to a Heckler and Koch 416 assault rifle which he'd retrieved from under his couch. A couple of years back he had given the rifle the name—Moe. Spending a lot of time working in his office, he'd often talk out loud to himself as kind of a sounding board anytime he wanted to walk through a deal or decision. Barbara would ask who he was talking to, and called him crazy when he answered truthfully. So, to appease his wife, as he always did, he would tell her he was talking to Moe on the phone.

Eventually, he took to the idea that he was really talking to someone else and his assault rifle became Moe.

Another soldier, hearing the wails of his fellow mercenary, gritted his teeth. This soldier, code-named Lincoln, would be damned if they were going to get him too. He wasn't about to feel sorry for his fallen comrade. The entire payout was just increased by another order of one-twelfth due to that soldier's ineptitude. Or so he could only assume. All he knew for sure was that there was adequate resistance being mounted on the part of their target.

Lincoln, laser focused, was ready for whatever the target threw at him.

But he wasn't ready for the invisible beam of light shining from an abstract clock on the wall, one with several lights shining out of it to indicate the hour, minutes, and seconds. Had he known better, he would have asked himself a simple question: Who hangs a piece like this in a narrow hallway?

Lincoln broke the beam projected by the hour light, and the entire clock panel slid up, revealing a box-like enclosure nestled inside the wall.

Like a rubbernecker passing an accident, Lincoln couldn't help but look for a split second.

Something sprang from the darkness within.

Something with teeth.

Lincoln screamed and flailed as the Australian brown snake sunk its fangs into a spot just below his chin strap.

Parelli's pet was kept on a very strict diet. One mouse, every two weeks. Angry and ravenous, it stayed attached to Lincoln's throat, injecting enough venom to drop a horse.

Parelli saw a shadow pass before him at the end of the hallway. The house was dark, as was planned with the arming of his various traps. Parelli donned a pair of night goggles and retreated into a nook that was cut into the wall. There he got down on one knee, assumed a firing position, and waited with the patience of a leopard.

The two men assigned to sweeping the upstairs walked right into Parelli's open window of sight. He sprayed the men with several 5.56 rounds, shredding them like paper dolls. To confuse the other men in the house, he hit the button of a garage door opener-like device. Guns mounted in the walls in three different locations throughout the house shot off several rounds. This was not designed to kill, but to confuse the men as to his real location. Ideally, this would force them to split up and lead some of the men to other traps.

Adams—not his real name—rounded the corner with a flashlight and revealed something truly hideous.

His buddy Lincoln was lying on the ground, flailing with what Adams assumed was a fatal gunshot wound. He took a panicked step toward him and was immediately seized with an altogether different kind of panic.

Adams was terrified of snakes, and there was a six-foot monstrosity rearing up not five feet in front of him, brown and slick.

He fumbled his flashlight. It fell to the ground.

The room went dark with hissing sounds.

Adams fired randomly into the blackness, the muzzle flashes created a strobe effect showing the snake's location. Some of his shots probably hit Lincoln, but the full-blown panic made him not care. What Adams didn't see was the owner of the house turning the corner. The gun blazed in the darkness.

Adams lay wheezing his last breaths of life, paralyzed, as the massive snake slithered up, its tongue flicking in and out inches from his eye. He wanted to scream but nothing came out except a guttural sound heard by him and no one else.

When Parelli had turned the key, something happened near the side door. A three-foot by three-foot section in the floor slid back to reveal a lattice of balsa wood slats painted black, all but invisible in the dark. Beneath those was a six-foot drop.

The soldier they called "Madison" was sent to inspect the gun shots fired in this section of the house.

He took no more than three steps in when he both heard and felt something crack beneath his feet.

Before he knew what had happened, he'd dropped down onto a jagged bed of metal spikes, each one-foot in length.

He emitted a scream that gurgled with blood.

Parelli stepped up to the floor trap and peered over the edge. The soldier within was gasping, each exhalation accompanied by dark red bubbles.

He took aim and said, "Say hello to Moe," then fired.

The face of the soldier exploded.

That was for Barbara.

Bullets snapped into the wall beside him. He returned fire as he retreated into the kitchen diving behind the island for cover.

He had to allow himself to pause, if only for a moment. There was no way to tell how many there still were. No doubt, they'd all close in now that they had pinpointed his location.

His wife was dead, but he wasn't leaving this house without her. Surrounded, as chunks of Italian Calacatta marble from the island countertop rained down on him from incoming fire, he held his ground.

Parelli returned fire involuntarily, spraying bullets at every half-face illuminated in the darkness. Everyone was Barbara's murderer.

He was running out of ammo and options, but he was not going to leave this house without his wife. At least that was his intention until he heard the unmistakable hollow thud of something solid landing and rolling on the countertop.

Grenade!

7

The men pinning Parelli down took quick cover to shield themselves from the blast. In that split-second, Parelli dove into the pantry.

With a thunderous flash, the kitchen was destroyed as if a wrecking ball went through it.

Code name "Jefferson" had seen Parelli's escape. "He's made it into the pantry, cover me," Jefferson said, reaching for another grenade. He ran forward through the smoke, up to the half-disintegrated island as he pulled the pin. Two men, one on each side of him fired steady shots into the pantry.

Jefferson threw the grenade perfectly, then took cover behind the island. By his estimation, everything in the six-by-eight room was about to be completely demolished.

The explosion was sharp, hot, violent, and left absolutely no doubt the job was done.

"Good work men," Jefferson said as he went to inspect for body parts. "Anyone seen Madison?" he asked with worry in his voice about his little brother.

The men replied in the negative.

"I'll be damned," Jefferson said.

Looking into the pantry, he saw that the walls and studs of the small room had been completely blown outward. Two-by-fours had snapped like toothpicks. The wood floor was incinerated, but there was no crater hole like he would have expected. Instead, exposed by the blast was a cement structure with a thick steel trapdoor. There was a spiderhole beneath the pantry.

"We didn't know about the traps and we sure didn't know about this!" Jefferson slammed the butt of his AR against the steel door.

"Come on out, you little rat."

"Concrete's over a foot thick," Kennedy said. "We might not be able to get at him in there."

"Anyone seen Madison?" Jefferson called out in frustration.

Nixon's voice came through the radio. "Madison's dead. Sorry, man."

Jefferson steeled his demeanor. "Kennedy, blow the door off with plastics."

"On it."

Jefferson moved carefully, shining his tactical light in every dark corner. He knew what to look for. Any single thing could be a trip wire, and anything could be a trap. He wouldn't open any doors that were closed even partially. Adrenaline buzzed in his veins, heightening every one of his senses. He was ready.

What he wasn't ready for was the headless body skewered like a shish kabob seven times over in the six-foot hole.

For a split second, he'd hoped it wasn't his little brother, but when he saw the watch he himself had given the kid on his twenty-second birthday, all hope was immediately extinguished.

He fell to his knees, realizing his baby brother was gone forever. "No, Bobby... no..."

He understood the logic of warfare. His brother had fallen into the trap and was bested and had to suffer the consequences. But coming by and blowing his head practically off his shoulders—that just made it personal.

"Plastics ready," Kennedy said over the radio.

Jefferson stood up, "Blow it. I want to be the one to put a bullet in this man's skull."

Six dead, six men still standing.

Jefferson, Kennedy, Nixon, Roosevelt, Eisenhower, and Reagan stood staring at the top of the impervious bomb shelter their target was safely inside.

"That C4 didn't even put a dent in it," Kennedy said.

"All our men dead for nothing," Nixon mumbled. "Cops will be here before we can get to him."

Jefferson was listening, but also observing his entire surroundings, waiting for the next shoe to drop. This mission had been a complete failure.

"Maybe we should cut our losses," Eisenhower said.

Jefferson could feel his men's eyes on him. But his eyes were on the security camera in the upper corner of the kitchen.

"He's watching us," Jefferson said, then walked out of the kitchen.

From the safe room, Parelli watched the man called Jefferson walk out of the kitchen. Sitting at the desk in the eight-by-eight cement box, he was pleased to see that most of the cameras in the house still worked. The infrared technology made it so he could see even in total darkness.

He would have rather killed all of these men and walked out of his house with Barbara. That would have been option number one. But that option was gone. Now his plan was to wait these men out. They were not going to be able to stay here forever. Surely, one of the neighbors had called the police by now.

Parelli became a little uncomfortable when he picked up Jefferson on camera in his living room, shining the light on Barbara. If he didn't know better, from the look of her rosey red cheeks, she looked like she was just taking a nap on the couch.

"You stinkin' little..." Parelli snarled as the man unexpectedly grabbed Barbara by the ankles.

Jefferson dragged Barbara across the living room and into the kitchen. Parelli watched carefully as the fire seed grew in his stomach. His skin sizzled as the man tore his beloved's blouse wide open.

"Have you lost it?" Kennedy said.

"He's watching us," Jefferson said, propping Barbara's body up at the kitchen table.

"I will kill you with my bare hands," Parelli mumbled at the monitor. The fire seed blossomed into dragon's breath, and it was ready to spew.

"I know you can hear me," Jefferson said, waving at the camera. "I bet you thought it was cute how you blew my brother's face off." He walked closer to the camera. "I saw how you took your dead wife from the floor and laid her on the couch, you even put a pillow under her head to make sure she was comfortable." Jefferson's face took on a greasy little smile. *"That was soooo sweet."*

Parelli sprung from his chair reaching for his rifle. "Don't touch her."

Jefferson shone the light onto Barbara's lifeless face. "What a pretty face. Isn't it? Makes me wanna mess it up a little. Nixon you have any rounds left in that M26?"

"Two," Nixon said.

"I'm going to count to ten. If our rat doesn't come out and fight, I want you to blow this pretty face to hell with those two 12-gauge shotgun rounds."

"10-4." Nixon pointed the barrel at Barbara, two feet from the woman's face.

"Alright, Mr. Rat, you have ten seconds to come out of your hole to stop Nixon. One, two..."

Something in Parelli snapped. He knew it was a suicide mission, but you just don't let someone shoot your wife in the face while you're hiding in a hole. He went to the ladder.

"...three, four..."

Parelli climbed the ladder up to the hatch. He looked back to the camera.

"...five, six..."

Parelli grabbed the latch handle, turned it open, and pushed.

It didn't budge.

"...seven, eight..."

Parelli gritted his teeth as he pushed with all of his might. It didn't budge. It must have been sealed shut by the explosion.

"...nine...."

He rammed his shoulder upwards.

"...ten..."

The M26 fired a 12-gauge round, obliterating Barbara's face into something truly horrific.

Parelli fell off the ladder onto his knees. His grating scream didn't let out any of the rage he'd felt. But what it did do was add to his decision to deploy the nuclear option.

He walked over to his desk, looked one last time at what was left of his wife, and with tears streaming from his eyes, he said, "Everyone will pay... everyone."

With that, he punched in the code.

The explosives wired throughout the whole house erupted.

All cameras went dead as the house became a firestorm.

The underground tunnel beneath the safe room leading out of and away from the house was damp, cramped, moldy, and covered in cobwebs. Things skittered past him in the dark and itched down the back of his neck.

Parelli made it to the backyard of his house, coming up from the ground through a portal beneath a moss-covered sundial.

He looked at the burning ruins of his house. "Barbara," he mumbled. "I'm so sorry."

Frozen, with the heat from the fire warming his face, he couldn't shake seeing his wife's head being blown off. He knew the memory was forever seared into his mind.

Sirens in the distance snapped him out of his trance.

He ran to the freestanding garage located within a grove of poplars in his backyard. He punched the code and entered. His custom Mercedes AMG G65 was waiting for him. The three-ton, matted black vehicle was outfitted with a number of little "toys", as Parelli called them--each one packing enough firepower to render the vehicle more of a tank than a SUV. He probably wouldn't be needing any of them at the moment, as his wife's grave was now burning to a crisp-- along with about 2,400 pounds of living garbage inside it.

He made a sign of the cross, asking for mercy on his wife's soul the best he knew how, then put the SUV in gear and took off through a path through the back woods.

The harder he pushed on the gas, the more his anger, hatred, and vengeance rose.

Everyone was going to die.

8

"If this bucket of bolts had Bluetooth I could connect my playlist." Mack said as he fumbled with the radio dial in the prisoner transport vehicle.

Caroline slapped his hand away. "Keep your eyes on the road. I'll find something palatable."

"Men don't want palatable, they want something with some hair on it. Right, Bic?"

"With Gracie safe back in Chicago, we can listen to yacht rock for all I care," Bic said from the back of the van.

"Yacht rock it is," Caroline said. She turned to speak to Bic through the barred window.

Bic shook his head and chuckled. "On second thought, maybe not."

"Bic knows what's up," Mack said, tapping the steering wheel for effect. "You tell this woman we wanna hear some Zeppelin."

"Stairway to a cat screaming in my ears?" Caroline said. "No thanks."

"You're talking about one of the greatest bands of all time," Mack said, his voice tight with incredulity.

"Stop."

"No, I'm serious. Find me a drummer who sounds like John Bonham. And those guitar solos. No one plays like Page. No one."

"He's a sloppy player."

Mack nearly swerved the van. "Jimmy Page? Are we talking about the same band?" He thought for a moment. "Alright, so he's a little sloppy. But he's got more heart in his worst solo than a thousand guitar players have in their entire careers."

"Yawn."

"And underneath it all, you have John Paul Jones keeping up in lock-step with *perfect* bass. Oh, and the lyrics? Hell, they're like Shakespeare. With the golden voice of Mr. Plant himself carrying them up *into the stratosphere*."

"Are you done?"

"No, but I'll stop there."

"Good. How about a little Jimmy Buffet?"

Mack put two fingers to his open mouth and made a gagging sound as his phone rang. "Be a dear and reach into my pocket, will you?" he said, still searching for the right song. "I need a dose of Pepto and 'Kashmir,' stat."

"You should have let me listen to my yacht rock. I might have reached into your pocket the way you like it," Caroline said with a smirk.

"Get a room," Bic said from the back.

Mack grabbed his phone and peaked at the screen. "It's Parelli." He answered. "Yeah... no, didn't read the text." He listened, then replied, "Uh, we're about two hours outside of Houston? Headed to LA, why...? Yeah, he's here..."

He looked at Caroline, muting the phone. "He's hysterical and wants to talk to Bic."

Caroline grabbed the phone, turned in her seat, and awkwardly slipped the phone through the bars.

"Parelli," Bic said into the phone. "Everything okay?"

Caroline watched Bic's white eyes widen.

"Alright," Bic said calmly after a moment. "So sorry about Barbara." He disconnected and handed the phone back to Caroline. "We've got a problem."

Caroline shook her head in disbelief. "It never ends, does it?"

"When you say problem, that can mean a lot of things," Mack said. "Problem like, she got my order wrong? Or problem like there's a nuclear bomb strapped to my ass and it's going to blow in five seconds kind of problem?"

Bic paused. "Tony said there's a two billion dollar hit on me."

Caroline and Mack both made similar choking sounds.

"Two billion what? Sunflower seeds?" Mack said.

"They tried to kill Tony so he wouldn't warn me." Bic paused. "They killed his wife."

Mack's voice was rising. "I'm a little confused. Two billion? That's not possible."

"We need to get off this highway ASAP," Bic said.

Caroline took Mack's phone and pulled up his GPS. "Okay. There's an exit in one mile. Get over."

A couple of Harleys roared past them on the right lane of three, going north.

"Hang on, hang on…" Mack said, waiting for the bikes to clear.

"Mack," Caroline said with some impatience, "get over. We're gonna pass it."

"I'm trying, but we're in the middle of some kind of Sturgis rally!"

Caroline looked to her right and saw that the two choppers that had roared past were now beginning to slow in front of them, while two more roared up on Mack's side, and two more on hers.

"These guys think they own the road," she said.

"Guys," Mack said through the window, "wanna maybe go play somewhere else?" He flicked on his turning signal and edged the vehicle toward the right lane.

The biker to Caroline's immediate right pulled out a gun.

"Mack!" she yelled as the biker shot out the front tire.

The vehicle swerved and skidded. The tires screeched as they laid rubber on the hot black pavement. Mack held it as tightly as he could. The van veered left, clipping one of the bikers on that side.

The bike dumped and threw its driver end over end into the grassy medium.

The van spun completely out of control the second it reached the grass.

"Brace yourselves," Mack yelled as the van's rear driver's side smacked into the concrete divider first. The front driver's side took the brunt of the collision in the continuation of the spin. A waterfall of glass from Mack's window cascaded down on him.

"Everyone okay?" Mack said, shaking the glass off him.

"Yes, but not for long," Caroline said, peering out at the approaching bikers. They were coming down the median area, which held the divider and the immobilized van.

Mack tried to open his door, but to no avail. It was crushed shut and up against the median.

Caroline drew her weapon and sprung out of the van using her door as a shield. She quickly unloaded a barrage of fire at the bikers. She hit two, both of whom went down fast.

The others squatted behind their bikes and returned fire, shooting up the van.

Mack crawled from the driver's side to the passenger's side.

Bic called to Mack, "Let me help."

"It's all smashed to hell, buddy. Sit tight." Mack continued to crawl out the passenger side door.

"I don't have a lot of ammo!" Caroline said, reloading.

Mack reached around her and returned fire. "We can't both be here, I'll flank around back."

"Be careful," she said.

He smiled with his eyes, then kissed her. "You too."

Mack ran to the back of the vehicle. When he made it to the back, he fired a couple of shots to help Caroline hold them in their current positions.

Mack then unlocked the back door in an attempt to let Bic out. "It's jammed, buddy," he said, pulling on the door handle with all his might. It didn't budge.

"A little help!" Caroline yelled.

Mack hopped over the median and made his way towards the bikers, staying below the vision line of the cement divider to stay hidden.

Caroline saw Mack peer out from behind the median and take a shot, taking out the man closest to him.

One of the other men immediately opened fire at Mack. He ducked.

The other got on his bike and charged toward Caroline just as she fired her last bullet. She missed her target. Her instincts told her not to go back into that van. She'd be a sitting duck. With that, she turned and ran towards the back of the van.

She felt the low, powerful, growl-like sound gaining quickly on her. She looked back to see a bearded man determined on running her over as he sped toward her like a torpedo.

A massive form sprung out from behind the van just as she cleared it. Bic threw his forearm out into the biker's chest, knocking him clear off his bike.

Caroline watched Bic lay a single, massive stomp to the prone biker's head, surely killing him.

Bic picked up the man's bike—it was still running—and revved it once before throwing it into gear. He lurched forward, springing him in the direction of the last biker.

Caroline popped up and followed Bic in a sprint.

The final biker stopped shooting at Mack and turned his attention towards Bic.

The man fired rounds at Bic as he closed in fast.

Shoot him, Caroline thought as Mack peered out from behind the cover of the median. But he didn't have his gun. He must have been out of ammo too. The next thing she saw made her heart lurch into her throat: It was Mack sprinting towards the biker that was shooting at Bic.

Caroline screamed. "*Mack!*"

Mack jumped onto the back of the biker moments before he shot Bic at almost point-blank range.

The biker threw Mack off his back just as Bic arrived, dumping his bike as he slid it towards the man.

As the biker's body flew, his gun discharged.

Bic grabbed the man by the head as he slid by him. He gave it a twist and something snapped.

Caroline ran up. Mack was on the ground, staring at her with a bloody splotch on his stomach growing bigger by the second.

9

Caroline screamed, running to his side.

Bic stood, frozen, staring.

"Mack, talk to me... oh, Jesus..."

She looked up at him. "We need to get him to the hosp--" She paused when she saw the look on Bic's face. "Bic, go get one of our phones from the van."

Bic sprinted to the van.

"You're going to be okay, I promise," she said rubbing his head gently.

Bic handed her the phone. She had to steady her hands from trembling as she dialed.

"This is Agent Maddox. We have a shooting incident. I have an agent down and need a MedEvac like ten seconds ago."

She looked up at Bic. "The prisoner... has *escaped*."

Bic nodded quickly and began heading toward the row of discarded motorcycles. He grabbed the biker with the snapped neck and ripped off his helmet and jacket. Throwing the latter over his arm, he picked up the most intact of all the bikes and wheeled it toward Caroline, who was finishing giving her coordinates.

"Tell the crew this needs to happen pronto!"

She disconnected the call. Mack had now fallen into a state of semi consciousness.

"Baby, they're coming. Hang in there, okay? I love you. Hang in there."

"What happened?" Mack moaned.

"You're going to be just fine. I promise."

Mack looked at her and slurred something.

"Don't try to speak now, baby." She tried to stay strong, but the chance of losing her soulmate brought tears to her eyes.

"I..." said Mack, a slight smile twisting on his face, "I guess I shoulda worn my vest?"

"Oh, God, Mack," she said, clutching his icy hand and kissing it.

She looked up at Bic. "You need to go."

He shook his head slowly. "Not until he's okay."

"Go, Bic! Just, go! Please!"

He turned, checked the pocket of the jacket for a wallet, then mounted the bike.

As he roared away toward the setting sun, Caroline whispered in Mack's ear. "I love you, my one and only..."

There was no response.

10

The woman stopped the 2013 Corolla hatchback in front of the large aluminum structure and noted the DOH logo on its door. She checked herself in the mirror.

She'd opted for the bangs, having allowed the rest of it to grow to chin length. It gave her the look of a hot 1920s flapper, and she dug it. She would go for herself, she thought. She pursed her lips and blew the mirror a kiss, her round, blue eyes full of innocence.

"That's the stuff."

She angled the rearview mirror down to check out her cleavage. She opened her shirt one more button, frowned, then buttoned it again. There was just enough here to drive those idiots out of their skulls.

She reached into her bag, grabbed the pink bottle of Narciso Rodriguez, and gave her neck a spritz. It covered the stench of garlic which, by now, must have seeped into the upholstery. She fanned her neck for a second, then exited the garlic-smelling car.

She headed around the vehicle, cursing silently at the gravel that was wrecking her new kicks. She adjusted her tube socks, gave her daisy dukes a tug at the butt, then grabbed the pizza from the back of the car and wiggled toward the entrance.

"Well now," said a biker who looked like a cross between a grizzly bear and a brick wall. "What have we here?"

"We have seven pizzas for y'all," she said, reeling in the flirtatiousness just enough to get the grizzly all steamed up inside.

"Where you from, darling?" the grizzly bear said.

"Georgia. What's your name, sugar?" She was laying the accent on thick.

"Milo," he said, chuffing out a breath of stale beer, "I'm all out of money, darling. Maybe there's something ever better you'd accept instead of payment?"

He smelled like a sow. It was all she could do not to gag. She smiled instead.

Milo pulled a small bag of white powder out of his front pocket and shook it like a dog treat. "How about I snort some of this off them nice big titties."

"Now, I'd love to, Milo, but…"

His eyes grew wide, and all traces of pig lust left his face. He obviously wasn't expecting that as an answer.

"But," she continued, "I kinda need the cash to show my boss. So maybe next time."

It was then that the joke hit home. Smiling maliciously, he threw a chin over his shoulder. "Hey Darius, someone order a pizza with extra poonanny?"

"We ordered," said a voice behind him. "Pay her so we can get our grub on."

The grizzly reached into his pocket and pulled out a wallet on a chain. From this he retrieved three bills. When she grabbed them he held on and gave them a yank backward.

"You sure you don't want to party?"

"I told you, next time."

He handed her the cash. "Keep the change. Let me see you stick it right between those puppies."

She giggled at that, turning her head slightly.

"Oh, hey," she said, "you gentlemen wouldn't happen to have a bathroom here I could use?"

"It ain't exactly fit for ladies, but if you don't mind, you can come on in."

He barely moved an inch as she sashayed past him.

A whistle came from the group. *"How about that?"*

She kept her eyes straight forward.

She stayed in the bathroom for as long as it took and no longer. The place stunk like every bit of foulness in the world bubbled up at once and collected there. She couldn't even admire herself in the mirror, caked as it was with blots of gray filth.

When she emerged, she sashayed across the room, feeling the full weight of the human male gaze on her backside.

"Hey!"

She turned, and there was Milo, standing there with a string of greasy cheese hanging from his mouth like baby drool.

"Come on, stick around and party a little." It sounded like a plea that came from loneliness.

She smiled and winked. "Catch you boys on the flip flop."

With that, she left to several jokes echoing throughout the room, all of which were poorly worded puns on the words "flip" and "flop".

She got back into the Corolla and breathed out a frustrated sigh. What she wouldn't give to lay waste to the entire room full of those bozos. And now here she was, back in this Italian Grandmamobile.

Just outside of Los Angeles, she stopped the Corolla and got out. It was a desolate area. And as the sun set, she wondered what kind of wildlife would be lurking here. Not too far away was the bustling city. Here, on the edge of the desert, civilization ended.

Her black Tesla was parked nearby within a patch of brush. She took out her fob and clicked open the front trunk.

The little pizza delivery dweeb was still there, mouth still taped shut, limbs still trussed like a piglet. Odd how he didn't make a sound when she opened the trunk. He merely stared at her with those little doe eyes that she found somewhat adorable.

She put a finger to her lips. "Sshhhhhh." And peeled the tape off slowly.

He let out a shaky, rasping breath.

She leaned down and planted a short, wet kiss on his lips.

"That's for being a good boy."

He stared at her with a mixture of confusion, horror, and--or so she liked to think--enduring love.

She pulled out a switchblade and began cutting the zip ties. "Now, here's the deal," she said, punctuating her words with violent cuts, and vice-versa. "I am going to let you go. I am going to give you your keys, and the money for the pizza, and a little something extra for your trouble. I had a little peek at your license, Mister Charlie Glick of 24B Rosevale Avenue. And if I get one whiff of your going to the cops, I'm going to seek out your family and skin them alive, and then I'm coming for you and I won't be as nice about it. Okay?"

Charlie Glick, his twenty-first birthday next week, nodded vigorously.

"Good," she said with a smile. She helped him out of the car, making sure he could stand alright. "Easy does it. Got your bearings?"

Again, the nod.

"Good. Now, as promised. Your cash." She handed him the three bills. "And this, for your trouble." She handed him twenty Ben Franklins.

The kid stared at his hands.

He *was* a cutie. If she were eight years younger, she'd probably go for it. But she didn't need any more reminders that she was approaching the hill. She herself looked young enough, and could, if she wanted to, make herself look even older than she was, but there was no hiding the fact that her intelligence would always expose her in the end. She had to live with that.

She took the boy's face in her hands and stared him in the eyes.

"Charlie," she cooed in her best Marilyn Monroe impression, "I'll love you till the day I am no longer roaming this earth."

And with that, she planted a *long*, wet kiss on his mouth. No tongue. All heart.

11

B ic pulled the Harley up to the gas pump and sputtered to a
stop, breathing a sigh of relief. He'd hit a stretch of road with
nothing on it for about twenty miles and was sure he'd done
the last half mile or so on fumes alone. He stomped down on the
kickstand and straddled himself on the tilted bike while he removed
his jacket. It was hot as hell out here. He hadn't felt it while riding.

He turned the jacket around and held it up, glancing over the patch
on the back. A nasty-looking dog chomping on a flaming bone.
DOGS OF HELL was stitched on above the ugly mascot.

He reached into the pocket and withdrew the dead man's wallet, a
black nylon thing with Velcro to hold it shut. *What kind of grown man
uses a wallet like this?* Strange how it hadn't struck him back at that
scene of carnage on the highway. All he thought back then was that it
was a wallet and it had cash and that was good enough. Now,
somewhat sober, he paused to allow reason to flow through his mind.
He tore it open and got a good look at the amount. There was enough
in here to last him for a little while at least.

That scene at the highway…

The events of the day wavered in his mind as if viewed through
desert heat.

Mack lay there, bleeding to death from a bullet to the gut.
Caroline's face, pleading.

He swatted the memory away, feeling the rise of rage in his blood.
He had a choice: get to the bottom of this or die trying. And die
trying was not part of Bic Green's diet.

He was about to head in to the station when he realized he ought
to wear the jacket in. He knew he stood out, and cameras didn't lie.
Begrudgingly, he put the jacket back on, only just realizing now that it

stunk like weed and booze and week-old b.o.

He strode confidently into the tiny convenience store wearing the dead man's sunglasses and made his way directly to the fridge. He grabbed himself a water and headed up to the clerk's area where there was a display of burner phones in clamshells hanging from a clip strip. He grabbed one and threw it and the water onto the counter.

"Twenty-one fifty on pump number one."

The clerk, looking like he slept in his clothes for days, could barely rouse himself out of his Instagram trance to conduct the transaction. When he finally did, he did so without eye contact. Bic felt a bit of luck. This guy didn't care a bit about this job, and was keeping his head down. No chance he'd notice him or the bike. If the police asked with his picture, he'd keep it simple for himself and say, nope, never saw him.

Bic pushed it over to the side of the building, where he peeled open the clamshell case.

Now to see if Mr. Dead Man has good credit.

He tore open the Velcro wallet, fished out a piece of plastic, and held it up for inspection.

The name read: Jane Kellner.

Bic shook his head. Sorry, Miss Kellner. Sorry you had to be Mr. Dead Man's last caper. Now to see if Jane had reported her card stolen yet.

In five minutes, it was done. Bic had an active phone. And Jane Kellner had another mysterious charge on her account. He chucked the card into the dumpster. No sense creating any more of a trail of his movements than he had to.

He dialed Parelli's number.

"Parelli" came the voice spoken cold and firm.

"Tony, it's Bic."

"There's nowhere on this earth they're going to be able to hide from me."

"I'm so sorry, Tony."

"Not your fault – it's whoever thought it was a good idea to come to my house and kill my wife."

"I know, but—"

"Did they come after you yet? Did you shake the FBI agents?"

Bic wiped his already beading forehead. "Yes, they came on bikes. Mack got shot and I'm now an escapee.

46

"Any idea who's after you?"

"The six guys on motorcycles were all wearing Dogs of Hell jackets." Bic turned to see the reflection of the jacket. "I'm wearing one of them. Says they're from Houston."

There was silence on the other end.

"Have you heard of them, Parelli?"

"Yeah, but I'm confused. The guys who came after me were a military, high-level professional crew. But the bikers, if I remember correctly, they're out of LA and do low level thug stuff. Street stuff, you know? This doesn't make any sense... where are you?"

"Tumbleweed town just west outside of Lubbock. Route 84."

"Head toward Albuquerque. I'll meet you there. Call me when you cross the New Mexico line."

"Got it."

The call disconnected.

Bic took a breath and stared off into the distance. A long stretch of straight, brown road, sparsely lined with trees and phone lines, disappearing into the horizon. He took a sip of his water. Cold and perfect. Then hopped on the bike and started it up.

12

Seth Braddick sat in the waiting room of the attorney's office, his eyes focused on the TV screen in the corner.

"We want to bring you the latest on the breaking news. A grisly scene on the highway, six people are dead, one critically injured in a shootout with police…"

FBI, morons, he thought. *Jesus, can the news get anything right?*

He'd been following the story intently ever since it broke. They had most of the details right, including the one about the prisoner, Bic Green, still at large.

That little bastard Nathaniel. He actually went and did it. Hired a gang of thugs to kill Bic Green.

"Mr. Braddick?"

He snapped to attention.

"Mr. Giblichman will see you now. Go right in."

He got up with a wince from his aching back and stretched. A few pops and cracks betrayed his age. He put on his game face and entered the attorney's office.

"How are you, Seth? Long time," said the attorney, a frost-haired man, dapper-dressed and smelling of tobacco and sandalwood.

"Long time, indeed," he said with a single shake of the man's hand.

"Have a seat, please. Hey, have you been following that story? Crazy stuff."

"Yeah, about that," Seth said, "listen, something's weighing heavily on my mind."

Giblichman's face went grave. "Of course."

Seth folded his hands on his lap. "I have reason to believe Nathaniel is involved in that stuff."

"Stuff?"

"That business on the highway."

Giblichman tilted his head. "Are you still... monitoring the children?"

Interesting choice of words, Seth thought. Funny how the family attorney avoided the dreaded word *surveillance.*

"It's not what you think."

"There's no judgment from me, Seth. I'm just asking."

"After what happened to their parents and the way it's affected them, I just can't--I have to know what they're up to. It's for their own good."

"I understand. But as the family attorney, they are my clients. You understand that. I'm concerned about their wellbeing. But back to this thing on the highway."

"Yeah, that," Seth said, feeling his mouth go dry. "There's a man on the loose. Name of Bic Green. I believe Nathaniel put a hit on him."

Giblichman leaned forward. "Excuse me?"

"I found some stuff..." Seth opened his briefcase and took out his evidence. "These are printouts of Nathaniel's activity on the dark web."

"Dark web."

"That's right. He's been actively searching for a way to hire someone to kill Bic. You can see here."

Giblichman perused the printouts. "Okay."

"I'm assuming my nephew has attorney-client privilege."

"Of course."

"So what do I do?"

"What do you do?"

"Yes, Robert. My nephew is hiring hit men. What the hell do I do? Can a minor get in trouble for this?"

"If this can all be linked, yes. Conspiracy to commit murder and also first-degree murder if the hit actually happens. Plus, in this specific case, there's a matter of collateral damage. If that cop winds up dying, both the person who pulled the trigger and the one who hired him can be charged with first degree murder."

Seth put his head in his hands.

"I can understand your worry," Giblichman said with care in his voice. "Just know that I'm there for Nathaniel. Okay? He'll have the best representation if anything leads to him."

Seth looked up. "There's just so much here. I mean, our whole life... the company, for instance."

Giblichman's brow furrowed. "What about the company?"

"He's about to inherit the controlling interest."

"Seth, if that's all you're concerned about--"

Seth rose from his chair. "Now hold on! I know what you're thinking and it's ridiculous. But the truth of the matter here is that the company is my brother's legacy, and it's important to not only protect the kids, but *also* the company, and anyone who doesn't realize that—"

"Easy, Seth. Sit down and get a hold of yourself." Giblichman held up his hands. "Our first order of business is ensuring that Nathaniel gets proper legal representation."

"Of course, that's why I'm here."

"We have the best in the world here to represent Nathaniel. The next step is to protect all of his assets. Seeing as how he's technically in no legal trouble as of this moment, we're okay. But I think it would be in his best interest to get... the guardian... in control as soon as possible."

Seth sat down and took a breath. "Okay."

Giblichman folded his hands and looked him in the eye. "In the future, Seth, it might benefit you to try not to look so relieved when you get news like this."

13

o cliché, she thought, *sitting here with my head in my hands next to my unconscious husband.* The machines answered her with Morse code robotic exactitude. She could grab his hand and tell him she loves him. Or she could pray aloud. Are you there, God? It's me, Caroline. Ridiculous thoughts in a ridiculous place.

She looked at her watch and felt a wave of agonizing anxiety overcome her. She grabbed her phone from her bag and stepped outside the room. The whole place stunk like sanitized sickness. How she wished for a fresh breeze to come and cleanse her lungs.

"Hey," said Gabby, her sitter, answering with typical singsong joviality.

"Hey. Listen there's something I need to tell you and I don't want Samantha to hear it. Okay? Keep your voice even and answer with neutral words if you can."

"Sure," the college student said with perfectly flat affect.

"Mack was shot. He's okay for now. They operated on him and he's on ventilation."

"Oh, my God…"

"Okay, see, that's the type of thing I don't want Samantha to hear."

"Right, of course," Gabby said, back to strange normality. "She's watching Paw Patrol."

"Great."

"Caroline, what's the deal?" Gabby said in a whisper.

"No doubt you saw the news about the highway shootout."

"That was *you*?"

"Mack was hit."

"Dear God."

"Enough, Gabby," Caroline said, her voice pinched and strained. "Can you put Samantha on?"

"Are you sure?"

"No, but do it anyway. I need to see my baby right now."

Caroline braced herself, feeling a bit of misery in her gut when she heard Gabby's voice cooing to little Samantha to come to the phone and talk to Mommy.

"Hi, Mommy," came the little voice.

She almost lost it, right then and there. What she wouldn't give to be home right now, her and Mack at the table, Samantha refusing to eat her broccoli. What she wouldn't give to have everything exactly the way it should be.

"Hey, baby, are you behaving for Gabby?"

"Yes."

"I don't believe you. Gabby said you're flying around the room like a dragon and breathing fire."

The tiny laugh that cut through her like a dull drill. "Noooooooo she didn't!"

"I'm just kidding. She said you're being the little angel you always are."

"Yeah."

"Listen, honey, me and Daddy are going to be late, okay?"

"Noooooo," Samantha said again, this time in a very different tone.

"Yeah, I'm sorry."

"Where's Daddy?"

Caroline's hand went instinctively to her heart. Samantha was Daddy's girl all the way. "He can't come to the phone right now."

"Whyyyyyy?"

"Because he can't. Samantha, you know what it's like when me and Daddy work late. We've done it many times."

"Nooooooooo…"

"Yes, we have. You're getting the pouty face."

A slight laugh. "No, I'm not."

"Yes, you are. I can hear it. Pouty face, pouty face, oh pouty, pouty, pouty, pouty face…" She finished with a pop of her finger in the cheek.

The child's giggle wrenched her like nothing else.

"Daddy loves you very much and I love you too and we'll see you soon, okay."

"Okay," the child said begrudgingly.

"Good. Now you be good for Gabby."

"I will."

"No more flying around the room and breathing fire."

That giggle again. "I didn't do that."

"Okay, sweetie, I love you."

"Love you too byyyeeeeee."

That last one put her over the edge. Thank God she disconnected before she broke down.

14

"Hello?"

Bic hardly recognized Caroline's voice over the phone. It was tired, worn. It sounded like it had been wrung of all its life.

"How is he?"

"He made it out of surgery. He's on a breathing tube. They're not sure."

"I'm so sorry, Caroline."

"You're on your own right now. You realize that," she said, her voice not without pity.

"Yes. I know he's going to pull through, he'll make it."

"I've got to go," she said.

Bic let the phone drop to his side. It was all he could do not to crush the thing like a walnut.

A warm breeze was blowing, earth-scented. Tiny tornadoes whirled dust across the road.

Bic looked around. Nothing but road and dirt and more road and more dirt, before him and out ahead. It felt as if he was looking at the entire stretch of his life. Everything he'd been through were mere appearances--mirages. There was nothingness to Bic Green, and this road was proof of it. It was as if the machinery that had projected all the events of his life had suddenly broken down, revealing the emptiness that was behind it all along.

There was a feeling that began in his gut. A rage. But it wasn't the same rage he'd felt all his life. This was something new. This was the rage of a man struggling in the void to be heard, to be noticed. He was more alone than he'd ever been in his life. And what's more, he was grateful for it. Not for himself, but for the people who came into his orbit. They were poor souls, every last one of them.

He was on the bike again, kicking up clouds of dust in the direction of his past. *Keep riding, Bic. You'll kick up enough of that dust to hide that fact that there's nothing behind you.*

He pulled on the accelerator.

No matter how many times he'd tried to make up for his sins, there was always another to account for. He was a disease, a virus. He infected everything, even when he tried to do good.

Very well then. He'd be a disease. Let all life wither away and die when he crossed it.

There was a battered Toyota ahead of him chugging along listlessly.

Something made him look at the driver. Perhaps it was the last vestige of his goodness asserting itself. Greet another man with a smile. Recognize a fellow human. You are Bic Green, you aren't…

Clarence?

His father's face.

Clarence let out an evil cackle, *"I'm comin' for you, boy."*

Then he raised his arm, which was torn off at the elbow joint, shreds of meat dangling.

He looked back to his father's eyes, they were reptilian, just like… an *alligator.*

The bike wobbled and swerved, slowing down just in time that he missed hitting the Toyota. Bic turned into the skid and fell—the bike went flying out from under him, scraping to a stop a good twenty yards away, still sputtering.

The Toyota was stopped. The driver was running over.

"You okay, friend?"

Bic looked up to see a middle-aged white man adjusting a pair of horn-rimmed glasses staring down at him. Not Clarence. His father was dead. Or alive inside his nightmares. Either way, there was no Clarence Green here.

"I'm alright," Bic said, taking his time to get up.

"You sure?" the man said. "You really took a spill. I saw it. I'm sorry. I know you were trying to pass me. Maybe I should have given you a little space. You sure you're alright?"

"I'm fine, thank you," Bic offered with grateful assurance.
"Okay, 'cause I can call 911 or something…"

"Nah, it's alright. I'm alright. Really. You go on and have a good day."

58

The man nodded. "Okay, friend. Take care."

And he was off, back in his Toyota, back to his life. And Bic Green got back on the bike, which had sputtered out. It started right back up. Good old Harley-Davidson. He revved out the gurgles and took off again, cautious and fighting the urge to just go and sail the thing right the hell off the edge of some cliff.

But as he always did, he kept moving despite it all.

And that's when it hit him.

Bic Green's real enemy was death itself.

15

As he lay on his bed reading the news story, Nathaniel's arm itched.

It wasn't supposed to be like this. There was supposed to be some dude with like a syringe or something, who'd walk up to Bic and stick him and walk away and that was it. Or maybe a Marine-grade sniper to pick him off from a distance. There wasn't supposed to be all this other crap. A massive shootout on the highway. Six dead. An FBI agent shot. All because of him.

He clapped his laptop shut, feeling his heart beginning to race. His breath was coming in hitches. The fear in his belly was raging now. And his arm was itching uncontrollably.

He leaned over and opened his nightstand drawer. The razor blade gleamed. With trembling fingers, he lifted it out. He should just do it. Get it over with. Slice deep and hard once and for all.

His reason for not doing so knocked lightly on his door.

He quickly put the razor blade back. Having Lucy find out about his little secret could be catastrophic to her psyche, or worse, give her a similar idea.

He opened the door to find her standing timidly, her head bowed slightly, her finger in the side of her mouth.

"You having nightmares again?" he said.

She nodded slowly.

"You wanna sleep with me, don't you?"

A slight smile appeared and she nodded more vigorously.

Nathaniel heaved a fake sigh--he had to at least keep up the appearance of the annoyed older brother after all--and moved aside to allow her entrance. "Come on, already. You better not toss and turn and keep me up all night."

Her smile grew wider and a squeaky sound like a stuck giggle came from her throat. She hopped into his bed and flopped over onto her side.

He climbed in after her. "Watch my laptop.."

She looked up and around at him, her smile still wide, her eyes glossy and tired. She was adorable. How could he even have thought about ending his own pain when she needed him?

"Go to sleep," he said lovingly.

She turned and he opened his laptop again, clicking off the news story about the massacre. A tinge of fear ignited through him as he caught the final glimpse of it. He fought the urge to cut. Not with her here. No way.

So, he wasn't going to get a good night's rest tonight. So be it. He started clicking around on other stories. His eyes fell on one item in particular, one that made the anxiety in his gut even more tangible: "BITCOIN DOWN 12 PERCENT"

Frantically, he clicked on the story. Sure enough, it was true. He did the calculation on his laptop.

Twelve percent of 1.9 billion, crap… he'd lost 220 million in the last six hours!

He had paid 100 million up front, he owed another 1.9. Now he had less than 1.7, but would owe 1.9 billion in a couple of days.

If Bitcoin went down another twelve percent, that's another 200 million gone.

This is bad real bad, he thought as his mind continued to process. What if the price went down another twelve percent, then another after that…?

He looked up the history of the Bitcoin price, and what he saw horrified him. The drawdowns in the charts were as much as ninety percent!

He began to beg the screen, plead at it with all the hope he could muster, to make Bitcoin rise in price again. But instead, the SOB dropped another five hundred points right before his eyes.

In the last ten seconds, he had lost another 15 million.

It dropped another 500 points. 30 million in *one damn minute.*

He closed the laptop in terror, unable to watch any longer.

The itch on his arm grew like a brush fire. And all the while, Bic Green was still out there, alive. And Nathaniel's life became more and more in danger with every downward tick of the coin.

16

There had been better days at the Dogs of Hell clubhouse. Most of the officers sat around the round table waiting for their leader to arrive. Usually the DOH did the killing, not the other way around. Sure, they had had a member or two killed over the years—back in the nineties, two members were shot down. *That* was a massive deal. *This* on the other hand, was like nothing that had ever happened in the club's history.

The talk was small and commiserate amongst the men, with lots of heavy drags of their cigarettes to calm their nerves.

All talk ceased with the sputtering growl of Roman Dog's Harley, heard in the distance. It grew louder until it culminated in one final roar before dying immediately. The leader entered the boardroom a moment later.

Red-faced, with a beer in hand, Roman stared down the officers in an intense uncomfortable silence. His eyes then wandered amongst them, and without warning, he whipped the bottle against the wall with a snarl. The glass bottle burst into a hundred pieces.

"Pop, take it easy," said Darius, the only one brave enough to try to calm their leader.

Roman glared at his son as if he was going to rip his head off, "Ah, ah… take at easy, I brought Sax into DOH while you were playing with the shit in your diapers. He and all his officers were killed. There's nothin' easy about it."

"Sax was a great president," Ugly Jesus mumbled. Then took a drag of his cigarette, burning it down to the filter.

"Hear, hear, to Sax," Milo said as he and Axl raised their beers in a salute. Ugly Jesus joined them.

Darius stood placing his hand on his father's shoulder, offering a cigarette from his pack. "Here, Pop, have a smoke. Let's sit down and figure out how to make this right."

Roman accepted and sat in his chair.

"There's no making this right," Axl said, his eyes fixated on the table.

"Ah, ah… the Houston chapter of the Dogs of Hell is no more! With all the officers killed, the rest of the club is patching over to the Killing Jokers."

"Gutless little turds," Milo said.

"Ah, ah… we're losing chapters instead of gaining." Roman slammed his fist on the table.

"Damn Jokers, bunch of bottom-dwelling, scum-sucking posers." Ugly Jesus said, lighting another cigarette.

"I think we should pay the LA Jokers a little visit," Milo added, placing his nine-millimeter on the table.

"We'll take care of the Jokers," Darius said, "but right now, Pop, we need to stay focused on Bic Green."

"The kid's right," Ugly Jesus said, raising his hand. "And can I raise a point at this juncture?"

"It better be good." Roman said, his eyes like hot pokers.

"Why the hell would they just ride up on this guy, just six of them?"

"Ah, ah… the hell you talking about?"

"Pres.," Ugly Jesus said, "we told them this bug was not going to be easy to kill. Instead of raining down on this guy with AKs and boomsticks, they came up on him with handguns."

Darius rubbed his fingers together. "My guess, they wanted the money for themselves, so the minute they got the word of the ten mil, they scatted with zero preparation."

"That cheapskate Sax, he's still got his communion money under his mattress," Axl added.

"Ah, ah… he always was one cheap SOB." Roman smirked for the first time, thinking about the time they were at Sturgis and Sax brought his sleeping bag, planning on going to sleep in the dirt with the scorpions to save money.

"Pop," Darius said, "we need to get a strong plan together and take this guy out."

Roman's mouth tightened as he shook his head. "Ah, ah… I can't believe it. You know what this makes me want to do, don't you? This makes me want to go out and nuke the sonofabitch." He paused, then looked to Milo. "Ah, ah… get me a map."

Road Captain Milo rose and went to a battered file cabinet in the corner of the room. From there he retrieved a stack of maps, rifled through them for a moment, then picked one out of the bunch and replaced the rest in the cabinet.

He spread the detailed map of Texas out across the table.

Roman's mannerisms turned calculated. "Ah, ah… where do you think he might be headed?"

Milo placed a finger on the map. "If I was him, I'd probably head up Route 84 toward New Mexico."

"They said he was heading East," Darius interjected.

"Balls to that. If you were running from the FBI, would you head back toward the largest city in Texas? Me personally? I'd head for the damn desert. Right along here." He traced a line along the map heading toward the New Mexican border.

"Ah, ah… now let's talk about a plan so we don't miss killing this sonofabitch a second time."

17

"Ah ah... now let's talk about a plan so we don't miss killing this sonofabitch a second time."

The girl sitting alone in the corner of the coffee shop almost snarfed her latte when she heard this over her earbuds. It was only yesterday that she'd planted the bug in their disgusting clubhouse. She'd gotten the tech from a guy she knew from her MI6 days. All it had taken was a dinner where he thought he had a chance of getting laid for him to fork over one of British Intelligence's most sophisticated listening devices, and give her his password to access the software to use it.

And here she was, listening to these yobbos talking about a plan. She couldn't suppress a chuckle.

"Cor, what a bunch of daft prats," she said to herself in her native British accent.

The two guys at the table adjacent to hers turned their heads at this. She felt their eyes on her, as she had when she walked past them, and then every two minutes after that.

"Hey, sexy," the big one said, "that's quite a nice accent you got there. Where you from, sweetheart?"

She pulled out one earbud. "Sorry?"

"I say, where you from with that accent?"

"Alabama," she said, replacing the ear bud and turning her attention back to the laptop.

She continued listening to the Dogs of Hell, tuning out the droning noise of the two at the next table. They looked over at her, and a loud laugh pierced the chatter in her ears.

She looked up. They were looking at her with greasy smiles.

She pulled an earbud out. "Are you two looking to be a nuisance?"

"I'm looking to hear you talk dirty to me in that sweet voice. Kind of a bucket list thing. You mind helping me out with that?" the big one said, followed by a chittering laugh from his crony.

"Listen," she said calmly, "perhaps some other day, yeah? Right now, I'm in the middle of something important."

"Oo, I say," the smaller one said in the worst British accent anyone had ever attempted.

She pulled out her other earbud. "If I throw a stick, will the two of you go chase it?"

The big one's mouth distended in mock indignation. "Whoa, good one!"

With a snarl of disgust, she closed her laptop and began gathering her things. "Unreal, this country."

"This is America, honey," the big one said. "Keep your knickers on."

Her things in hand, she walked by them, knowing exactly what was about to transpire next. As if on cue, the big one grabbed her bum.

In anticipation, she grabbed his hand. Specifically, she grabbed a pressure point just opposite his palm.

He drew a sharp breath, his eyes bulging, his mouth in a painful yawn. A small sound came from his throat.

"Now let's see if I can fill that bucket list for you, yeah?" she said calmly. She turned her voice sexy. "Do you like how that hurts, darling? Oh darling, tell me how much you like it to hurt..." She applied more pressure. "It hurts like a bugger, doesn't it?" She turned to the smaller one. "Do you want to get in on this pain, big boy? Make it a threeway?"

The smaller one, paralyzed, staring dumbly, nodded no.

She smiled. "I hope it was as good for you as it was for me, honey."

With that, she threw the hand onto his half-eaten omelet, cracking the plate beneath it.

As if reacting on instinct, he sprang up. The move surprised her. Perhaps she was losing her touch. That little pressure point move usually incapacitated them. The meathead tackled her around the waist, causing her laptop to drop and lose a few keys.

In her peripheral vision, she caught sight of a patron ready to help her.

Not today, Judge Dredd. But thanks.

She used the meathead's own momentum against him, moving herself back and to the side, throwing him to the floor. She then walked over and slowly pierced his palm with her heel. She had them made special for just such an occasion. As an added bonus, they happened to be damned sexy.

He yowled in pain, struggling to get her to release, going so far as to chomp his jaws at her leg in an effort to bite her.

"Down, boy! Down!" she said, punctuating the last syllable by kicking his nose with her free foot. With that same foot, she stepped on his hand and withdrew the spike.

As he twisted and cried, she removed her heel and swiped it across his shirt a few times, leaving behind several thin, messy smears of his blood.

"Go home, clean up, and forget about me, darling. I'm thinking I'm no good for you," she said, then collected her broken laptop and left to applause from some rather easily entertained coffee shop patrons.

18

The low, deep-throated, *potato-potato-potato-potato* rumble of his Harley at 70-plus decibels made Bic feel like he was calling for everyone to look at him as he rolled into the parking lot of Tio Bobby's Diner just off Route 66. The bike charismatically announced its presence. He could definitely see the appeal for someone who wanted that type of attention, but this was the opposite of what he was looking to achieve. He'd made the chess move of skirting onto 66 from 84, figuring that his pursuers would expect him to avoid the storied highway. Once over the border, he'd called Parelli, and was given this spot.

The place sat on the edge of one of the pockets of civilization that dot the landscape every five miles or so. Bic stopped the bike, taking care to avoid raising too much of a dust cloud out of the unpaved lot. Tio Bobby's was a tiny little hole, one of those places that probably served the best damned huevos rancheros on the planet and only three people on earth knew of it, proud to keep the secret to themselves.

Parelli had told him to keep an eye out for his Mercedes. Bic had once witnessed the tank, stunned at Parelli's resources and a little perplexed at how the man thought he'd ever need such a vehicle. But ultimately, he knew in their business, one day it would come.

A bug appeared on the horizon and grew slightly, turning into a blinding dot of sunlight. It came into focus. It was the black tank alright. Bic shook his head.

The vehicle pulled in, bringing a cloud with it that damn near choked out the sunlight. Parelli got out.

Sometimes you can read a man's mind in his walk.

Parelli was stooped, defeated. He walked as if his legs were weighted. His arms hardly moved. His face was older, more decrepit. He was like an old mafia don dying in prison, having lost his entire empire, as well as his notoriety. He was a walking dead man fueled by hate.

He stepped up to Bic without a word. He looked like he was searching for something to say.

"She's gone," he said at last, tears in his eyes.

Bic knew right away that the man had not even paused to consider the fate of his wife until this very moment. Knowing Parelli, the man probably hadn't thought of anything else but revenge. And now, face to face with his old friend, he finally allowed himself the luxury of grief.

He fell into Bic's arms and wept silently.

Over a chipped mug of excellent coffee, Parelli had just recounted the entire grisly story, from discovering the hit on Bic to the home invasion to its fiery conclusion.

"She was an amazing woman, Tony."

"I'm gonna kill every last one of those *stugots*. I give you my word on that."

"Where would we even start?"

"It's on the back of your jacket," Parelli said flatly. "I had my guys do some diggin' on the Dogs of Hell on my way over. They got 17 chapters, heavy in Cali. They got presence in every major city across the Southwest, all the way into Texas. They're not the largest motorcycle gang in the country, but they're known to be willing to get their hands real dirty. The leader of the gang is a guy named Roman Dog. Ex-military. At least one or two stints in prison. His son is Darius Dog, a kind of Michael Corleone-type genius. Word has it, if it wasn't for the son's instinct, they'd all be locked up by now."

Bic nodded his head carefully, taking in the information.

"They take low-level hits," Parelli continued between sips of coffee. "They actually have fun with it. They've built a reputation of being real sickos."

"Why go after you?" Bic asked.

Parelli's mouth twisted into a strange half-smile. "To make *you* more vulnerable." Parelli leaned forward but was interrupted by a server with an armload of plates.

"One omelet with bacon and pepper jack, and one huevos rancheros. Can I get you gentlemen anything else?"

"No, thanks," Bic said, avoiding eye contact.

Parelli leaned in again. "What do you think their strategy is, Bic? They know about you and want you isolated. They are going to take everyone out who surrounds you, leave you naked in the cold, then put you in the ground." Parelli picked up his fork and cleared his throat wryly, his brown eyes narrowed to slits. "But, whoever they are, Bic, they've gravely underestimated who we are."

Parelli shoveled a heaping fork load of omelet into his mouth. Bic dug into his huevos rancheros. True to form, they were the best things he'd ever tasted.

"What's next?" he said.

Staring down at his plate, Parelli shrugged. "What's next is not the question, my friend." He looked up at Bic, the resolve of absolute revenge coated in his voice. "The question is *who*."

Bic waited for Parelli to continue as he shoveled more food into his mouth.

"The who I've been thinking about a lot," Parelli said as he continued to chew. "The hit is for two billion. I've got eyes on the twenty-two ."

Parelli didn't need to explain the meaning behind that number. The twenty-two hits that Bic was wanted for by the FBI as a USUB, all linked together by a pork chop left at the scene. Bic's identity was discovered when FBI agent Max Maddox figured it out.

"Even though all of those hits were underworld types," Parelli continued, "none of them have two billion laying around. So that leads us to the nine."

It was another number Parelli didn't need to explain. The nine wealthiest families in the country. Eleven more graves Bic had personally carved.

"Any one of those can have the coin," Parelli said. "But I've had eyes on them as well. Money in and money out. Nothing on this scale."

"Could be a conspiracy," Bic said, his voice low.

Parelli nodded. "Could be. I could have my guys checking for corresponding end points of cash flows. If more than one flow is emptying into the same spot, that could be a lead." The man's eyes changed in an instant. They became stony and dark, with a dead glare to them that turned Bic's heart cold. "But," he said with an emptiness that matched his expression, "I think our first order of business is debt collection. Second order, we cripple the organization. Then we can get Roman and Darius. Bottom up and then top down. That's our strategy. I'll personally beat Roman with a crowbar until he squeals."

There was no hatred in Parelli's voice now. It was colder than hate. It was business, pure and simple. The business of blood for blood.

As for Bic, there was a sensation he'd never felt. Everything was in perspective. These little men on this ball of dirt, him included, were warring over the land--a little slice of mud they could claim as their own for a short time. That was it. Try as he might, Bic couldn't find it in his heart to feel any real animosity toward whoever it was that had put the hit on him. It was the circle of life. It was to be expected.

But a friend was a friend. Parelli had been there for him more times than he could count, and that stood for something in the heart of Bic Green. He thought of Gracie, about how everything he'd ever done in his life was in service of protecting that one, sweet soul. The rest of them were damned. Parelli had helped her too. He owed it to this man sitting across from him, this defeated, decrepit, mournful old man.

"So, we're on the offense," Bic said. "What's the next move?"

Parelli put down his fork and folded his hands.

It was obvious he'd given this *a lot* of thought.

19

About an hour East of Albuquerque, just North of Route 66, was a town that the world had forgotten about, one with the long, seedy history of a place where outlaws go to hide. Years back, Roman Dog was one of those outlaws, passing through town hunting a man down. He came across a group of bikers laying low after a heist. Roman and a man given the nickname "Saint Steve" hit it off, and the rest was history. A DOH chapter was formed that would be responsible, along with the Tucson DOH chapter, for being the organization's mainline of drugs into the US from the Mexican border.

Under the setting sun, the AMG G65 rolled into this ghost town. Since they'd eaten, they made one stop in Tucumcari, where a contact of Parelli's supplied them with everything they needed for this particular operation. The talk between them was specific: Parelli wanted revenge. Bic grew steadily more and more concerned about the air his friend was giving off. Pheromones of danger. Every physical movement of Parelli's, right down to his nibbling at a hangnail on his pinky, seemed bent toward his new, dark purpose that had swallowed up his soul.

"Up there," was the single phrase Parelli uttered, accompanied by a motion of the chin.

Vandals and time had ravaged the entire little town with equal severity. The crumbling stone structure Parelli had motioned toward stood isolated from the other ruined buildings in the area. It was obvious the one they were headed toward had once been the local jail. And if it wasn't for the collection of motorcycles out front, no one would have any idea this was the headquarters of the local chapter of the Dogs of Hell.

Heavy metal music blared from within. Perfect cover.

Spach looked over to his fellow Dog, a fifty-something by the name of Sicko, sitting beneath a rather enterprising woman half his age. The poor thing was trying hard, working just for the free drugs. There were plenty of ladies in the club tonight, though most had a good bit more mileage than this one. That's why Spach had had his eye on her from the get-go.

"Hey! Pass the bitch!" a stoned-out-of-his-gourd Spach yelled from his seat on the stone bench. Several women hopped off the men they were straddling, including Spach's female. They all went to the bar—some half-clothed—for shots of tequila that were waiting for them. Instead of licking salt, the DOH did their shots a little differently. There were white lines of coke next to the shot. For many, it was the sixth or seventh shot for the night. They all snorted their lines, took the shot, and then bit the lime. Heads were bopping, devil horns high with hoots and hollers as Black Sabbath's 'Iron Man' riff began on the boom box.

Spach was just undoing his pants, his heart beating fast—maybe it was from the coke or maybe the hot girl he was about to get freaky with—when the wooden door—the one he'd proudly built when DOH claimed this abandoned old jail house as their own—slowly began to creep open.

A large black man entered, brandishing a Heckler & Koch 9mm submachine gun.

It was Spach's habit, when confronting the unusual, to think coldly about the problem. But there was something about this scene unfolding before him that caused his mind to react in a slightly different way.

High as a kite, the first thing that went through his mind was, "Damn, I want one of those for Christmas."

"Nobody move!" Bic growled. His gaze fell on the mp3 player that was connected to a set of high-end speakers mounted in the corners of the large room. And even though his baritone voice had cut through the music, he figured he'd rather not have it. He turned the gun on the player and opened fire. A rapid spit of bullets put a halt to 'Iron Man' in a split second. And it had the effect of clearing the space around the thing pretty fast.

Screams came from the women, followed by shouts from the men telling them to shut the hell up.

Bic caught sight of a biker charging him with a knife in his right peripheral vision. He turned and opened fire. The guy dropped in a misty spray of blood. A command came from a single voice that destroyed all the others.

"Sit tight, Dogs!"

It had to be the leader.

"Good advice," Bic said calmly. "Anyone who moves, it won't end well for you."

A man came forth, his hands up. "Easy does it, big guy. I'm Saint Steve. What's your beef that you're coming in here with that type of hardware?"

"My friend's wife."

Saint Steve looked around with a chuckle. "She's not in here is she?"

Bic shook his head. "He just has some questions."

"Okay, I'm sure I can help, where is he?"

"The women need to get out first."

A tiny chorus of pleas rose from the females in the group.

"Calm down!" Saint Steve yelled. He looked at Bic. "How do you wanna handle this?"

"I want the ladies to come with me," Bic said. "I'll bring them outside and my partner will come in and you can talk."

"Why can't they stay in here? Your partner don't like ladies? Is that what kind of partner he is?"

The bikers laughed.

Bic smirked. "Something like that."

"Just so I got this, you're going to take the girls outside, then your friend is going to come in here and ask some questions?"

"That's right."

Saint Steve kept his eyes fixed on Bic. Then that strange smile on his face grew into a delighted smirk. "I want everything that has a vagina to follow Blade here outside. Now!"

Slowly at first, and then quickly, the girls grabbed what clothes they could and corralled behind Bic, who was blocking the door. He took a half step forward to let them pass, all the while keeping watch on the men, moving his gun from side to side in a slow sweep.

Once the place was empty of women, Bic backed up until he was standing in the stone threshold of the doorway.

He backed out and closed the door.

20

Did he really just back out of here and close the door behind him? Or am I so high I'm just seeing things? Spach thought as he watched the huge dude with the dark glasses back out of the place. He felt no fear, only confusion. He was ready for a fight, as he knew instinctively there was going to be one. Poor Sicko had bought it in a blaze of glory, or so the old bastard probably thought in his last dying seconds.

Seconds after the door closed, the DOH, led by Saint Steve, scrambled in the silence to get their hands on a weapon. Luckily, they were everywhere. None of the thirteen outlaws had his weapon of choice, but considering ten seconds ago they'd had an automatic rifle pointed at them with nothing in their hands, a random assortment of handguns and two shotguns felt like a decent upgrade right about now.

Spach took aim with a pistol. "I'm gonna light this dude up if he's stupid enough to walk through that door."

"Yeah, for Sicko," another Dog said, taking cover behind a table and readying his weapon.

"Whatever walks through that door, were going to fill it with lead," Saint Steve commanded in a low, even tone. He'd turned toward the group, deadly seriousness in his eyes. "He's a dead man."

What was twenty seconds had already felt like an hour to Spach as he stared at the door like it was a portal to the unknown. *Was this guy going to just walk back in and get shot?*

Just as Spach's anxiety about the door was building, it opened at a slow and steady speed to reveal nothing. Just that outside, the sun had set and it was nighttime.

The men were ready for anything. It was going to be killed the second it walked through that door.

What they didn't expect was a hellish *wooshing* sound, followed by what could best be described by Spach as the roar of a dragon, as a thirty-foot flame shot through the door and into the room.

The two men on a direct line in front of the door, even though deep into the room, were ravaged as if a fiery god had sentenced them to a 3000-degree punishment.

A man dressed like some kind of sci-fi spaceman walked the flame deeper into the room. A couple of shots were fired at the man, but it didn't slow him down a bit as he did a left to right side of the room.

Spach felt the first blast of heat from the thing as the flames began on the left side of the room. Before they made it to his side, he dove beneath a sun bench built into the wall, the same one Sicko was perched on while trying in vain to get it up for that little tease. Spach pulled his knees to his chest and there he lay, a fetal biker feeling the heat from a spray of hellfire and hearing the screams of men as they burned.

His mind raced. The only other exits were barred with ancient rods of iron. He noticed two helmets on the ground. He grabbed them both, put one on and used the other as feeble cover for his knees, which were sticking out of the bottom of the bench. *Funny*, Spach thought, *that helmet's got a flame design on it. I almost got that on mine.*

His nostrils filled with the stench of burning flesh and spent fuel. It was a sickly combination, like jet exhaust at a pig roast. He felt his lungs constricting.

If he could just wait it out till the next spray of flames passed, he could roll out of here and make a run. He'd come up against that goon with the gun, but so be it. It was better than burning.

It was like timing a lawn sprinkler. A continuous spray of fire fanned across the room from one side to the other and back again. There were no more screams, just the end of the world and the smell of death. And searing heat.

It was over now. Bodies were burning all around him in a monotonous roar.

Now was his moment. He rolled out, narrowly missing the glowing ember body of one of his now-former clubmates. *Interesting*, he thought, *the body looks like a turd.*

He got to his feet and was about to make his way to the door when the figure appeared before him, looking like a sci-fi angel of death.

"Welcome to hell," it said.

Light. Heat. More heat. Pain beyond belief.

The girls, panicked and hysterical, had fled at the sight of Parelli igniting the flamethrower. Bic allowed them to go. Some hopped on bikes while others took off into the dark, unforgiving desert.

Parelli emerged from the building, turned, and filled the doorway with one last gush of fire. He stared into his finished work of utter destruction for a moment, then turned away.

He took off his helmet and face shield. His face was sweaty, his hair comically matted in some places and spiked in others. He stared silently at Bic, his dark brown eyes void of emotion.

"The girls?" he asked numbly, removing his body armor suit.

"Gone," Bic said.

"They saw your face, you know."

"That's the last thing I'm worried about," Bic said, motioning toward the flaming grave that was once the old jail. "It's time for us to go."

Parelli squinted at the stone building with its flames lapping through the barred windows. "This is just the beginning."

That's what I'm most afraid of, Bic thought to himself.

21

Nathaniel stared at his computer screen in horror. He got up, paced around the room once, then sat back down and stared. Then he got back up and repeated the process. He'd been doing this for the last hour, non-stop.

Bitcoin was going down hard.

He was now doing mental calculations obsessively. He'd already paid 100 million up front. Now, due to the price drop, that left him with 900 million. And in three days, 1.9 *billion* would be due in escrow.

He was a billion dollars short.

"Come on," he said, his voice wracked with angst, "go up... go *up*..." He picked the laptop up off the desk and shook it. "Come *on!*"

He had to get ahold of himself. Otherwise he'd be short one billion and one laptop. This thought reignited the fire of anxiety in his belly and he placed the thing gingerly onto the desk. He got up again and paced.

There was only one solution right now. He paced a bit more, trying to come up with the words. After formulating an idea made up of broken sentences, he sat back down and logged into the Tor browser.

He navigated over to the private messaging service he and his broker had agreed upon and began:

Hey, a little problem here. I had the money all set to go into escrow and I don't know if you saw it but the price of Bitcoin is dropping like a bitch. Will you take 900 mil?

He stared at the message, his finger hovering over the enter button.

Here goes. He tapped it and off the message went.

He got up from his seat, anxiety so bad his right eye had begun to twitch. He held up his hands. They were visibly shaking. His palms were clammy.

He looked over at the message box. Three dots had appeared. A message was coming through. Nathaniel felt his heart in his throat. The reply popped up:

That is unfortunate.

He felt his heart sink back down into his chest and keep going. He put his trembling fingers on the keys, trying to think of a reply.

Another three dots appeared. Nathaniel froze, then withdrew his hands.

The message appeared:

1.9 BILLION IN THREE DAYS OR YOUR FAMILY IS DEAD

Nathaniel sat back, feeling as though he was about to pass out. He clapped the laptop shut and began to cry.

22

Silence was key to the element of surprise. Silence and brutality.

Bic lay on his belly, the crossbow steadied, watching Parelli.

The DOH of Mesa Arizona had taken over a tiny sports bar called "Dougie's" and converted it into their own private headquarters. No one went to Dougie's for a drink anymore, and if they did, they stood a very poor chance of leaving the place satisfied.

Dougie's stood as part of a small complex within a strip of four stores, two of which were closed. The only other one in business was a real estate office that rumor had it was merely a front for a prostitution ring. But the land was still cared for by the landlord. Parelli's homework had revealed as much. And so it was very little trouble for him to procure a pair of overalls and set aside a few minutes to perfect his best Mexican accent. These idiots wouldn't know the difference anyway.

He set about in his disguise with a weed whacker, working the perimeter of the building. A couple of Dogs had exited the building and were chatting it up in the sun. They paid him no mind as he stooped down and yanked up a couple of weeds, placing them in a bag.

He went along methodically until he reached the DOH building.

"Get lost, beaner," said one.

Parelli looked pleadingly at the men. "Senor Garrone, he say… he say to plant and pull weed."

"You can pull my weed and get lost."

His buddy tapped his arm. "Let him go. We don't wanna mess with Garrone."

It was just as Parelli had expected. Dave Garrone was the landlord of this lovely strip who accepted a nice fat wad of cash by both the

DOH and the real estate business in order to keep things as tidy as possible. Literally and figuratively. In the literal sense, that meant a periodic beautifying of the place so as not to draw too much attention down on it from the city.

Parelli bowed sycophantically and went back to the ratty pickup truck he'd bought for a song first thing this morning. From there he retrieved a battered case and a few gardening tools.

He went back to where the bikers were, feeling Bic's eyes on him the entire time.

"Senor, please..." he said to them, motioning. "I plant... I plant..."

"Go on and do it, then!" the first guy said belligerently.

Parelli bowed again. "Gracias."

He moved behind the men and stooped at the perimeter. There he began to dig with a spade, setting aside clumps of dry, hard dirt.

Good thing these morons knew nothing about gardening. You couldn't even plant a wish in this ground.

But Parelli wasn't planting wishes. He opened his battered metal case and pulled out a brick of C4, which he stuck into the hole he'd just excavated. He took out a plastic baby cactus--99 cents at Walmart--and stuck it on top for camouflage.

He moved over a foot or so and repeated the process. Then again.

"Hey!" said the nuisance who'd been harassing him. "What the hell are those?"

"Is plants," Parelli said.

"Yeah, no. What's that underneath?"

Parelli looked perplexedly at his work. "Is plants," he repeated.

"*Underneath* the plants, dumbass!"

The biker moved in, crouched down, and yanked up the plastic plant, uncovering the block of C4 in the process.

"What the..." the biker said, shooting back up while simultaneously pulling a large hunting knife from its sheath. "This guy's planting C—"

An arrow came through his neck at that very moment, cutting off his speech in a gurgling mess of gibberish before he could take a stab at Parelli.

"What?" the other said, just as he was struck in the eye with an identical arrow.

This ended the silent portion of the strategy. Now it was on to the brutality portion.

Parelli turned on his weed whacker to cover the gurgling screams of the men. It would be over soon, but not soon enough. Parelli gave the signal, and Bic fired two more arrows each into both men. Parelli turned off the weed whacker. Silence again.

He made short work of the final C4 plant--no need for camouflage now.

The blasting caps in place, he retreated to where Bic lay with his weapon. Dressed in desert camouflage, he looked like he'd just returned from a tour in Syria.

"Nice shot," Parelli said, crouching down to Bic's level. "All set for Phase Two?"

Bic switched out his crossbow for an AR-15 and nodded.

Parelli picked up a matching gun and readied for the explosion.

A mere typing of a code into a burner phone sent a radio signal to the blasting caps, and it was a messy damnation for the DOH chapter of Mesa, Arizona.

The place erupted in a mushroom of flame that rose into the sky and blotted out the sun for a moment. The sound nearly collapsed both men's eardrums.

They readied their weapons.

Parelli caught a sight off to the left. Two bikers were speeding up to the place. He tracked them for a moment, then opened fire. The bodies flew from the bikes as if flicked off by a giant finger.

"That's two more. Now it's time for some fish in a barrel," Parelli said.

What he was referring to happened in the next thirty seconds. Bikers began to pour out of the flaming wreckage. They stumbled and fell. Some were in flames and were rolling on the ground.

Parelli wasted no time, opening fire on any and all movement outside that bar. He mowed down rolling bodies and upright ones alike. He even plugged away at the bodies that lay still on the ground.

Parelli's rifle fire filled Bic's ears. With every additional pop, Bic watched the massacre, but he hadn't fired one shot.

When it was done, Parelli kept firing. Bodies exploded on the ground.

He took another shot and *POW,* a still body on the ground burst in a spray of red.

"That one's deader than dead."

"Tony!" Bic said, grabbing his friend's arm. "That's enough."

Parelli looked at him with a sneer. "For what they did. It's not even close to enough."

He took his time taking his gaze off Bic. Then went back and plugged a few more bodies. After about the fifth one, he stopped and put down his weapon. "Now it's enough," he said plainly, as if leaving the last remnant of dessert on the plate after a large meal. "Let's go," he added.

Bic got up and both men headed back toward the Mercedes. Wise choice to leave it back here, as the pickup was now in flames.

Once in the SUV, they stared at the disaster.

"That will send a message," Parelli said.

Bic turned to Parelli for clarification.

"They picked the wrong guys to kill," Parelli said, then put the car in gear and left the mess for the Mesa authorities to deal with.

23

There was something bizarre in Parelli's eyes as they drove. They were dead and yet stirring, a strange mix of life and lifelessness. Bic recognized the look. It was one he'd seen in others, and it was one he himself had shown to the world many times. It was a loop of death men like he and Parelli were trapped in. No matter how hard he'd try to change it, it didn't matter, his past sins had cemented him in this loop. Be killed or kill, and regardless if you make it, people you care about will wind up dead. Now his lifelong friend had him back in this loop of revenge. A loop he had spent the better part of his life in chasing after his father. Somehow, the hit was on him, but because of Tony's own loop of sins, his wife wound up dead. Only God knew what new loops of death and destruction he and his friend would create in the next couple days.

"We're gonna skip the Phoenix chapter," Parelli said as he took the I-10 exit to go east toward Phoenix.

"I'm glad the plan is not to kill everyone," Bic said with hope.

"They'll be expecting us there next," Parelli said as he turned sharply onto the ramp. "So far, we've drawn a neat little line heading straight toward Phoenix. So, we're gonna throw those *stronzos* off, keep them guessing."

Bic kept his eyes out the window. "Don't get me wrong, Tony. I understand your vengeance over Barbara, and feel it too, but what's the end game here?"

"What are you talking about?" Parelli sped onto I-10, cutting in front of a pickup truck, giving the guy the finger immediately after the guy flashed his headlights.

Bic turned to Parelli. "I thought we were going to figure out who's behind this and end it. I'm not in the mood to go on an endless killing spree."

Parelli waved a dismissive hand. "We're just stirring up the worker bees to get the queen bee to come out from hiding. And when we flush that bitch out," Parelli squeezed the steering wheel so tight, he could have choked the life out of it, "sweet revenge I will definitely get."

"Listen, Tony," Bic said, waiting for the man's full attention.

"I'm listening."

"You need to hear me out on this."

"Save the self-righteous bullshit because you've had this religious experience. You may have delusions of purity now, my friend, but you're still not pure. Your past, *our* past, will never let us out."

"I know..." Bic felt a wave of contempt rising in him. "But revenge isn't all it's cracked up to be. It's just an endless dark path. Please, Tony, trust me here, you think there's light at the end of the tunnel, but the damn darkness is just sitting there waiting for you." Bic clenched his fists, his forearm muscles bulging. "It's waiting there every-damn-time."

"Alright, enough, I get it. I'll go to church when this is over. Until then, it's an eye for an eye all the way."

Bic pounded the dash with his fist. "You're not listening, instead of killing the evil you're after, you're just feeding it. And it'll grow bigger and bigger until it's all you're left with."

Parelli looked at him and shook his head slowly. "When did you become such a self-righteous pussy?"

The two men glared at each other in the type of way men do right before someone throws the first punch.

"I'm still waiting for the word 'cat' at the end of that sentence," Bic said, smirking.

Parelli cracked a smile. "Fine, when did you become such a pussycat?"

The men laughed.

Parelli swerved into the right lane to pass the vehicle in front of them, "Here's where you don't give yourself enough credit, Bic. You beat the darkness. You were man enough to stay on that dark path until you killed that SOB."

Bic turned his head back to the road. The road swished by in a dusty brown blur. He felt an ugly sensation in him, not unlike the rage that used to rise up and take over his entire being. Now it was rage mixed with fear and dread. It made him want to vomit.

"You okay?" Parelli said with genuine concern.

Bic breathed heavily through his nose, leaving little patches of fog on the window.

"Bic?" Parelli repeated. He tapped Bic's leg. "You look like your head's about to explode. What's going on?"

"I see him."

"Him? Who him?"

He turned back to Parelli. "Clarence."

"You're seeing your father."

"A couple times now."

Parelli nodded, turning his attention back to the road. "Just your mind playing tricks on you friend, that's all."

"You don't know what that man's capable of."

Parelli shifted uncomfortably in his seat. "Your father is dead."

"Maybe, maybe not." Bic rolled down the window for some air.

"What do you mean, maybe not?"

Bic ran a dry tongue over his lips. "I left him hanging upside down in the swamp."

Parelli turned to him, a perplexed look on his face. "You mean after almost fifty years of wanting to kill that man you didn't watch the gator tear his every last limb?"

"I felt a peace within, I didn't need to see it. I heard the splash, but—"

The men looked at each other, Bic deep in thought.

"My father used to keep a knife strapped to his ankle. He could have--"

Parelli waved him off. "Aw, come on, Bic."

"He could have cut himself loose. That splash could have been him falling into the water."

"Aw, hell, Bic. The one person you actually wanted to kill and you..." Parelli shook his head, his mouth holding a grim line in the center of his stubble.

Bic turned back to the road.

Parelli was silent for a full minute, then finally spoke. "Listen."

Bic was silent.

"Your father is dead. Unless there are such things as zombies. Which, let's face it, if anyone can become a zombie, it's *that* rotten son of a bitch. But more than likely," he rolled his hand in the air, searching for the word, "it's an apparition. You know? Like guys we knew when they came back from war. They see stuff, right?"

"Maybe," Bic said, noticing a bug that appeared in his side-view mirror.

"Remember all the crap they used to see? They thought it was all real, but it wasn't."

The bug grew larger. "What'd you say?"

"It wasn't real."

"I think we might have company."

"What is it?" Parelli looked into his rearview mirror. "Another biker rat?"

Parelli reached for the hand cannon tucked between the seat and the center console.

"You don't need that," Bic said, "I'm sure it's just an apparition."

Parelli didn't answer. Instead, he gunned the Mercedes. And Bic kept a watchful eye on the movements of the fast-approaching motorcycle behind them.

24

Parelli slowed the vehicle, allowing the motorcycle to catch up. Bic readied his weapon. "We really should try to get this guy to talk."

Parelli smirked as he clicked off the safety button. "Sure thing Bic."

Bic kept a keen focus on the fast-approaching motorcycle.

"Shoot that rat right between the eyes."

Bic leaned to the side view mirror. "*What?*"

"What is it?"

"He's waving."

Parelli pulled the AMG onto the shoulder and crawled to a stop. The motorcycle followed in lock-step. The rider pulled off his helmet.

"Hawk," Bic said.

"Say again?" Parelli said, his voice wracked with confusion.

Hawk sidled up onto the driver's side. "Whatd'ya say, besties? Whoo-wee! Fine day for a ride!"

Breathing a heavy sigh of relief, Parelli relaxed in his seat. "You dumbass."

"What?" a confused Hawk said.

Bic leaned forward. "You nearly got yourself blown in half."

"Gnarly! You serious?"

"Considerin' what's going down, you think rolling up on us with a motorcycle is a good idea?" Parelli said with annoyance.

"Got to keep you old men on your toes, that's all."

Good ol' Hawk, Bic thought. Still stuck in the 80s. Even after all those head surgeries, he still kept his professionally styled mullet, spiky on top, long and bushy in the back.

"Well," Hawk said, scratching the baby chick fuzz on his head, "I don't know about you gentlemen, but I could go for a veggie wrap. There's a totally awesome diner just off this exit here."

Parelli looked at Bic, who shrugged by way of response.

"Hell, I'll pay," Hawk said.

Bic motioned toward the exit.

"You seem like you've recovered pretty well," Bic said, leaning back in the banquet and raising his coffee cup to his lips.

Hawk gestured his sandwich. "Mostly."

Bic was surprised at how matter-of-fact Hawk seemed with this particular subject. Hawk's run-in with the Farmer was no joke. By all accounts, the man sitting before him waving his whole wheat veggie wrap like he was using it to land a plane should have been dead by now.

"I still get stiff, and not in a good way. Although that's returned in full force. The ladies of the American South are grateful for that. And I wake up every morning with an aching back until I get up and realize it's actually my legs that are hurting. And I got a ringing in my ears that's tuned to G-flat and won't ever stop. Other than that, life's been good."

"Sorry I let that happen," Bic muttered into his cup.

Hawk smiled at Bic, letting him know he wouldn't have had it any other way, then wiped his mouth with his napkin and dropped it on the table. "If you boys don't mind, I gotta go find a tree." With this, he got up and headed toward the bathroom.

Noticing the man's slight limp as he walked, Bic shook his head. "That's a good man right there."

"Pure as snow." Parelli sipped his coffee, instinctually his eyes scanned the diner for danger.

"Why didn't you tell me you contacted him?"

"I didn't think the nutbag would stalk us and nearly get himself killed."

"You think it's wise he's involved in this?" Bic said.

"What do you mean?"

"You don't think he's been through enough?"

Parelli leaned in. "Not for nothing, Bic, but Hawk felt kinda slighted when he found out about your trouble in New Orleans. He wanted to know why you didn't call on him for help."

"Really? That's his gripe?"

"That's true friendship, my friend."

Bic shook his head. "He's been through enough. I mean, I'm happy he's here. But he's been through enough."

"Relax."

Hawk returned. "Whoo-wee, a piss is one of life's greatest rewards for keeping the body healthy. You boys talking about me?"

"I don't want you involved," Bic said, "but Parelli here seems to think you can handle yourself."

Hawk's face went grave. "I can, Bic. What's the matter, man? Did I do anything to offend you?"

"It's not like that."

"Then what is it?"

Bic stared at him for a hot moment. "You took a beating for me and Gracie, and I am forever indebted to you for it, but—"

"But what? You think I'm not capable of physically helping?"

"Nothing like that. I think I'm the one that should be doing you the next favor, that's all." Bic reached over the table and put his hand on Hawk's shoulder. "I owe you everything and I don't just want to keep taking from you."

"Let me ask you something, Bic. Is there a limit to the times you'd stop showing up for me?"

Bic shook his head.

"Then why should there be a limit for the times I show up for you?"

"Bic," Parelli said, "How about this. We'll do the dirty work while Hawk stays at a safe distance. He'll be our ace in the hole, the wizard behind the curtain keeping an eye on our backs for us as he always was."

Hawk stared, a slight smirk on his face. He spread his palms as if waiting for an answer.

Bic nodded. "I love you, my friend."

She opted for a red wig that fell over her shoulders in a smooth splash. And she really did up the makeup this time, going for cherry red lips--no smear, and perfect for blowing bubblegum bubbles. Her five-inch heel Gladiators probably weren't the best choice, but what the hell; they were red and they were hot. She kept her ear buds in and her horn-rimmed shades on as she strutted from car to car in the diner parking lot, placing yellow flyers on each windshield that advertised BIG BILL'S CARWASH--LOW LOW PRICES!!! PRESENT THIS FLYER FOR HALF OFF!!!

She hummed along with the music in her ears. Bach's Partita in E Major, Third Movement.

She got to the matte-black Mercedes G65 AMG. The heels came in handy here as she reached up and placed the flyer on its windshield. She took note that the glass was at least an inch thick, as opposed to your typical windshield at a quarter of an inch. A dead giveaway that it was bulletproof. With the owner paying over two-hundred K for the car, she assumed he spared no expense going with the glass-clad polycarbonate layered construction, a design, when this thick, would protect against high-powered rifle ammunition.

Finally, some professionals, she thought as she went around to the back, her strut never faltering. There she purposely dropped some of the flyers. As she bent down to pick them up, she fumbled the paper around for a second, giving her time to discreetly place a tracking beacon under the rear passenger's side bumper.

Two cars down, two men sat in a dusty pickup, looking like they'd just gotten off the line. Construction tools were heaped like hoarded garbage in the bed. They were ogling her, passing comments back and forth. She moved carefully toward the vehicle, never slowing her pace. When she got to it, she handed the flyer to the driver.

"Hello yourself," he said, a slick smile on his face.

She blew an immense bubble and allowed it to pop on her lips and chin. She licked off the remains of it in one swoop, gnawed on it noisily for a moment, then removed the gum from her mouth with her thumb and forefinger. By now, as expected, both men were hypnotized. She placed the gum in the driver's gaping mouth and he chewed it slowly. She left them there and returned to her car, humming.

25

Bitcoin had fallen another nineteen percent. Nathaniel's stash was down to 729 million. No small sum, but peanuts considering what he'd started out with--and what he was now short. He needed to recover 1.17 billion. And all indications pointed to the fact that Bitcoin was going to fall even more in the next couple days.

Nathaniel needed help. For the last several hours he'd fallen into an Internet hole researching how to recover from crypto losses. Maybe there was something he was missing, a way he could play the market into performing to his advantage. His searches led him to a YouTuber with 1.25 million followers, who sprang out of a cheesy coffin in front of an obvious green screen projection of the classic Tales From the Crypt TV series. His street cred had risen significantly with Nathaniel since watching him these last couple of days. He had been predicting the massive drop of Bitcoin. If Nathaniel had listened, he would have saved a billion dollars! The show about to go live was titled, "Buy the Rumor, Sell the News—Bart Simpson pattern confirmed...R. I. P."

> "Hey guys, it's me, the Crypto-keeper, here with everything... you need... to know... about crypto. We got a great show for you today, but first, if you like making money in crypto, smashy-smash that like and subscribe button for me. Also, don't forget to follow me on Twitter. @Crypto_Keeper3. Go to it. Now let's do it. Buy the rumor, sell the news, Bart Simpson. Here's what you need to do right now to recover. Of course not investment advice. Do your own research."

Nathaniel sat before his laptop watching the man gesticulate before the camera, graphics popping up in ADD succession around him.

Nathaniel quickly learned what it was all about. A certain type of investor buys a coin on rumors of that coin's impending rise—say, a partnership or some other major investor making a whale-type purchase. This generates a buzz that causes retail investors to go in. When the price inflates, everyone goes all FOMO and recklessly piles into the coin at any price. What these retail investors don't know is that Big Money is selling it to them. Then, when the news breaks that it was just all a big nothing burger, the coin falls in price and investors sell off in a frenzy.

"You guys have no doubt heard the recent news of Bitcoin dropping like crazy…"

Nathaniel's ears perked up.

"The retail investors once again fell victim to the classic pump and dump by institutions and whales. Not our community though, I've kept you guys safe from the Crypto-Reeper."

A huge, animated grim reaper character popped onto the screen and cut the head off a cartoon donkey with its eyes crossed, presumably a clueless retail investor.

"The institutions wanted you to think a spot Bitcoin ETF was being approved this week and then found out that it was bogus. We all know the SEC is in the pocket of the big banks. Then comes the FUD, and when investors found this out, they dumped their Bitcoin like a cheating spouse…"

A big tombstone with "Bitcoin R.I.P" writing on it appeared on the screen. Below the tombstone was Bitcoin's price chart.

"For my loyal followers, I've been banging on my coffin about this Bart Simpson pattern forming. Now I have no doubt…"

He pulled up Bitcoin's bear market chart from 2018. Its pattern looked just like an outline of the cartoon character profile.

"Just like in the bear market of 2018, Bart Simpson is confirmed."

"What happened last time, and what the charts are showing me support the notion that we have a minimum of another forty percent down in Bitcoin from here. But, I got my loyal listeners out before then! If you're new to the channel or didn't act on my info you still have time to save your asses."

"C'mon guys, we have only nine hundred likes and fourteen thousand watching. Crypto-Keeper is bringing the alpha every day. Smash those likes and—I tell you what—if we get to 5,000 likes—I'm gonna do it. I'm going to share with you guys a little known ALT coin even before I buy it that's gonna 10X in the next couple of days! When I tell you it's a can't miss, you know it's the goods! Of course, not financial advice and do your own research."

Nathaniel watched the likes on the live feed and smashed it himself. As he watched the likes climb over 2,700, he did the easy math. If he were to invest two-hundred-million and it multiplied by ten, he'd have two billion.

The likes got over 4,200 and he messaged into the chat. "Come on guys, smash those likes! I need this to save my life!"

And then it happened—the likes zoomed past 5,000.

"Hell yeah. I've got the most loyal community in the world! The Keeper Fam is just the best! So even before I buy it or any of the whales, I'm going to get you guys into this alt coin. Everyone knows how corporations are vowing to go green. Well, in order to go green, they need to be carbon neutral. The problem is it's impossible for them to do so in their core business. So, what they are all doing is buying carbon credits. The issue with carbon credits is it is very hard to verify them. It is a super shady business. But that's all about to change with what I believe is going to be one of the first huge use cases for the blockchain. A certain small company has created a decentralized and open market for carbon credits. Guys, it's a digital currency backed by real carbon assets!"

Nathaniel wasn't one to drool, but his mouth was gaping wide open as Crypto-Keeper made the case for how this coin was going to be the world center for climate change. This had to be a sign. His dad had been a huge supporter of the climate movement. He hit the button and sold the two-hundred-million of Bitcoin. He had his order box ready. All he needed was the token and he was all in. This was his Hail Mary to bail him and Lucy out of this mess.

"So, are the most loyal followers in the world ready for the coin that will be at the center of a new green economy? GreenCOIN, token symbol GRN."

Nathaniel typed in the symbol, hellbent on getting this order in as fast as possible before all of Crypto-Keeper's other users. The coin was at 2 cents already, up fifteen percent for the day. He put the order in, and a frenzy of activity followed. The price climbed all the way from two cents to twenty-two cents. He quickly realized he was buying shares with an open market order all the way up. He had purchased 2,150,537,634 coins at an average price of 9.3 cents per coin. Nathaniel smiled as he saw he had already doubled his money in a matter of two minutes from two hundred million to over four hundred and seventy three million.

He did a bit more math and figured he needed GreenCOIN to go up about another 42 cents and he would be back at two billion. By the time he finished his calculation, he looked back up at the screen and it was up another ten cents already.

He sat back in his chair, feeling an odd combination of relief and anxiety, as if the two were sparring for domination inside him with every tick of GreenCOIN's price change.

"Nathaniel?" came the voice from outside his room.

The door opened and Uncle Seth poked his head in.

"Can't you see I'm busy," Nathaniel said, unable to hide his frustration and annoyance.

"Not for this, you're not," his uncle said, barging in with a stack of papers.

The boy stood up. "I don't like people in my room!"

"Your room is in *my house*, you understand? And things that take place in my house concern *me*. You need to get that through your head. Case in point..." He shoved the papers under Nathaniel's nose.

"What about them?"

"I was just about to ask you the same thing."

Nathaniel glanced down and saw to his horror that Uncle Seth had printed out a number of emails discussing the assassination of Bic Green.

Nathaniel rifled through the pages, then handed them back. "It was just a joke."

"Just a joke? You think killing a man is a joke? You're talking about payment here."

"I told you, I was kidding, I don't even have any money!"

"Then how do you explain the FBI agent vehicle transporting Bic Green a couple days ago being attacked by six bikers?"

Nathaniel avoided eye contact with his uncle. "Coincidence? How should I know?"

"The FBI agent is on life support. He was shot in the stomach. If he dies, the person who paid the bikers to kill Bic Green can also be charged with murder. Did you know that?"

"I had nothing to do with that."

Uncle Seth flaunted the papers in front of him, "That's not what these messages convey Nathaniel. A case could easily be made that you were deadly serious. In fact, I think it's pretty obvious you were."

Nathaniel's collarbone flared. "Why can't we just forget about this? I won't send any more messages like that. No one would connect this to me, it's all on the dark web."

"I don't think you understand how powerful you are going to become when you turn eighteen, Nathaniel." Again, he shook the damn papers. "The person you sent these messages to could blackmail you. Or just sell these to a tabloid."

Nathaniel's chin dropped to his chest. "What, now?"

Uncle Seth let out a sigh. "Nathaniel," he said, his voice calm and full of concern, "this is enough to get you thrown in jail for a very long time. At best, it can ruin your life."

All words stopped in the boy's throat.

Uncle Seth dropped the papers to his side. "I'm on your side kiddo, and I think I know the best way to protect you, but I need you to walk straight, you hear?"

Nathaniel nodded his head.

"The best way to get ahead of this is to bring this matter to your father's company…"

Nathaniel picked his head up.

"The boys in your father's legal department are a bunch of sharks. The thing you have going for you is this: since you own the majority of the company, anything that hurts you hurts the company. They will do their best to bury it for sure."

"You sure this is a good idea?"

Uncle Seth nodded. "They've taken on the federal government in antitrust and won, for goodness sakes, they can surely figure this out. I will go to them personally. I'm not sending anything over email. I don't want any record of this. I'll get the nanny to stay with you both overnight while I'm gone. This may take a couple of days."

Nathaniel nodded in agreement. Uncle Seth was making a lot of sense about how his dad's company would definitely protect him. If for no other reason than it was in their best interest to do so.

Uncle Seth spread his arms and received a hug from his nephew.

26

"**D**ude," Hawk said, lowering his binoculars, "are they hiding nuclear secrets in there or something?"

He raised the binocs to his eyes again. Confirmed: the San Diego chapter of the Dogs of Hell was hiding *something* important. Maybe not nuclear secrets, but something.

"They're prepared for an ambush," Bic said.

Hawk looked at him sarcastically. "Wonder why?"

"Might have something to do with Tony barbequing their friends."

"They ain't seen nothin' yet," Parelli said.

The three were flat on their bellies, scoping out the DOH clubhouse. Constructed of tin and located in the middle of a junkyard, it looked a lot like a large mechanic's shop with six garage doors. The door on the end was oversized, big enough for a Mack truck to enter. A brick wall, every bit of ten feet, surrounded the entirety of the lot, save for a fortified front gate. DOH members patrolled the flat roof with automatic weapons, others were stationed outside the closed gate, through which the stealth threesome could see the piles of scrap cars and parts which lay strewn about the place as if dropped from above.

"This place is the Camelot of junkyards," Hawk said. "Any suggestions?"

Parelli lowered his binoculars and thought for a moment. "A couple. What do you suppose is going on in that last garage?"

Hawk took another look. "Which side?"

"The right. They're carrying those sheets of metal into it."

Hawk shrugged. "Custom bikes maybe?"

"They're working awfully hard at dusk, don't you think?"

"Chop shop," Bic said. "Drugs, ammo. You name it."

"I was not expecting this good of a setup from these *momos*," Parelli said, frustration in his voice. "There's gotta be a way in without sounding the alarm bells."

Bic lifted his binocs to his eyes and focused. "There."

Parelli followed suit. "Where?"

"Nine o'clock. See that pile of cars poking a couple of feet above the wall? We can climb over there. That pile of junk will make for some pretty good cover from those shooters on the roof."

"Bic," Hawk said, "you are a fine man and a snappy dresser and all, but your plan kinda stops short of suicide."

Bic looked at his friend.

"No offense, dude," Hawk said, "just sayin', we don't have a lotta wiggle room once we're in. We'd be surrounded."

"Who said you're going in?"

"Hawk's staying put," Parelli said suddenly, belly crawling backwards.

Bic and Hawk exchanged glances and, after a shared shrug, followed him back to the AMG, which was safely camouflaged within an overgrowth of weeds and shrubbery.

Parelli was already enacting his plan, pulling a drone out of the back of the vehicle.

"Mint!" Hawk exclaimed.

Bic stopped and stared. "I hope that thing shoots missiles."

"My stuff's good, but not that good," Parelli said, setting the drone on the ground carefully. "This little baby has four cameras attached to it. Hawk, you'll stay behind and fly it over the place. You'll be able to keep surveillance via my laptop. You'll be safe and Mama Bear Bic here doesn't have to worry about you."

"Um," Hawk began.

"Mama Bear, huh?" Bic said, chuckling.

"Hawk, you'll even get to play a little FBI." Parelli opened a case with sets of ear buds and wrist mics."

"Totally rad," Hawk said, scratching his head. "Does it matter that the one time I flew a drone I crashed it into the neighbor's pool in about twenty-three seconds?"

"What are you saying?"

"I'm saying you'd be better off handing that chore to a jittery crackhead who's missing three fingers."

"It's got an autopilot feature," Parelli said. "Can you handle at least flying it into position?"

"I can handle watching *you* fly it into position."

Parelli looked at Bic. "It's like dealing with a kid."

Bic smiled and turned away. He looked out at the DOH compound in the distance, and his smile disappeared. Why did he feel as though it would be the scene of his last stand on earth?

Hearing a whirring noise behind him, he turned and saw the drone rising into the air. Hawk stood gaping up at it as Parelli manned the controls.

"I can fly this thing into your girlfriend's shower undetected."

"Smells like teen spirit," Hawk said.

Bic was amused. "I see someone's moving into the 90's."

Hawk took his eyes off the drone. "That decade had some good music, I admit it."

"There she goes, gentleman. Say *bon voyage*."

The drone soared high up and over the compound. It became a mere fly speck in the sky as Parelli maneuvered it over the center of the lot.

"And," he said after a moment, "we are on autopilot." He looked at the two men. "And now, gentlemen, the sun is going down. We shall enter Phase Two of the operation."

27

Scaling the wall itself was easy. Both men had served and had done more difficult scaling in their military days. Remaining invisible, that was the hard part. They had the cover of night, but knowing the paranoia of their adversaries, it was a safe bet to assume they had night vision.

"Should have waited till a new moon," Bic whispered. "Or a rainy night."

"Maybe you're right."

Hawk's voice squawked through over their earpieces. "All clear, boys. Nice climbing there. Totally tubular."

"He's gotten worse with that," Bic said.

"The eighties stuff? I agree. Think it was the head injury?"

"Probably not."

"Listen up," Hawk said. "You have a clear path to your left as long as you lay low. You're gonna move in an upside-down J when I say go. About ten seconds until our shooters on the roof are out of position."

"Copy that," Parelli said into his wrist. He looked at Bic. "I'll take the lead. Cover me."

"I got you."

Parelli took a deep breath and let it out as he turned back to Bic. "I promise, this time we'll get some answers from these guys."

Bic nodded, then repeated, "I got you."

"Okay," Hawk said, "ready... go."

Parelli crouched and began a duckwalk to his left.

Bic came around the corner of a stack of cars, then took a knee and aimed his M27 machine gun, ready to take anything out as Parelli made his way through the small break in the junk scrap cover.

In addition to his M27 machine gun, Parelli carried an M136 single shot anti-tank weapon slung around his shoulder like a street busker's guitar. The twenty-five pounds of weaponry definitely slowed his duckwalk more than he would have liked.

If all went as planned, Parelli would get close enough to shoot the M136 into the heart of the clubhouse where most of the members were likely to be hanging out.

Parelli was feet away from getting to a nice area of cover, when every flood light in the place lit up at once, followed by a buzzing alarm.

"Tripped a laser sensor," Bic said, holding firm in his position to protect Parelli who was completely vulnerable.

One of the garage doors opened up, releasing a couple of junkyard dogs who charged like they were lusting for the taste of human flesh.

Parelli made a move toward cover, but the men from the roof started firing at him with automatic weapons of their own.

Bic returned fire, hitting one of the men. The other dove for cover. This gave Parelli a window to get behind cover.

"Boys," Hawk said, "there's a coupla mad puppies on their way toward you."

The men ran from junk pile to junk pile to avoid the snarling dogs. Bic continued to spray fire at the man left on the roof to keep him at bay. As Bic prepared to get a good shot, a second garage door was opening. The massive one on the end.

Something like a cross between a bulldozer and a tank rolled out.

"What the hell is that?" Parelli said, trying to catch his breath.

"Looks like a CAT bulldozer—fortified." Bic looked through his scope, trying to see if he had a shot to take out the driver.

Hawk's voice interrupted. "So that's what they were doing with all that metal."

They'd underestimated the bikers' ingenuity. The dozer was fortified with giant sheets of metal surrounding the cab on three sides, protecting the driver from gunfire, reflecting the flood lights and making the thing glow like a rolling yellow and black beacon. A beacon with a massive dirt-pushing blade in the front and a big DOH logo in the middle of it.

"I can't get a shot," Bic said, "that things impenetrable."

As if reading Bic's mind, Parelli was crouched and readying the M136 rocket, taking dead aim at the tank dozer. Just as he fired, a dog launched itself at Parelli, teeth-first. He fell over sideways, his screams echoing throughout the compound.

The missile had missed. And now Parelli was getting mauled. He thrashed back and forth, trying to throw the snarling beast off him.

Bic moved to help his friend, but the second dog charged at Bic. With his back against a rusted out 1980's Monte Carlo, Bic reached back, grabbing the door handle, and in a fluid motion, opened the door and redirected the attacking dog into the car as it jumped at him. He then slammed the door shut as the angry animal champed at him through the glass.

Parelli was getting mauled while the guy on the roof was shooting at him. The shots were getting too close for anyone's comfort.

Bic fired at the shooter on the roof as he crept up closer to line up a shot at the dog.

The sound of crunching metal caught his attention, as a pile of cars stacked eight high suddenly tumbled over towards him.

Bic dove out of the way as the cars atop the pile came tumbling down to the ground.

Bic, now with the dozer in full sight, fired at the beast, but it was no use. There was just a small hole about two-by-four inches for the driver to see out of. From the ground, the shot was impossible.

The CAT dozer's diesel engine roared, and suddenly the pile of vehicles were being pushed toward him. Behind him was the brick wall, to his right and left were stacks of junk. He was trapped. The junk lurched forward at him. Bic jumped up onto the first vehicle, moments before it crashed into the wall. He ran across the smashing pile of cars as the dozer pushed forward. He was four cars away from making it to the front of the dozer when the shooter on the roof opened fire at him.

A bullet grazed his leg, and he dove off the pile of cars onto the ground in a rolling motion to the side. Bic quickly reloaded as he rushed towards Parelli, firing in all directions, making sure he held off the now-swarming militia of bikers in the junkyard.

Bic punted the dog off Parelli without ever stopping his strategic fire at the attacking men.

Parelli's face was a mask of pain and panic, his arm a bloody mess. But he wasted no time grabbing his M27 off the ground and grunting through the pain as he joined the fight.

The two men retreated their way behind a single vehicle close to the wall as the rumbling roar of the dozer grew louder.

"Guys? Guys?" Hawk said. "Not sure if you can hear me, but all the men are gathering behind that there dozer. I think they're getting ready for it to flush you out. You guys are…ah shit, I'm comin'."

The dozer pushing a mountain of scrap edged forward toward the car they were using for cover, Bic came out from behind the vehicle firing, but took on heavy gunfire from the men flanked just behind the dozer. They now scattered in positions of cover from their pinned-down location.

Bic retreated back behind the car. "It's either get smashed against this wall or get showered in bullets. What say you, old friend?"

Parelli gasped as the eight-foot wall of scrap pushed up against their car. "I say it's time for a little *NÓ LÀ MA ĐEN.*"

"The Black Ghost is gone," Bic said as their vehicle they were hiding behind inched them toward the wall.

It became painfully obvious to both men that they had been outsmarted by a bunch of bikers, as the gap between them and the crushing wall was reduced to about four feet.

The machine gun fire began, spraying the ground and the walls on both sides of them. The bikers were toying with them, just begging them to come out and get sprayed with a hail of bullets.

Bic's mind was racing as he searched in vain for a way out. So much so that he almost didn't notice the figure climbing over the wall in the distance.

"*Oh no,*" he grunted with frustration and disbelief. *"That stupid, 80's-lovin' SOB is gonna die here with us too."*

28

The gunfire from the DOH ripped into all parts of the vehicle Bic and Parelli hid behind, as their four feet of space turned into two and the dozer's exhaust flooded the area with gray smoke.

The booming roar of the dozer was the foreshadowing of their imminent end, right up until the death machine went silent and the junk suddenly stopped moving forward.

"And he's down!" Hawk said over their earpieces.

"Where the hell are you?" Parelli said.

"Behind a lot of junk flanked to your left."

"Cover me," Parelli said to Bic as he jumped on top of the first vehicle in front of him, which was the beginning of about ten yards of scrap to the front of the dozer. As he did, Bic did exactly as he'd asked, popping up and firing along with Hawk to keep the DOH from getting an easy shot at Parelli.

Bic dropped out his magazine and reloaded another in under a second as he continued to fire with precision, hitting some of the men who had gotten the same idea to get control of the dozer.

Parelli climbed the front of the machine, leaving streaks of dirty blood on the front of the dozer. When Parelli got to the side, Bic, having reloaded yet again, came out from behind his cover on the right and charged, killing anyone who continued to fire.

Parelli climbed into the cab. The dozer immediately came to life as the massive steel-treaded track propelled the machine backwards. The DOH scattered out from behind. Bic picked off several of them as they fled.

The blade of the dozer rose as Parelli swung the thing around and accelerated forward.

The San Diego chapter of the Dogs of Hell was known for many things, but war strategy wasn't one of them. In the melee, they'd poured out into the lot. Figuring Bic and Parelli were trapped, they'd been stupid enough to advance.

And now Parelli was mowing them down like he was clearing trash. Bic walked behind the dozer for cover. It was the DOH's strategy in reverse. Now they were either getting picked off by Bic and Hawk or getting run over by the dozer.

"Good work, Hawk," Parelli said into the earpieces.

"Just clearing some biker trash out of your way," Hawk said with joviality in his voice, "Keep on keepin' on."

As if this were Hawk's benediction, the tractor lurched forward and tore through the tin garage that served as the DOH clubhouse, ripping a gaping hole in the structure. Parelli continued to plow deep into the structure, and the whole building began to collapse.

Bic ran after a weaponless man attempting to flee from the wreckage. He dove head first at the man, checking him into the ruined pile of metal and concrete, hearing the crack of bones in the guy's leg as he did. The guy shrieked in pain. Bic got up and lifted him up by the collar. It was then he noticed the patch on his chest. It read, "JR -- President."

The tractor stopped and Parelli climbed out. "Mr. President, we'd like a word with you."

President JR responded with speculation about Parelli's mother.

Parelli raised his M27. "Bic, go find Hawk and sweep the outside. Make sure there are no stragglers. I'm going to politely ask Mr. President who hired the Dogs of Hell for this job. And then I'm going to destroy what's left of his legs.

Bic released the president onto his broken leg. JR cried out and instantly collapsed.

"Better call your *goomah* and tell her you're gonna be late," Parelli said with a smirk. "I don't think tonight you're gonna get the type of action you'll like."

29

Roman Dog's mistress told him she had a headache, and so he was about to show her what a headache really felt like. No woman ever refused Roman Dog and got away without getting roughed up a bit.

His phone rang, enraging him. There was nothing worse than blue balls.

It was a Facetime from his cousin JR. What the hell?

He clicked on it. The picture of JR sprang up before him.

It was his cousin alright, and he was sucking on the barrel of a gun.

"Ah, ah… what the hell's going on?"

The camera swung away and revealed the face of a hard, desperate man.

"My name is Anthony Parelli and I'd like to know who hired your little gang of ballet dancers to kill Bic Green."

Roman heard muffled sounds of protest coming from his cousin. Then he smiled. "Ah, ah… you've been quite a busy guy the last couple of days."

"You killed the wrong guy's wife."

Roman smiled again. "Ah, ah… why don't you come visit me here in LA and I'll tell you who hired me."

Parelli, flipped the camera to reveal a full shot of JR strapped into a chair with duct tape. It panned down to reveal JR's dirty bare feet. The camera steadied and Parelli's legs appeared in the frame. He crouched down and held up a jagged piece of concrete with two hands.

Roman heard more protests from his cousin right before Parelli brought down the chunk onto JR's foot. Blood and bone spattered every which way, and the camera's microphone overmodulated with the sounds of his agonized cries.

"Who put the two-billion-dollar contract on Bic Green? What agency hired you?"

Roman sat still, listening to the sounds of his cousin's pain.

"No answer?" Parelli said. "I don't like to have to ask twice." Again, he brought the chunk down onto the already broken foot, messing it up beyond recognition. "Roman, I want you to know I'm going to work my way up your cousin's body until I get to his head."

Roman Dog did know how the game worked, and he enjoyed it.

"The escrow account," Parelli said. "The account number. What is it?"

"Roman!" JR screamed. "Tell him, for God's sake!"

As much as Roman enjoyed hearing the pleas of the tortured, he had things to do. "Ah, ah… I'm sorry, JR," he said, and disconnected the call.

He was in a bind. The call had angered him, but then again, the painful cries of his cousin invigorated him to new heights of energy.

Maybe he'd go a little harder on that teasing bitch of a mistress than he was originally going to.

Parelli stared at the phone in his hands, almost disbelieving that Roman ended the call so soon.

"Call him back!" JR shouted through tears and spit. "Call him back! He'll talk!"

"He's not going to talk," Parelli said calmly.

With this, he shot the man square in the chest. His pain ended, the body slumped.

Parelli turned away from the sight and dialed Roman back, this time on a voice call.

It went to voicemail. So, that's how it was going to be.

"Leave a message at the tone…"

Beep

"No one on this earth can imagine what I'm going to do to your son, right before I rip your heart out of your chest."

30

Parelli exited the shack, feeling a strange mix of exhilaration and disappointment. Over to his right, Bic was keeping a keen watch, his gun at the ready. Over to his left, Hawk was on his knees petting one of the vicious attack dogs.

"There ya go, buddy. Snap into a Slim Jim."

"That better not be the one that attacked me," Parelli said, suddenly aware of the screaming pain in his arm.

"Not this sweetie," said Hawk. "Who's a good boy?"

"You always carry Slim Jims?"

"Found 'em in one of the packs on the back of the bike. There ya go, ohhhh, you big boy, you big boy..."

Parelli rolled his eyes. "Hawk, come here a minute."

"Now you wait right there and Uncle Hawk'll see if he can't rustle you up another Slim Jim. Ohhhh, who's a good boy, yeah..." He stood up and pointed at the beast, whose tail was wagging like it had just gotten a fresh set of batteries. "Stay. Good boy." He approached Parelli. "That was a close one, huh?"

Parelli threw his arms around him in a tight, back-patting hug.

"Well, I love you too. What's the occasion?"

"That shot you took back there. You saved our asses. Thank you for that."

"Which one? I took a few of them."

Bic sidled up to the two men. "The one that took out the driver of the bulldozer."

"Listen, folks," Hawk said, holding up his hands, "I appreciate you giving me the credit for another man's work and all, but that wasn't me."

Bic and Parelli exchanged glances.

"You had to have, from up on the wall. It was the only possible angle that could have had a shot," Bic said.

"No, I had just scaled the wall and landed in a pile of dead rats when that happened."

Without another word, Bic turned and headed toward the bulldozer. The other two followed.

Bic climbed into the cab. The spatter of the dead man's blood formed a neat fan outward and up to the top of the passenger's side window. He held his hands in a V formation, mimicking the spatter pattern, and moved them back and forth. He looked behind him, trying his best to follow the bullet trajectory indicated by the pattern. Then he jumped out of the cab, landing on the ground and throwing up a cloud of dust.

He moved around to the back of the monster dozer to the location it was when the man was shot. He panned back and forth along the perimeter of the lot and suddenly pointed to a specific spot.

"There," he said.

"What?" Parelli said.

"That's where the shot came from. Hawk, is that where you were?"

"Nah. I mean, I was *sorta* near there? Like maybe fifty yards away?"

"Fifty yards isn't sorta near there," Parelli said. "Bic, you sure about that?"

"I'm sure."

The three men looked with utter confusion at the spot where Bic was pointing. There was nothing there but brick wall. Nothing to hide behind. No obstructions. What's more, the area was fully lit by flood lights.

"If there was a guy there," Bic said, "*someone* would have seen him and taken him out." He focused on the spot for a minute more.

"What are you thinking, Bic?" Parelli said.

Bic pointed at the spot—or moreover, at a spot beyond the spot. "There."

"Where?" Parelli said.

"That building. What is that? Apartments?"

"Looks it," Hawk said, training his eye on the five-story building that lay beyond the lot, at a distance of over five hundred yards.

"It can't be," Parelli said.

"It has to be," Bic replied, scrutinizing every window of the place.

Parelli shook his head. "Who took the shot then, Lee Harvey

Oswald?"

The men stood in silence for a moment.

"Well gentlemen," Hawk said, putting his hands on his hips, "looks like we got ourselves a guardian angel. I just have one question."

"What's that?" Parelli said.

Hawk spread his arms. "Can I have another hug?"

31

The three men sat in the Mercedes, six eyes boring into the laptop screen, the drone footage from the battle unfolding before them.

"Gnarly," Hawk shouted at the screen during the scene of Parelli's anti-tank misfire.

"What do you mean, *gnarly*? I missed. And I got attacked by a dog."

Hawk slapped his knee. "Look at that poochie go!"

"Fast forward," Bic said. "We ain't got time for this."

Parelli snarled, fast forwarding through the footage. "I've gotta get this arm stitched up."

"Stop here," Bic said. "Watch..."

The scene unfolded before them. The monster bulldozer was bearing down about to crush Bic and Parelli.

"There I am," Hawk said. "Scaling the wall like a boss."

"We see you," Bic said.

"And there I go behind the rat pile."

Bic focused on the apartment building. "Zoom in there."

Parelli zoomed in best he could. A fuzzy pixel vibrated on top of the building. "That can't be anything. It's interference."

Hawk too was now caught in rapt attention. "How far away is that building?"

Parelli shook his head in disbelief. "It's gotta be at least five or six hundred yards away. Maybe more. Nah, that's just video interference." Parelli zoomed out again.

"Wait," Bic said. "Watch. It should be any second now... there! Did you see it?"

"See what?" Parelli said. "I missed it."

"There was a flash. Hard to see, but it was there. Rewind."

Parelli rewound the footage a few seconds.

Bic pointed. "Zoom in there."

Parelli zoomed in again. "That's video interf-"

His words caught in his throat as an unmistakable flash appeared on screen for but a moment.

"Can you slow it down?" Bic said.

"Yeah," Parelli said softly.

Hawk was shaking his head. "I'll be damned."

Parelli rolled it again. Sure enough, there was the flash. He backed it up frame by frame and froze it right at the moment. All three men sat back.

"We need to get on that roof," Bic said.

The Breeze Development was one of the Emerson Housing Project's less-celebrated attempts to gentrify the area. The five-story apartment building stood as a testament to blind political optimism. In no way, shape, or form was this development ever going to achieve what its planners hoped it would. When the build went millions over budget, the money dried up and the semi-finished building was left to rot next to a junkyard. Bought at action, the new owner did what was minimally required for Section-8 status.

The original plan had called for a finished rooftop patio complete with a children's play area. As Bic, Parelli, and Hawk stepped out onto the results of this failed project, avoiding discarded needles and puddles of dried vomit, it became obvious that anyone up here was bound to be left alone.

Bic pointed to the southwest corner. "Over there."

They made their way to the corner, lit by cellphone flashlights. There was a breech in between the glass wind shields in the corner, and this just happened to overlook the junkyard that up until a little while ago served as the DOH San Diego chapter headquarters.

"No way can anyone make a shot from here into that ten-inch slit," Parelli said.

Bic pointed. "I could have. And if you remember right before we got crushed, the angle from right here would have been perfect."

"Yeah, but... there's no way."

"And yet," Bic began as he moved in for a closer look at the breech, "if I'm not mistaken, this is blowback from the gunshot right here along the edge." Bic bent down, his nose inches away from the roof's edge. He took a deep inhale. "You can smell powder. Yeah, I'm sure he took a shot from right here."

Parelli made a sound of wonderment.

Hawk put a hand to his forehead. "Gnarly, another assassin."

"High-level, no doubt," Bic said.

Parelli paced for a moment, then turned. "Bic, you and I need to go talk, figure this out."

"I agree."

"Hang on," Hawk said. "Don't I get in on this action?"

"Hopefully this joker," Parelli pointed where the shot was taken from, "doesn't know about you. So I think it's best if we split up for now. You start shadowing us. If we're lucky, you'll be able to flush him out."

"Got it. Good idea," Hawk said.

Bic nodded. "I like it."

Parelli began speaking with his hands before he actually spoke. "Start by talking to some residents here. Judging by the condition of this place, I doubt you'll get anyone to talk. But you never know. If we can even get a height or a skin color, that would help. Grease a palm here and there if you need to. Don't look like a narc though."

"This ain't my first rodeo," Hawk said.

Parelli looked out. "Hopefully he's not watching us right now."

"Professionals don't stick around," Bic said.

"I take your word for it. Hawk, Bic and I are gonna split. You hang back for a while snooping around and we'll figure out our next meet-up point."

Parelli and Bic left the rooftop to its lonely night and didn't speak another word.

32

The tides had turned, and the Dogs of Hell were now being hunted.

Roman used some of the ten million to upgrade the weaponry of the gang. The place for the pickup was Ricky D's tattoo shop. In a seedier part of LA, bikers were in and out for new ink into the wee hours of the night. There was hardly a time when there weren't at least a couple of bikes parked out front of the old single-story brick building. Built in the fifties, this small rectangular storefront had a basement that didn't show up on the county records. The same size as the first level, the twelve-hundred square foot cellar was perfect for stashing things that didn't want to be found.

Roman and Darius's hogs grumbled to a stop as they parked their bikes. Milo and Ugly Jesus made their way around to the back alley in a van.

Roman sat on his bike, staring at Ricky D's big neon sign in the window under the moonless night.

"You okay, Pop?" Darius asked.

Roman gazed for a second longer. Without taking his eyes off the sign, he asked, "Ah, ah… something's not right."

"Yeah, well, DOH are dropping like flies. So there's that."

"Ah, ah… it was something he said before he killed JR. He asked who hired us for a two-billion-dollar contract."

"You sure about that?"

Roman nodded.

"Could mean a lot of things, pop. I thought something was off with the billion in the first place, so I did some digging. Bic Green killed the heads of nine of the wealthiest families in America a couple years back."

"Ah, ah… dumb it down for me, son."

"Knowing he wronged people that wealthy, the billion makes a little more sense. My guess is that someone from those nine families put out the contract."

"Ah, ah… think they hired someone else for the job besides us?"

"It wouldn't surprise me. To be honest, Pop, the more I dig up on this Black Ghost, the more worried it makes me. This guy is a cross between a serial killer and a war machine. They say he can dodge bullets.

"Ah, ah… you need to stay off the internet, son. It's rotting out your brain. But let's say it's all true. We're picking up some new toys that oughta give us the edge on anybody." Roman got off his bike and reached into one of his saddlebags to retrieve a brown paper bag.

Roman and Darius made their way through Ricky D's, past walls covered with artwork of tattoo ideas. The place had the odd smell of tobacco and bleach. It was set up like a barber shop, with six chairs. A steady buzzing sound came from the needle jabbing into the arm of an oversized man in the chair. It was the beginnings of some type of skull design.

Roman handed the paper bag to Ricky, an older man with a gray handlebar mustache. Ricky had on a tank top exposing sleeves of tattoos which ran all the way up his massive arms.

Ricky took a peek into the bag, saw several bundles of hundred-dollar bills within, then said with a smile, "Want to get a little ink while you're here? On the house."

"Ah, ah… I'll be back, to get something special when I finish a job I gotta do."

"Special, huh? Anything you want me to be sketching out for you?"

Roman paused, scanning the artwork on the wall. "Ah, ah… yeah, start coming up with something that looks like a dead, black ghost."

"Alright, alright, alright," Ricky said, waving him to the back. "You know where to go, brother. Make sure to stack everything back just the way you found it. My back's been killing me."

"Will do," Darius said.

The men walked to the back of the shop. On the right was a door marked 'Bathroom' and on the left, 'Supply Room.'

The supply room carried a hoarder vibe. There were boxes and old supplies, some probably left there from a couple of decades ago.

"Ah, ah… all that crap in the corner needs to be moved."

Space was a commodity in this room. Darius began moving random items, including a mannequin covered in marker tattoos, into the center of the room. As he worked on the pile, the small trap door on the floor came into view.

The basement, just like the closet, was filled with junk. Roman walked to a stack of old crates. He opened one of them and saw what he was looking for: brand new, black, shiny MP5s. AKs and other assault rifles were impossible to hide when you're riding a motorcycle, but an MP5, at about 22 inches with the stock retracted, can fit right into a satchel or saddlebag.

"I see you found the candy," Ugly Jesus said as he and Milo came down the old ladder.

"Ah, ah… I want every Dog to be armed with one of these." Roman passed the submachine gun to Ugly Jesus for inspection.

He looked over the weapon. "Welds look perfect." He ejected the magazine. "Strong tension. These are top notch."

Roman took the weapon and aimed it like he was about to shoot someone. "Ah, ah… JR and I used to ride minibikes together when we were kids. Four of our clubs have been totally wiped out."

"These guys gotta pay." Milo said.

"Ah, ah… it's no longer just a job, it's personal."

As Roman dry-fired the weapon, Darius sidled up next to him.

"I just hope you…"

"Ah, ah… what? Think before I act?"

"Pop, it might not seem like it, but these guys are strategic. I don't want to give them the upper hand again."

"Ah, ah… revenge *is a dirty business*, son."

"Time to get into the mud," Milo said, transferring a couple of MP5s from the crate to a duffle bag.

Roman smiled. "Ah, ah… we are going to create a moving target. Our strategy is this: No one, and I mean *no one* is to stay in any clubhouse anywhere. We're a mobile club from now on. No more sitting duck targets for these guys to hit."

"That's a good move, Pop."

Roman looked at Ugly Jesus and Milo filling the bags with MP5s. "Ah, ah… we're going to unite everyone. All chapters need to be on board for this. I want our club swarming the roads, mobile-ready at all times. At the command, we attack from all angles and smash these two!"

"I've talked to the other road captains," Milo said with a touch of hesitancy.

"Ah, ah... I know that voice. What is it?"

Milo looked at the ground with embarrassment. "The Dallas, Portland, and Vegas clubs are out."

"They're just a bunch of Chickenshits," Ugly Jesus said.

"Did they give a reason?" Darius asked.

Again, Milo paused. "They don't think it's worth dying for a job they're not getting paid for."

Roman's eyes felt like hot pokers. "Ah, ah... ah, ah... you put it out, anyone who questions my word, I'll tie them to my bike and drag their naked bodies on the pavement for a hundred miles!"

Milo nodded. "Done."

"Ah, ah... one more thing," Roman growled. "Put it out there to all the channels—I don't give a shit. Any scumbag, killer for hire, even a one-eyed pirate for all I care. There's now a twenty million bounty for the heads of Bic Green and that Parelli character."

"You sure about that, Pop?"

"Ah, ah... I know what you're thinking. You're worried we only have ten."

"Simple math."

"Ah, ah... well then, you fix the math."

A look of confusion masked Darius's face.

Roman put a hand on his son's shoulder. "Ah, ah... you figured out who hired us. I'm putting you in charge of getting us more money up front."

"They usually don't like that."

"Ah, ah... if they balk, tell them that's the cost for hiding important shit from us, like another contract."

"Got it, Pop."

"Ah, ah... Jesus and Milo, I want you to map out a route to gather up the entirety of the California club membership in one place. The word's going out that anyone who wants to join has a place at our table."

"Yes, sir!"

"Ah, ah... I want an army of killers raining down on them the next time we meet." He smiled sadistically. "It'll be an assassin's ball!"

33

"Gimme a big ol' bloody piece of meat," Parelli said to the server. "I want you to walk the cow past the campfire once. And I want a martini so cold it'll make a polar bear cry."

They were at The Good Steer, a fancy steakhouse in the heart of San Diego. They had slept at a paisan of Parelli's from his younger days in New York named Jimmy Clean. Of course Clean wasn't his real last name, that was his nickname he got from his reputation of being able to wipe any crime scene clean of evidence. The accommodations were great, except he only had one extra bed. It was a king bed, but when you're used to a stillness like Bic was it was hard to sleep with anyone, let alone a violent snorer like Parelli. Bic had laid low for the day while Parelli saw a guy to get his arm properly stitched up. Parelli insisted they hash out their next move over a fine meal.

"And for you, sir?"

Bic handed her the menu. "Same. But medium and hold the martini. I'll stick with the water."

Parelli folded his hands, waited for the girl to leave, then spoke in a low voice. "I've heard from all my contacts. No one knows anything about this hit."

"Not one, huh?"

Parelli shook his head.

Bic thought for a moment. "Think any of them could be lying?"

Parelli shrugged. "The thought did cross my mind, if I'm being honest. So, it's possible, not probable."

Parelli's drink arrived. He held up his glass. "To our mystery superhero."

Bic clinked his glass and the two men sipped. There was at least another minute of silence, as something heavy lay between the two men. Uncertainty.

"I'll tell you what's bothering me," Bic said after another minute. "These Dogs of Hell are low-level. Why them?"

"Seventeen chapters," Parelli added by way of correction.

"They're not professionals."

Parelli nodded slowly. "Okay."

"So, again." Bic spread his hands. "Why them?"

Parelli had no answer.

Bic took a deep breath. "I've been rolling this over in my brain. Over and over. You don't think it's..."

"Don't say it," Parelli said.

"What am I going to say."

"Your dear old dad," Parelli said plainly.

Bic chewed his lip.

Parelli leaned in. "Now get one thing clear. Clarence Green is dead and gone. Forever. Pushing up daisies, or swamp grass is more likely. Understand?"

"Yeah, we had this discussion already."

"Then it should have been done when we had it."

They left it at that, feeling the tension to its fullest as the din of the restaurant swirled around their ears.

Minutes later, the steaks arrived. Parelli dug into his like a lion.

"My tech guy told me," he said with a mouthful, "that the whole thing was done by someone who encrypted everything from top to bottom. Completely untraceable. It's almost like they wanted the hit to go out to give it some kind of paper trail even though it had already been put in motion."

Bic nodded slowly.

"I mean," Parelli said, stabbing his steak at a 90-degree angle with his fork. "I got the fax, then seconds later there was an entire team of hitmen at my door." He pointed his knife at Bic. "Not bikers, by the way, professionals."

"Listen," Bic said, suddenly realizing he had very little appetite, "maybe it's time we go on a nice vacation."

Parelli froze mid-chew. "You mean hide."

"Visit our friends in the islands. You know, give us both a chance to cool off and rest up. And..." He paused, unsure of how to put it, then decided to go for broke, "It'll give you time to grieve."

Parelli resumed chewing, breathing heavily through his nose. "I got a better idea. How about I grieve by killing every last punk sonofabitch that had even the smallest role in killing my Barbara? Is that R&R enough for you, Bic? Or do you have any other therapy ideas?"

He took another stab at his steak, sliced it only partially, and tore the rest with his fork. Shoving the stringy piece into his mouth, he said, "And another thing, I'm not about to take lessons on vengeance from a guy who spent decades tracking down his Daddy, if you please. No offense, Bic. You're a good friend. Maybe even my best friend. Who knows. And I appreciate you looking out for me. But please, no more advice on how I'm going to handle my feelings on this one. Okay?"

"Point taken."

Parelli nodded to his plate. "Good."

Bic paused for a moment. "So who is it?"

"That's the two billion dollar question."

"Someone from... my past." The word *past* was bitter in Bic's mouth.

"I thought a lot about that. Let's talk about the billionaires." He put down his fork and began ticking off the names on his fingers. "We got Vorg, the Benningtons, Henry Barron, Killebrew..."

Bic felt a shudder of ghostly regret go through him. He didn't like the man he was when he killed those innocent billionaires. Having Parelli reciting the list made him sick to his stomach.

Parelli continued. "Uh, let's see, the Wilkeses, Virginia... Peppermint? Pepperpot? No, wait... Peppercorn! Virginia Peppercorn. The Braddicks, Deeds..."

The Braddicks...

There was an awful memory that haunted him.

It had to do with eyes. The little boy and girl that he locked in the movie room right before he killed their parents. The girl seemed to be none the wiser. Or maybe she was. There was something questioning in her eyes. But the boy...

He stared at Bic like he saw through to his soul--if there was even any soul to see. The eyes were hateful, hurting, and they pleaded for life and sympathy.

The haunting screams the boy made in an attempt to save his parents.

The screams pierced through his skin from the inside, like a parasite having done its job of eating its fill and then worming its way out. More screams…

They were *his* screams. Bic Green, age seven.

His mother's screams. The screams of his father. The taste of that raw, rubbery pork chop in his mouth, gagging him half to death. And the little boy Braddick. They all coalesced in his mind as one giant symphony of hate and anguish.

"Bic? You here?" Parelli said, his voice full of genuine concern.

"Huh?"

"Have some water, take a deep breath. You look like you're gonna yak your steak back up on your plate or somethin'."

"I'm okay."

But he wasn't okay. He grabbed his water with a shaky hand and brought it to his lips. It was cool and he felt it coursing on down along his esophagus and into his stomach, where it pooled and settled him, bringing him back to the here and now.

"You sure you're okay? I can call the guy who patched up my arm earlier today. Good guy. No questions asked."

"I said I'm fine, Tony. It's just that… I know who it is."

Parelli cocked his head. "You do?"

Bic nodded slowly. "Yeah. I don't know why this didn't hit me sooner. It makes so much sense and is at the height of irony considering what my father did to me and now I…"

"Enough with the riddles, who?"

"Did it to him… It's the Braddick kid."

Parelli's vicious stabs at the steak had finally given way to thoughtful slicing and spearing. He put one last piece in his mouth and chewed it thoroughly. He sipped at his martini, rolled it around his mouth, and swallowed.

"Bic," Parelli said at last, "What do you say you and I take a little trip to LA. We'll kill that punk, Roman Dog. And then, once that's all taken care of, we'll go and straighten things out with that little Braddick brat."

34

She wore the same heels she wore when she stomped that bugger's bollocks in the cafe. They suited her personality, or at least who she was *most* of the time. She entered the bar. To her surprise, knowing what she knew of her prospective company, it wasn't a dive. It was a fairly nice establishment done in shabby chic, with rustic signage--hand-painted aphorisms and pithy quotes.

She sidled up to the bar, two seats down from him.

"Beefeater and tonic," she said loudly, knowing that order was an efficient way of bringing out her accent.

The waft of jasmine coming off her helped for sure.

"You English?"

She looked at him. "A subject of the queen, at your service."

He put out his hand. "They call me Hawk."

"Hawk?" she said, laying on the Brit.

"Whoo-wee, I like the way you say that," he said. He was not without charm.

"Do you? What other things do you like, Hawk?"

"Well, I'll tell you what I *don't* like. I don't like ordering a beer and having it served to me in a mason jar. To a redneck, a mason jar's got two purposes: Storing the peaches and pissin' in when the toilet's backed up. That's it."

"Charming," she said with a smirk. And he was, aiming for the gross-out like an eleven-year-old with a puppy crush. She liked it when they had a hint of innocence about them.

"Ya think so?" He raised his glass. "Cheers."

"Cheers," she said.

He sipped carefully, then put down his glass thoughtfully. "Hey, let me ask you something. Do you really pronounce it '*sshhedule*'?"

She chuckled. "I'm afraid so. And don't forget *aluMINium*."

Hawk shook his head. "Cute as hell. I love English people. Hey, what's the difference between English and British?"

"One's a muffin, I'm told."

Hawk slapped his knee. "Radical! Sexy and a sense of humor."

"Humour with a 'u'."

"Exactly."

She cocked her head at him. "My turn to ask you a question."

"Shoot."

"Where did you get those scars on your head?"

He looked flummoxed. She knew exactly where he'd gotten them, of course. A guy they called the Farmer screwed his fingers to his face with a screw gun. But he was an experiment to her, and she knew there was no better way to know a man than by how he acts when he's self-conscious.

"Oh... that," he said, rubbing at his forehead as if according to a textbook on human behavior. "You see, it was a bear attack gone horribly wrong. For the bear, I mean."

"Do go on."

"Well, you see I was camping and he came up and insulted my mother."

She issued a thoroughly fake chuckle. "My, that must have been exciting."

"Honey, for me, it was a slow Tuesday."

"Really," she said, running a hand through her hair for maximum effect. "Is your life that interesting?"

He looked her in the eye. "It can be if you let me buy you another drink."

"Tell me the truth about your scar and I'll let you buy me another after that."

"Barkeep! Another round for me and... I'm sorry, what was your name again?"

"I didn't tell you in the first place," she said. "It's Millie."

"Millie, I like that. Short for...?"

"Mildred."

"Mildred. Old school. I like it. Totally awesome."

"Now that," she said, "is a phrase I haven't heard in a while."

"Honey, you're looking at a latter-day Jeff Spicoli."

"I'm afraid I don't follow."

Hawk put a thoughtful hand to his chin. "Hmmmm, so you're not an eighties girl."

"Oh, you mean Duran Duran? Spandau Ballet?"

Hawk slapped the bar. "Now that's what I'm talking about. Def Leppard?"

"Pour some sugar on me."

"Hell yeah, I will if you want."

They shared a flirtatious laugh over that.

"Okay," he said, "I made you a promise. The truth. I got into... well, let's say I pissed off the wrong guy. He duct-taped my hands to my head and started screwing them to me."

She widened her eyes and leaned in. "Screwed them to you? Like, actual screws?"

"He wasn't what you'd call a nice guy."

"No, I don't suppose he was. And what did you do to run afoul of such a creature?"

"Long story, honey, but I assure you, there's nothing to fear. Guy's long gone and Hawk here is as strong as ever. No danger to me, honey."

"No danger at all? Pity that," she said with a wink. She could have sworn she saw him flush a bit.

"Well anyway," he said by way of recovery, "bygones are bygones. Know what I mean?"

"That's an incredible story. Makes the bear one look tame."

"Guess so. So, how about you? Quid pro quo, doctor."

"Hm?"

"Silence of the Lambs?"

"Ah, yes, of course. Quid pro quo. Right, what would you like to know, Hawk?"

"Well, for starters, I don't see a ring on that finger, which says to me that you're either cheating or you got the plague."

She laughed at this, and was sorry to admit to herself that half of it was genuine. "No plague, and not married. Rather, I *was* married."

"And he left you?" He slapped the bar in mock anger. "Come on, we're gonna find him right now and beat him senseless. Let's go."

She smiled. "It's nothing like that, actually. No, in actuality... he was the love of my life. He stopped at a red light and the drunk behind him didn't. Slammed him into the middle of an intersection where he was hit by a semi. A few hours later, he was gone. Taken from me. No one asked me if I wanted to be rid of him. No one told me I needed to savor our last conversation, or the last time he looked me in the eye. That was it. Gone. I was two months pregnant at the time. I miscarried shortly after. Grief does a lot of damage."

She stared at him. His face was grave.

He swallowed hard. "Well, now, first of all, I owe you a heartfelt apology for not having the brains that the good Lord gave a jackass to keep my mouth shut and saying what I said."

"Hawk, it's okay, please don't apologize."

"And second, I'd like to offer my condolences. Stories like yours sure make a good case for atheism. I'm so sorry to hear that."

Again, she smiled. "I've recovered… almost."

"What was his name?"

"Christopher."

Hawk held up his glass. "To Christopher."

"To Christopher." *Clink.*

"Almost recovered, huh?" he said after a moment. "What was the thing about him you loved most?"

"He wanted to have six children with me."

"That's love for sure! God bless him."

She needed an out. She focused on the song playing. "Do you hear that?"

"Do I?" Hawk said, hopping off the stool. "I love me some Prince."

"Hawk, are you about to hit the dance floor?"

"If there's one advantage to having your fingers drilled to your head, it's that I'm left with a strange kinda twitch when I dance."

"This I have to see."

"Care to join me, Ginger?"

"After you, Fred."

They exited the bar having closed it down. His arm was around her and she was fine with that.

"Hawk, you are the most interesting human I have ever had the pleasure of twitching with."

"The pleasure is all mine, my dear." He took her hand and kissed it regally. "That how they do it?"

"Close. You need a haughty accent and about a hundred years of inbreeding, but it's pretty close. So, is that it?"

"Is what it?"

"The night is over?"

Hawk smiled. "It ain't over till Yogi Berra says it is."

"Then perhaps Yogi Berra would like to come back to my place?"

Hawk suddenly lost his smile. "Hey, um, about that…"

"What is it?"

"Listen, I like you, Millie. I mean, I really, really like you. And if I was two years younger, you know, I'd… aw, hell. When that guy roughed me up, he did a number on me and… some things don't really work as well as they used to. I don't mean to let you down or nothing, I just didn't want to start something I couldn't finish and then have you think it was you, you know?"

She took his face in her hands and placed a gentle, dry kiss on his lips.

"That's what I think of your damned chivalry, Hawk. Now come back to my place for more drinking and dancing. And if I hear one more word about shagging, I'm calling the house mistress."

"After you, my lady," Hawk said.

35

Bic stared at Jimmy Clean's guest room ceiling in the darkness just before dawn. Parelli had kept him up snoring for half the night. The other half was spent tossing and turning, his mind a jumble of chaotic thoughts. He'd gotten out of bed a couple of times to check Parelli's phone for any response from Hawk, whom they'd tried to contact several times last night. Nothing. Maybe it was this that worried him.

Or maybe it was something else. Like Parelli.

His old friend had undergone some sort of change since losing his wife. A man losing someone close does change him. Bic could attest to that. His own mother smashed to death before his eyes had set him on a violent course forever. But there was still hope. He'd always kept that in mind. As long as he had Gracie, there was hope.

And then there was Mack and Caroline. Strange how he thought of them as family now. They'd been mortal enemies at one time. Some divine hand had flipped the script. He thought of Mack lying there, shot. He wished he could be there for them, especially Caroline.

"You're up," Parelli said from his side of the bed.

Bic continued staring at the ceiling. "I've been up."

"Told you not to have the coffee last night."

"It wasn't the coffee. It was your thunderous snoring."

Parelli stretched and rose from the bed. "I didn't realize the guy who slept in wet jungles and prison would be perturbed by an old Italian's faulty sinuses."

Parelli walked into the bathroom, hacked up half a lung, and relieved himself noisily. A moment later he emerged.

"Any response from Hawk?"

"How would I know?"

"Because you were up checking my phone."

Bic turned to him and gave him a look.

Parelli shot a finger at him. "I was bluffing and you fell for it."

Bic shook his head. "I'm concerned."

"Well?"

"Well, what?"

"Anything from Hawk?"

"Nothing."

Parelli grabbed his phone and frowned down at the screen. "I hope he hasn't gone and gotten his fingers screwed into his skull again."

Bic shrugged. "He's probably drunk. Or forgot to plug in his phone and it died. Or maybe some combination of the two. He's not exactly the punctual type."

"No, he's not," Parelli conceded. "But he is reliable in just about every other way. I'm worried. The likelihood that he's sleeping off a drunk or he forgot to charge his phone is just as great as something bad happening to him. Considering what we're into now."

"Yeah," Bic said, wanting to continue the discussion about what it was they were actually into. And whether it was really necessary for them to be into it. He wanted out. He wanted it all to end.

Parelli was on the phone, in the midst of a terse conversation.

"Right," he said, and disconnected the call. He grabbed his clothes and started to dress.

"Where are you going?"

"To a bar. Care to join me?"

"Do I have a choice?"

Parelli continued buttoning his dress shirt. "You always have a choice, Bic."

Bic looked into his friend's eyes. The implication was all-too obvious. He *didn't* have a choice. He was going to be coerced into seeing this to its very messy end.

"Relax, that was my guy I called last night. He traced Hawk's phone to its last ping," Parelli said. "He figures it came from a bar called The Rusty Hinge. Again, care to join me?"

"Gimme a quick minute," Bic said, popping out of bed.

Any doubts as to whether Hawk was actually at The Rusty Hinge were quickly dispelled the minute they laid eyes on the place. It looked like it had been transported through time from 1986. It was about 7 am, and they could just make out the flashy decor within, complete with Patrick Nagel prints on the walls and gaudy leather couches in a lounge area off to the side.

"So what are we looking for?" Bic said, squinting through the window at the darkened interior.

Parelli had his phone out. "Anything."

"Thanks for clarifying that," Bic said. "Who you calling?"

"Well, I'd like to take a look inside but the sign says they're protected by Secure ONE. That's good news. I have a guy there..." He put the phone to his ear and held up his finger. "Yeah, it's me... I know, I know, I only call for favors. Just one more and I promise it'll be worth your while. At a bar here called The Rusty Hinge. I'll text you coordinates. I just need ten minutes tops, if you can arrange it. Thank you, darling. Bye now."

"Darling?" Bic said. "I thought you said it was a guy."

"It is. He happens to like Broadway a lot. I like to keep him happy."

"How far do you go to do that?"

"That's enough outta you," Parelli said, texting his Secure ONE contact. "Okay, should be a couple of minutes."

Bic shook his head and peeked again through the windows, trying to look for, as Parelli had said, anything. The bar looked drab and depressing, as every bar does in the morning.

Something moved in front of the wall of spirits. He could see his own reflection in the mirror, staring. The thing stirred.

"You see something, Bic?"

"I don't know. Looks like..."

A cast iron frying pan rose up, clutched by a dark hand. It went down behind the bar.

Clarence Green stood up, a satanic grin on his face.

"You're next, boy."

Bic pushed Parelli out of the way, nearly knocking the man to the ground. He aimed a swift kick at the door of the bar, caving it in like it had been ajar the whole time.

"Are you out of your mind?" Parelli screamed, following him in with his hand on his pistol tucked under his jacket.

Bic stood at the bar before the mirrored wall of spirits. He looked over the bar at the floor. Nothing. He spun around.

"You're lucky my guy just came through with the alarm deactivation. Damn lucky. You mind telling me what the hell that was all about?"

Bic's heart was thumping in his chest. His stomach was tight. His breath came in adrenaline-fueled gusts.

"I don't know," he said. "I thought…"

"You thought what?"

"I thought I saw someone."

Parelli stared, a look of concern on his face. "You okay?" His voice was full of concern.

"Yeah. I saw a body. I thought maybe it was Hawk's."

"Behind the bar," Parelli said.

"Yeah."

Parelli moistened his lips. "Okay. Well, while we're here. Let's give a quick look around for Hawk's phone."

"Yeah," Bic said again, turning away and walking toward the lounge area. "We ought to come back here later and ask if they've seen him."

"Good idea," Parelli said, his voice uneasy.

"Question," Bic said, turning to Parelli. "What do we do if we don't find his phone?"

"Well," Parelli said, "I was thinking of paying Roman Dog a visit."

Bic nodded, turned, and scoured the area for a cellphone, feeling a phantom of the old rage swirling inside him.

36

Hawk opened his eyes to blinding light and shut them again. He groaned once. His head felt like something had crawled in there with a sledgehammer and was now trying to get out. He opened his eyes again, this time bracing himself against what he knew would be a yellow and orange waking nightmare. When he did, and when the light speared his brain through both eyeballs, he instinctively brought his elbow up to shield them.

But something stopped him.

"Huh?"

He looked over to his left. The picture came slowly into focus.

A handcuff on his wrist.

The whole picture came into view, a little at a time.

First, the handcuff. Then, what was on the other end of it. A radiator.

What the hell?

He looked around and recognized the meager decor of an Airbnb. He was on the floor, hurting all over—the old aches from his near-death beating by the Farmer asserting themselves proudly.

His phone was ringing. He looked around. Where the hell was it?

It was coming from somewhere nearby. On the bed? No, on the floor. He peeked under his cuffed wrist and saw it glowing beneath the radiator. With a strain that taxed his battered body, he finally grabbed it. The number was unlisted. He answered it.

"Hello darling," she said. "Don't answer. This is a recording..." She giggled playfully. "Would you believe me if I told you that last night was the most fun I've had in a very long time? No? I don't blame you. But it was. And you know what? A shag would've been nice, after all. It's just that I would've wanted a bit of brekkie and, well, you were in no position to order up, as you can see. Anyway, last night was the second time I decided not to kill you. Third time's the charm, so it's probably best if we don't see each other again." Here, her voice switched to a flawless American valley girl accent. "But, like, you know, it was, like, totally rad and you're cute and all and you rrrreally do remind me of him, so like, whateverrrrr." The British accent returned after a sigh. "Hawk, you just sit tight there, okay? What's about to happen does not involve you in the least. I mean it. I mean, I meant what I said when I said I had fun last night. You know." There was the sound of a wet, smacking kiss. "Ta!"

The call ended. Hawk looked at his phone.

It wasn't his. In his dazed state he hadn't even realized it.

He tapped at the screen. The thing had died completely.

What?

He let it drop to the floor and stared straight ahead. Millie, if that really was her name, had drugged him. That was obvious. That ten-plus chick being into him. He should have known. She was pretty good at a story. That stupid thing about her… what was it? Her ex-boyfriend? Husband? *Christopher.* That was it. That was probably fake. Her accent was obviously real. Or was it? That American accent she put on, if it was a put on, was pretty damn good.

Last night was the second time I decided not to kill you…

When was the first?

No, that couldn't have been her.

The sniper.

He rested his head against the wall and began putting the pieces together. A sniper, and a damn good one. If it was her, she was as good a sniper as she was at doing an American accent. Or a British one.

And if she was actually British, and she was that good with a gun, and at telling stories, and disguising herself, and slipping him a drug, and calculating exactly when he'd wake up from it so that she could play him a message on some random cellphone that automatically went dead once it was done…

"MI6," he said to the room, his voice deep and grated.

Hawk took a deep breath, he still smelled her jasmine scent on him. He quickly remembered how close they were dancing last night as a simple thought came to him. *My new girlfriend is British Intelligence.*

37

The public library was quiet. Usually that made it a peaceful place. But as Darius sat at one of the many computer terminals, he felt as though he was being watched. He knew that was highly unlikely, but he had arranged for an emergency online chat at 10:00 am today with their employer. The free internet access at the library made it untraceable to link anything back to him or his father legally in the event the conversation he was about to have was obtained by the authorities.

As he looked at his watch, a couple of minutes to, memories surfaced of his mother taking him to a library just like this one as a kid. This brought mixed emotions. An avid reader growing up, coming to the library was like a normal kid going to a toy store. Only here, everything in the store was for free. All the books, thousands of them to choose from. He remembered when he was about nine, looking up at the shelves stacked almost to the ceiling. Unfortunately, his mother, who never read a book in her life, only took him to find books so that he'd get so wrapped up in them in the house alone while she was out partying on all-nighters. One time, he remembered finding her hiding in a private reading room at the library, trying to shoot heroin, her drug of choice. When she OD'd a couple years later, he moved back to LA to live with his dad, Roman.

The private chat came to life:

--Hello...

--Hello, Darius typed.

--We are hopeful you have more success filling our order. Thus far we have

been very disappointed at your performance.

Darius thought a moment, he didn't even consider they'd be on the aggressive. Total curve ball.

--I can assure you the order will be completed. However, we do need an additional ten million up front to cover expenses.

--Our expectations are for you to fill our order with the terms agreed upon by both parties.

Darius responded, *The terms we agreed upon didn't include another supplier trying to fill the same order!*

There was no response for what seemed like several seconds.

--Your information is incorrect. Your contract is exclusive, but if you cannot fill the order, we will be happy to collect our deposit plus interest and hire another supplier.

--We will fill the order, we just don't like our employer hiding any details.

--Nothing to hide — But our patience is running out on your lack of performance.

--You say nothing to hide, I say you are hiding something. Like, we know who your employer is.

--Now you are playing a very dangerous game.

--Does the phrase "nine billionaire families" ring a bell?

--That's a pretty smart guess. Maybe all of those books around you are increasing your IQ.

Darius sprung away from the computer, then discreetly pulled his pistol out from behind his jacket and put it in his pocket. While still holding his nine, he scanned the place, looking for anything suspicious. He picked up more typing on the computer screen.

--Please, sit back down. Just wanted to make sure you understood who you were dealing with. I see your organization has been committed and have had severe disruptions but you still continue to work hard at delivering. We will see what we can do, we might have a small side delivery that we can advance additional funds.

The employer left the chat before Darius could respond. He sat back and wondered what possibly could be a small side delivery. This was already way above their pay grade, and he may just have really complicated things by getting them deeper into the quicksand they were already stuck in.

38

Nathaniel hopped out of bed with an 'I can' attitude. Today would be the day he would begin to make things right. He'd gone to bed last night with GreenCOIN only two cents from his target sale price of sixty-four. He pulled up his coin, and immediately a smile pulled at his face. GreenCOIN had climbed to seventy-one cents overnight just as Crypto-Keeper had predicted it would. On Twitter they were talking about a #GodWhale who bought up almost all the liquidity of the low-market cap ALT coin, basically assuring its ascent to a buck.

Nathaniel didn't care about a dollar price. All he wanted was to be able to pay his debt and make sure Lucy would be safe. As he put the order in to sell it, all he felt was relief knowing this was almost over.

He sat there and waited for the cash to be settled into his account. After a few seconds, he realized only a hundred thousand shares had filled at seventy-one cents.

Then the price started dropping like a rock.

155,000 shares filled at sixty-three cents...

477,000 shares filled at fifty-one cents...

374,000 shares filled at forty-seven cents...

1,080,734 shares filled at thirty-one cents...

He received a Twitter alert, it was from Crypto-Keeper. "#GodWhale is selling! Get out of GreenCOIN now!!!!"

Nathaniel felt numb inside as GreenCOIN dropped like it had jumped out of a building. In a matter of minutes, GreenCOIN fell all the way back to less than a penny a share. Out of his 2,150,537,634 shares, he had only been able to sell thirty-four million. Even at a price less than a penny, no one wanted them. They were all but worthless.

He couldn't bear to watch anymore. His stash of Bitcoin and GreenCOIN were down to 397 million.

He clicked off his computer and sat back, feeling the itch on his arm again. He rubbed it a few times, feeling the scar there from a recent slice.

He logged on to his Tor browser and, with hands trembling, messaged his contact.

I'm cancelling the contract. CRYPTO has crashed. I no longer have the money.

He paused before sending, reading and re-reading the message. There was nothing more to say. He hit send and waited with excruciating patience.

A moment later, the reply came.

Commitments have been made. You have 2 hours. If the money isn't in escrow by then there will be new targets added to the contract.

Nathaniel felt his bladder begin to loosen. Then ellipses appeared on the screen. He was getting another message.

It was an image. A picture of Lucy.

Nathaniel froze in horror. Hot tears came. He shut the computer. It was a few minutes before he was able to rise from his chair and move about the room.

He had to do something. Then he remembered Uncle Seth going to see his dad's company lawyers. There was hope there. There wasn't any hope in this situation. But that's just what hope was for, wasn't it? When there wasn't anything left?

He called his uncle.

"Yeah?"

"Hey, how's it going?"

"The meeting's in an hour. Just having some coffee. Hang on, let me pay the girl…"

Nathaniel licked his dry, cracked lips as he listened to Uncle Seth flirt with the girl behind the Starbucks counter.

A train of thought began in his mind. Coffee. Spilled. In the middle of a fight.

His parents arguing.

"I warned you about Seth," Mom said. "You can't trust him as far as you can throw him!"

The argument had been about Seth leaving Dad's company for his chief competitor. Nathaniel's child brain processed what it could. Mom was mad, so mad she spilled her coffee. That made her cry. He always wondered why spilling her coffee made her cry like that.

"Ok, so what's up, Nathaniel?"

Snapping out of his thoughts, Nathaniel stammered his reply. "I'm... hey, why did you leave Dad's company?"

A chuckle on the other end. "That's what you called me for?"

"No, I mean, yeah, I was just curious."

A pause. "Listen, Nathaniel. Forcing your father to buy me out and leaving was the worst mistake of my life. Why did I do it?" He sighed heavily. "At the time, it really seemed like it was the right thing to do. It pained me to do it. The last thing I wanted to do was hurt my brother. So I'm afraid that's the best answer I can give you. I was a selfish idiot who was afraid we would fail and went to the bigger company at the time for security. I arranged for your father to come with me by the way and buy us both out, but he believed in what we had started."

Nathaniel was silent as he digested the words.

"That all?"

"Yeah," Nathaniel said softly.

"Everything okay?"

"Yeah. I was just missing my parents, that's all."

Uncle Seth sighed again. It sounded phony. "Yeah, I miss them too, kiddo. I really do. Good folks, the both of them. Real good folks. The best."

Nathaniel was silent again.

"Is there something else?" Uncle Seth said.

"No."

"Okay. Cuz if there is anything else, you need to let me know. We have to be honest with each other now. Understand? You're in some trouble and we're gonna get you out of it. But you can't be withholding anything, otherwise that can only get us in deeper and make it harder to get out. Understand?"

"I understand."

"Good. Now, if you don't mind, I'm gonna get off now so I can drink my java and go over some stuff. We cool?"

"Yeah, we're cool."

"Good. See ya later. Hotdogs for dinner. Whatd'ya say?"

"Sounds good." He disconnected the call and paced slowly across the room, his mind a mess.

It had been a lie on the phone, but now it was the truth: He really did miss his parents. Right now, it was his mom, and more than ever. And he couldn't help but think one salient thought over and over again:

Mom didn't trust you. So I don't either...

39

Bic and Parelli arrived at the DOH clubhouse in LA just after 3:00 pm. The parking lot looked like a ghost town. Bic felt beads of perspiration rolling down his scalp under the hot sun. M27 in hand, he was hopeful he could break the loop of death in which Parelli had confined him.

"Well," Parelli said, almost as if taunting to someone hiding in the bushes to come out, "what a bunch of chickens."

"Looks like they got word somehow we were on our way," Bic said.

"Either this is a trap," Parelli said as he moved the barrel of his automatic rifle to areas where one might hide, "or these punks are mobilizing. Rounding up every chapter from here to Timbuktu because they're scared little boys. I'll wager the little rabbits got afraid and hopped off to gather up all their friends."

Parelli gave Bic the signal to stay outside as he entered the clubhouse.

Still alert, Bic nodded his head slowly, careful not to let on that the whole situation was making him extremely uneasy. By Parelli's actions, it was clear this had little to do with Bic Green and everything to do with cold revenge. However this played out, in the end, Bic was a wanted man in the eyes of both law enforcement and the criminal element. He could end this now by turning himself in or sailing a boat into a hurricane. Either way, the only true ending to this was him as a dead man. The hit was on, and in prison they'd eventually find a way to get at him. He was actually safer unconfined. As for disappearing, well, there was Gracie. She was everything to him. The last thing he needed was for them to flush him out by getting to her.

There were also Caroline and Mack, who'd helped him when he

didn't deserve help. That got him thinking. Maybe he could—

"Right," Parelli said. He was holding a map in his hand and a phone to his ear when he emerged from the clubhouse in mid-conversation. "Good work, my friend. I owe you a bottle of Pappy. No, you deserve it. Take care." He disconnected the call. "Well, we found the Braddick kid. He's in Los Altos. Practically right around the corner from me. Also, if my guy's right, and it usually is, there's another player joining the chess match. They call him the Irishman. Mean sonofabitch."

"You know him?"

"Works mostly international jobs. A real pro." He held up a road map. "Looks like the idiots are mobilizing after all. Probably a scratch plan, but it reveals quite a bit. There's a route here. I think if I spend some time with it I can map out exactly what's going on. In the meantime, I'm gonna plant a little surprise for our friends in case they return to their little roach motel here. When I'm done, we'll head on out to Los Altos."

"Hang on," Bic said. "We need to go back and look for Hawk."

Parelli cocked his head. "I guarantee going to see the kid is the best way to find Hawk."

Bic knew his next response would be a huge risk to his friendship with Parelli. But it had been bothering him ever since he figured out the kid was behind it. "You need to make me a promise first."

Parelli cocked his head. "Promises. You got a lot of nerve. My wife is dead because of a hit on you."

"No Tony, let's set one thing straight. Your wife is dead because you sent me in to kill the Braddicks, not telling me I'd have to murder them in front of their little kids." Bic paced away, then came back, gritting his teeth as he spoke. "You knew I wouldn't have done the job, so you hid that from me, didn't you?"

Parelli narrowed his eyes. "Our business is a messy one, Bic."

"Good, you got my point...What's the endgame here, Tony? Because, honestly, I'm not in the mood to keep killing people. I've got to move past it."

"Gettin' past it? Your life, my life, they're soaked in blood. It's what we do. There's no escaping who we are, except in a box." Parelli licked his lips. "So it's gotta happen, Bic, because the only way out of this is to fight. First, we're going to lay waste to every one of these chickenshit bikers. They're all going to be put into the dirt. And second, we're going to get to the bottom of this hit. They gotta go down too. No lousy little fetus with a trust fund can get my wife killed and…" He stopped and his face went grave, as if he'd said too much.

"And what, Tony?" Bic said, his voice hard. "And live?"

Parelli's smile disappeared. "Okay. Okay, Bic. We'll play it your way. We'll let this kid live. Hell, we'll set him up with ice cream and cotton candy too, if it'll make you happy. But we're gonna get info out of him one way or another and you're not going to stop that from happening. *Comprende?*"

Bic nodded. "I want your word."

Parelli glared at Bic with the type of intensity two male lions do right before they rip each other apart. "You have my word."

"One more thing."

"Don't push it."

"I need Caroline's number. I don't have it on this burner."

Parelli shook his head and took out his phone. "You're turning soft as ice cream, you know that?"

Bic's phone dinged with a text. Caroline's number.

"Give me a minute," Bic said.

Parelli opened the trunk to the AMG grabbing a satchel. "You get fifteen."

Pacing around the back of the clubhouse, Bic felt a strange sensation listening to the phone ringing on the other end of the line. It was a feeling he only reserved for Gracie, the feeling that he would do anything he needed to do good by her. He didn't know why he felt that way about Caroline now. He felt like rushing to her side. Maybe it was the fact that, if Mack were to die, she'd be on her own. And Bic Green just wasn't okay with that.

"Agent Maddox," she answered.

"Hey, it's me."

Her voice lower. "Bic?"

"Yeah."

Colder now. "Now's not a good time."

"How is he?"

He heard her moving, as if walking to a location out of earshot of others. "How is he? Is that what you just asked?"

"Yeah."

She made a breathy sound like one who's fed up with everything. "Well, Bic, funny you should ask, because it looks like he's got a fifty-fifty shot and those odds may decrease in the next twenty-four hours. So that's how he is, no thanks to you."

"Caroline—"

"No, no, no, Bic. You don't get to pull any heartstring garbage with me. And you got some nerve calling me. You realize we took a chance on you? Somehow, we thought when your father was gone, the madness would stop, but the reality I've realized while watching my husband on a machine twenty-four-seven is that it was you, Bic. It was *always* you and it will never leave you. Stay far, *far* away from me and my family."

The call disconnected. Bic stood with the phone glued to his ear. He let it drop slowly and took a deep breath.

She was right. He'd all but ruined her life by now. There wasn't anyone he could touch without some terrible thing befalling them. Even Auntie Elodie, the voodoo mamba who'd helped lift his father's curse from his head, even someone as good-hearted as that wound up nearly dead because of her involvement with him. It hurt bad. This is what it felt like to have feelings for someone.

He walked back around to the front of the clubhouse, thinking to himself it wasn't much fun to care about people. Being dead inside was easier.

Parelli was crouched before the entrance, a small device in his hand.

"You wired the place?"

Parelli smirked like the devil. "I got a hunka C4 under one of their ugly couches big enough to turn this entire area into a meteor crater. And this..." He held up the device. "This is a laser trip wire..."

"I can see that."

"What you can't see is that this little sucker is a counter. I set it at nine. It won't detonate the C4 until it counts nine people inside. When the ninth crosses, the little rabbits are gonna get a nice welcome home." Parelli stood up, dusted off his knees, and looked at Bic. "Well?"

"Well, what?"

"You get in touch with them?"

"Mack's got a fifty-fifty chance."

Parelli pulled out his phone, looked up a number and called. "Yeah, I need a favor. There's an FBI agent by the name of Mack Maddox in bad shape. I need you to reach out and make sure he got the best docs in the world working on him...thanks, I owe you one." Parelli walked over to Bic and put his hand on his shoulder. "You know I hate the heat, but I like those two agents. If he's anything like his wife, he'll pull through. You ready, pal?"

Bic looked into his old friend's shark-like eyes. Even though he was poison to everyone else, he and Parelli were actually good for one another. He found a renewed sense of purpose with the prospect of them cleaning up this mess together. "Thanks for making the call, Tony."

They hopped into the AMG G65 and set off for Los Altos with the blinding sun in their eyes.

40

Hawk remembered Houdini.

When he was a kid, his family had gone to the Houdini Museum in Scranton, Pennsylvania. It was a pure delight to the eight-year-old boy, enthralled as he was with the incredible magician and his real-life escapes, which had nothing to do with actual magic and everything to do with the perseverance of the human spirit.

Here was Houdini, chained from head to toe, encased in a chest and submerged in sub-freezing waters. Little did the audience know that the wily magician had stashed a set of lock picks inside a false lock that fastened a part of his fetters. Little did they know that the magician stuck his fingers down his throat and subsequently vomited up a key he had swallowed not moments before taking the stage. And little did they know that the miraculous straight jacket and handcuff escapes were due to the fact that Houdini dislocated his shoulders from their sockets and his thumbs from theirs, enabling him to slip out of those confiscations with the greatest of ease.

Hawk loved Houdini.

What would Houdini do now, chained by the wrist to a radiator in a nasty little Airbnb in God-knows-where? That was indeed a question.

He looked at his wrist. It was a nice wrist, if a bit bony and unevenly hairy. How would he detach his thumb from its socket if he needed or wanted to? He remembered the debilitating pain he'd been in during his recovery. The endless hours of excruciating misery while he struggled to walk again, to raise his arms above shoulder height, and to wiggle his hands. He was no stranger to pain, but he couldn't bear any more of it. The very thought of dislocating a thumb was the last—the very last—thing he could imagine doing. He couldn't dislocate a thumb any more than he could willingly puncture a lung. He'd try every last damn thing first before he did that.

He looked at the radiator. It was an old, ornate thing, painted white a long, long time ago. It stood on antique-looking feet, curvy and steadfast. The feet themselves were bolted to the floor. Whoever had done so ensured that they would stay secure for several lifetimes. He gave a couple of yanks on it. Nothing but the arrhythmic clanking of metal against metal. He tried to turn the bolt, and realized after but a few tries that he would have a better chance of pulling out one of his own teeth. Even a fairly clever tactic of wrapping a link of handcuff chain around the bolt and pulling it back and forth in a sawing motion in an attempt to catch the threads failed before it even began.

Hawk put his head back against the wall. He felt like crying. He'd been in worse situations. But pain has a way of creating hopelessness when all you can think about is your pain. All Hawk could think about was hopelessness.

Livin' on a prayer, he thought, and began to hum the Bon Jovi song to himself. Soon he was singing full-throated in the emptiness of the room. For all he knew, he was alone in the entire building.

He began to thump his heel against the floor in accompaniment to the tune.

Whoa, we're halfway there...

Thump... thump...

Livin' on a prayer...

An idea occurred to him: What if he wasn't alone after all?

He began to thump his heel against the floor. Over and over again. Both heels. Thump... thump...

Boy, if the Great Houdini could see him now, what the hell would he say?

Good job, kid. They'll never suspect a thing. Thump harder.

41

Alone in the world, Millie stood in the steamy hot attic of a stately two-story colonial. Usually she'd be cutting a small hole with limited peripheral view, but this nest would be set up in one of three large dormer windows. It was perfect. On her stomach, to a person on the ground outside, she would be all but invisible.

She yawned unexpectedly. Her sleep had been restless and agitated the previous night. In her dreams, she replayed several bad scenarios. The one that bothered her, most oddly enough, was having to put Hawk down. In just one night, she had become really fond of that bloke.

She fell back on her arse. It was a purposeful move. A fake "I give up," as she let out a very real sigh of exasperation. She put her elbows onto her knees and sat there, staring out the dormer at the peaceful house across the street, the one she'd be watching. It had taken a bit of wheeling and dealing, but she'd gotten the place clean with a little help of a phony call from the gas company:

We have detected a gas leak. You and your family must evacuate until we get out and inspect your house.

She felt an itch in her throat. It had to be the insulation. *Don't let that pink stuff get into your head, it will turn minutes into hours*, she thought as her mind began to race. It was these dreadful moments of realization, when it was all waiting—this is what she considered quitting over. Every. Sodding. Time. The wait.

What would Christopher say? "It's *all* waiting, love. Didn't you ever wonder why it is that all MI6 agents have nervous tics? Tapping fingers, eh? Grinding teeth?"

Cheeky bastard. He was perfect. That was the joke. No tics. No tells. Poker face to the last.

She shuddered to think of him and the avenging angel she'd become because of him. She'd better not go there. She was getting dangerously close in her memory to that day she found him, when the agent died and the killer was born—no, stop it. Once you injected emotion into the job, it was over. Maybe that's what had got him— *stop it, stop it, stop it!*

This job reminded her of those days. They were muddy. Unclear who the targets were, assignments changed on the drop of a dime. Now that she had freedom of choice, she vowed never to work under these circumstances again. Only take the straightforward ones. Here's a picture, a location, a payment, now go take him out. But the payout for this one was too big to pass up. Big enough to buy all the information she'd been chasing for the last several years.

No sense in setting up the rest of the nest when confirmation of the targets was still pending. She might have to break down. She'd learned this rather early in life, having nearly assassinated a would-be dictator on the rise in Myanmar. At the last minute, she'd gotten word that it was to be an inside job and was ordered to beat it back to HQ before the rival junta found out about her presence. In breaking down, one of the clamps holding the rifle in place had stuck. Cue the panic. She'd gotten the gun off the tripod but not before ripping open her trigger finger.

No tripod necessary for this job. It would be a detriment, actually. She looked over at the case that contained her rifle. It had a shamrock engraved into it. She smiled.

Edward, she thought. That would be a good name for her notorious hitman character. She liked the name. It was a proper name. Sturdy. Better than "the Irishman," as she was already known. It was the best cover, and it was so easy to pull off. Most of the Neanderthals in her business would never even suspect that a woman could kill all of these men. Even the word *hitman* made one assume it was a man. Couple that with "the Irishman" and *voila*, you had yourself a man, no questions asked. But if "the Irishman" had a first name, it would definitely be Edward. This way, she could go by Eddie the Mick. That had a nice ring to it. Cosa Nostra meets Looney Tunes.

She ran a hand through her cropped hair. It was soft and silky. Thank you, Biolage. She had an assortment of goodies—a wig, glasses, a police uniform, and some tape for her boobs—packed in the duffel. She'd need them soon enough. Right now, it was good to be a girl. Something about that juxtaposition of soft flesh and hard, destructive steel. She didn't like to analyze it too much. Too much analysis meant it was waiting time, and waiting sucked bollocks.

She pulled out her phone and opened the chess app. There was a problem she'd been working on for a good five days now. White to move and mate in two. Black king in a8 guarded by two pawns and a bishop with the white king in c8. White rook in a1.

Bloody impossible.

She let out a huff and put the phone down.

Waiting sucked *great bollocks*.

42

In the five-hour drive from LA to Los Altos, Bic had a lot of time to think. The car was pretty much dead silent between him and Parelli. Gazing out at the matte-black hood of the AMG G65 as it ate up highway, there was only one question he tried to answer: What he would say to the boy whose mother and father he had killed? Ironically enough, he should have been more qualified to answer this question than anyone else. What would he have wanted his father to say to him if he'd come and asked for forgiveness? Bic remembered the letter he'd believed to be a true heartfelt letter from his deceased father.

The thing he remembered was not to insult the kid by asking for forgiveness. That was just wrong, and he had no right to do so. Trying to figure out what to actually say when he looked into that boy's eyes became a swirl of screaming confusion. Bic's mind jumped from the image of the screaming kid pounding on the movie room door, to the thud of the frying pan smashing his mother's skull. The thoughts went back and forth, back and forth, setting a chain reaction as if an atom bomb just went off in his head.

"You ready, pal? We're here," Parelli said, stopping in front of the Braddicks' house.

Bic turned to Parelli. He could feel the moisture in his eyes.

"Mother of God," Parelli said, with the look on his face as if he'd seen a black ghost.

Bic's head felt like it was burning above ten million degrees. He looked at his reflection in the windshield. His eyes were amber white. Everything about him was unstable.

Parelli handed Bic his water. "Drink some."

Bic did, and he started to cool down.

"Good, we need to turn those babies down a little. I haven't seen those eyes since way back in 'Nam. You sure you're okay?"

"I stole a lot from these kids."

"I know. I thought a lot about what you said earlier. You had a rule never to kill innocent people. I should never have brought you the billionaire deal. I just knew—"

"Let me just try to make this right, and hopefully this kid will move on with his life."

"Okay."

With this, the men exited the G65 and headed toward the front porch of the house, where they rang the bell and waited.

After a time, the door opened, and a young boy peered out. He was pale and skinny, and his hair was a tangle of black. He looked like an anime character.

"You Nathaniel?" Parelli said.

The kid stood frozen, staring at Bic as if he saw the grim reaper himself standing on his porch.

Parelli broke the awkward silence. "Is your uncle home?"

His words broke Nathaniel out of his trance. The kid took off like a bullet.

"Sonofabitch," Parelli muttered to himself. He went into the house and Bic followed.

Bic breathed heavily, feeling like he was hyperventilating. He put a hand on the back of the living room couch and focused on deep, slow breaths.

Parelli turned to Bic. "Man, this has got you all kinds of messed up."

Bic nodded in pain. He just wanted to weep. Seeing the boy was just too much. He could tell the boy wasn't right. He didn't know how, but when he looked into that boy's eyes, there was an instant connection to his soul. And all he could see was that he was broken beyond healing.

A gunshot exploded the air in the room, as the sofa took a hit in one of its cushions, missing Bic by inches.

Both heads turned to see Nathaniel holding a shotgun on top of the stairs.

"I knew you'd come back," he snarled at Bic.

"Nathaniel," Bic said gently, showing his palms, "I'm not here to hurt you."

"Yeah, kid, we're just here to talk."

Bic saw Parelli inch his hand inside his jacket, obviously reaching for the hand cannon resting in his shoulder holster.

Bic walked in front of Parelli, creating a shield between him and the shotgun, hoping it would calm him down. "Nathaniel, I deserve to die for what I did. And there's nothing I can do to heal the pain or your hatred of me. But what you got yourself involved in doesn't end with me dead." Bic could tell he struck a nerve with the boy. "Whoever you hired will own someone like you for the rest of your life. They'll threaten to hurt your sister. We can help you get out of this mess."

"My uncle's talking to the lawyers at my dad's company right now," the boy said, the shotgun trembling in his arms. "They'll sort this out."

"Nathaniel, no lawyers can help with the type of people you got yourself involved with," Bic said, his voice pleading, being mindful to stay in front of Parelli. "Please, put the gun down so we can talk. Nathaniel… we just want to find out who you hired and stop those bad men."

"Kid could have at least six more rounds in that pump-action," Parelli muttered from behind Bic.

"Nathaniel, remember when I gave your parents my word that I wouldn't hurt you if they did what I said?"

Nathaniel nodded.

"That still stands, and I won't break it."

Nathaniel lowered his weapon. Bic's heart filled with hope.

"Good, Nathaniel. The next thing we're going to do is sit down and figure out how to get you out of this mess. Would you like that?"

Tears filled the boy's eyes as he nodded again. This was a giveaway. Things had already gone terribly wrong and he needed Bic. And it certainly seemed like Bic was his only hope. But right at his highest moment, out of the corner of his eye, he caught a movement from the kitchen. Bic turned his head, realizing that Parelli had caught it too. Only Parelli had caught it first and was now gripping the little girl with his pistol against her temple.

"Curious little kitten here," Parelli said. "Don't you know curiosity killed the cat?"

"Let her go!" Nathaniel screamed, training the shotgun on Parelli.

Bic held up his hands. "Nathaniel, hold on!"

Nathaniel's gun went to Bic, then back to Parelli.

"Don't do it, Nathaniel," Bic said, his tone urgent. "Let me handle this. Parelli, let the girl go."

"Bic. I'm tired of listening to you beg this kid like he's got the upper hand here."

"I'll shoot you," Nathaniel said.

"Then do it, you little mouse turd," Parelli hissed. Then he chuckled. "You're a real badass with that thing. A threat to sofas everywhere."

"Nathaniel," Bic said, edging again toward Parelli to block him from shooting Lucy. "If you pull that trigger, you're going to give this man a reason to act! Don't do it!" Bic was almost in front of Lucy, but he didn't want to move too fast. In this type a situation, any twinge could cause a trigger finger to squeeze. "Or worse, what if you hit Lucy?"

Tears were streaming down the boy's face. "Let my sister go!"

"*Only chance is to put that gun down*," Bic shouted, enunciating every word. "Nothing is worth losing your sister! Dammit, Nathaniel! Listen to me!" Bic suddenly realized that his voice was beginning to break. Hot tears were pooling in the corner of his eyes. He didn't want to cry, but all the emotions, the mixture of his pain with the boy's pain, were coming to a head.

"Kid," Parelli snarled, "I'm done messing around."

"Nathaniel!"

All heads turned toward the sound, which had come from the little girl in Parelli's arms. It was high, dry, and cracking—scratchy and full of pain.

"I trust him!" she said, her crying eyes focused laser-like on her brother.

"You talked," the boy said, stunned, as he lowered his shotgun.

"Good girl," Parelli said, letting her go.

Lucy ran past Bic, who was walking slowly toward Nathaniel. She flew up the stairs and he dropped the shotgun as she jumped into his arms.

"I love you so much," he said, sob-sucking and sniffling while squeezing her in his arms.

Standing over the two kids, Bic felt like a giant. They were so small so helpless. All his anxiety seeing the sibling embrace brought back memories of Chandra, his big sister and Gracie's mom. The little girl looked up at Bic. Lost in her larger-than-life blue eyes, he forgot for a second who he was to these kids, and before he knew it, they were both wrapped in his massive arms.

"It's going to be okay," Bic said as his heart filled with something he hadn't felt in a long time: Hope.

43

The second the wonderful moment was over, Nathaniel tore his sister out of Bic's arms.

"Don't ever touch us again, you murderer!" Nathaniel spat. "Ever!"

"Well, great, now that we've reestablished who everyone is, I've got some questions that need answering," Parelli said.

The four sat at the kitchen table. The scene was like a Bizarro World Norman Rockwell painting: Two hardened killers, legends of the underworld for decades, on one side, and two little kids on the other.

"What do you want to know?" Nathaniel asked, his voice reserved.

"For starters," Parelli said, "I'd like to know who you contracted."

"It was on the dark web," Nathaniel said, desperation coming into his voice as he remembered something, "but I'm short on money now, and..."

"And now it's a mess," Parelli said. "All because of some rando you found on the dark web—probably not even a real broker. Which explains the low-level bikers."

"I just..." Nathaniel began, choking back a sob as he looked to Bic, "I just wanted you dead. I wasn't thinking straight."

Lucy huffed and squeaked at her brother in both disbelief and disappointment.

Bic noticed Nathaniel scratching his inner forearm. It was covered in scars left from recent cuts. He remembered a girl from back in foster care who used to cut herself. The more depressed she got, the deeper the cuts. Until one day...

"Your actions were just," Bic said. "Help us figure this out and we will make it all go away."

"Who is your contact on the dark web?" Parelli said, all business.

"I... I don't know."

"Let me get this straight. You gave someone two billion dollars and you don't know who you're dealing with?"

Nathaniel hesitantly nodded. "I sent a hundred million, but lost most of the rest in crypto."

"A hundred mil to a stranger." Without warning, Parelli reached across the table and slapped the kid across the face, hard. "Do I look like Bozo the friggin' Clown to you?"

Nathaniel held his face. Parelli's meaty red hand print on his cheek dwarfed his own. "No, you look more like Bozo the bitch to me."

Parelli popped out of his seat, so quick the chair flew out from behind him. "I'm gonna teach you the meaning of that word by bitch-slapping you until you give me a name."

Lucy hid under the table, but Nathaniel didn't move. He was either stubborn or frozen in terror. Either way, Parelli wound up to slap him so hard his head was going to spin 360 degrees.

Bic grabbed Parelli's wrist, stopping him from swinging. "Enough, Tony. Let me handle this."

"This little punk got Barbara killed. He needs to be taught some manners."

"I know, but you gave me your word." Bic said firmly. He let go of Parelli's wrist.

Parelli fixed his jacket sleeve. "Back in the Bronx, we used to have a simple rule on the streets, us enforcers. If you're old enough to pull the trigger, then you're old enough to get one snapped back at ya."

"I'm not going to let you hurt this kid, not when it was our fault for what he did."

"One of two outcomes are happening here: The kid gives us something useful, or I work him over good."

"Tony, please. You will get revenge, I promise you. But, dammit, not on the boy. Can't you see something happening behind the scenes here? It wasn't him who went after you."

The men glared at one another, Bic broke the silence, "I'm asking you to do this for me. I can't take something happening to him."

"You'll see it to the end?"

"You have my word."

"Okay," Parelli agreed, as he continued to fix his jacket.

No later than Bic could celebrate defusing the situation, Parelli caught a glimpse of his cufflink, it triggered something from within and he pulled out his pistol.

"You killed the wrong man's wife, you little motherfuc-"

Bic rammed into Parelli as he fired at the kid. The shot went errant and Parelli flew into the wall.

"Stand down, Tony!" Bic stood between him and his target.

"You're gonna have to do a lot more than a little shove." Parelli aimed the weapon at Bic. "You have two seconds to get out of my way."

Pure instincts took over as Bic simultaneously snatched the pistol and rammed Parelli in the face with the butt of the gun. Parelli went flying back. The gun discharged at the floor, causing Lucy to scream. The sound went through Bic like a knife.

Staring down at Parelli, he pointed. "You gave me your word, Tony. I told you I would see this through. Just let me handle the kid."

"This is what I get. My most trusted friend turns on me to protect the person trying to kill him," Parelli said, his face a mess of bright red blood that gushed from his nose.

"I know what revenge can do to a person," Bic countered. "I'm willing to chalk it up to pain." Here, he shot a glance at Nathaniel, and keeping his eyes on the boy, he said, "It ruins you from the inside, warps your mind, makes you into a shell that can only hurt and nothing else."

Parelli hopped to his feet and rushed.

He was no match for Bic Green.

Bic merely had to put up a defensive blow with his right to send Parelli back down to the floor groaning.

Parelli got up slowly. "Your punches are getting soft too."

"Don't do this Tony," Bic said.

Panting, Parelli got to his feet. "Guess you learned well from your old man how to treat family."

"I'm begging you."

Parelli charged again, this time more aggressively. He launched his body off the ground, driving his shoulder into Bic's midsection. Then his feet found the ground running and he drove Bic into a China cabinet. The front glass shattered and plates spilled off the shelves on to the floor.

Unfortunately for Parelli Bic not only absorbed the blow, but had caught him in a guillotine chokehold.

It was tight, Bic knew it and so did Parelli.

"You tap." Bic growled.

"Not a chance." Parelli said as he punched Bic in the kidney area.

With no leverage, the blow was weak. Bic squeezed tighter cutting off all blood flow to the brain. Parelli went red, then blue, then limp.

Bic sat Parelli on the chair, making sure he didn't fall.

Parelli quickly came to and made his way to his feet. A little wobbly, but too proud to use anything to help him balance.

"Families can disagree, we'll figure this out," Bic pleaded. "Not on this one, Bic. You just flushed forty years of brotherhood down the toilet," Parelli said with a dismissive wave. "Have a nice life with your new adopted kids."

With this, Parelli turned his back on Bic and limped out of the house, not even bothering to close the door behind him.

44

"**G**it your arse in soight, ya daft prat," she said, her voice guttural and dripping with Celtic pride. It helped every so often to speak like this to herself. It aided in the role play. She was the Irishman, after all. She needed to feel it in her throat.

She'd been watching the front door of the house ever since the text came to "stand by." That usually meant the target info was imminent. "Hang tight" meant more info was needed. Those were the worst messages to get. You spend an hour or so keeping your adrenaline at bay, all to have it gush in one giant tsunami once that little alert buzzer buzzed. Then you check your text and it tells you, well, hm, maybe or maybe not. Just wait a little longer. And now your hands and legs are shaking because there's no focus. And the only thing you can do in that situation is feel it buzzing through you like a current.

But the text came and told her to stand by. She was ready. She'd assembled her rifle, named 'Lucky,' for obvious reasons, and waited. Periodically she'd stare through the scope, getting a feel for the view. Even though it was night, between the moon and all the uplighting of the houses, she opted for day vision.

And then Parelli came out of the house, and his face was a mess of blood.

"Look at you, ya manky old dosser. What happened? Ya git yerself fluthered and fall down?"

She watched him stumble to his AMG G65. Before he entered, he turned back and spit on the ground. And that's when her phone buzzed, igniting another current in her.

Target confirmed. Bic Green. 2 children. Nathaniel and Lucy. A picture of the latter two followed. A second text arrived: *When this is all wrapped up, $5,000,000 bonus if scene investigation concludes Bic Green killed the kids.*

Kids. Really? *Sick feck*

It was a dirty, slimy game, her business, but the money would get her closer to Christopher's murderers. At any rate, she had a feeling it was going to be Bic Green.

She peered through the sight. Parelli was just driving off in his SUV. She could have blown his head off easily had he been the target.

She swept the gun a few degrees to the left and aimed at the open door. No one was there. Shifting slightly, she caught sight of Bic at the window. He was watching the bleeding old man drive away. She was readying the kill shot when the bugger moved away from the window.

"Feck off," she said, wondering if the kids were already dead.

She was going to have to play the waiting game some more.

45

Bic got down on one knee and stared at the boy, keeping a comfortable distance between them. Parelli's blood on his shirt was a stark reminder of what had just happened between them. He was devastated by it. Parelli was his oldest friend. They had been through a lot, stretching all the way back to the jungles of 'Nam. But he had made up his mind about these two kids. There was a debt to pay and he was going to pay it, at any cost. Unfortunately, the cost was already beginning to reveal itself. Losing his best friend was a hefty price. And it was only the start.

"I know how you feel about me…"

"No, you don't," the boy said through gritted teeth.

"It's not safe here. I need you to let me help you."

"I'm not gonna believe a murdering bastard."

"I can't bring your parents back. But what I can do now is protect you and Lucy."

"Why?"

"Nathaniel!" said the girl, her voice in shreds.

Nathaniel looked at her.

"Please," Lucy said.

"He murdered Mom and Dad and you want to go with him?"

She nodded her head. She'd never been more confident.

Nathaniel shook his head no. Bic could tell he felt a little betrayed by his sister.

"What was the last thing the men you hired said to you?"

Nathaniel looked at Lucy. "They said they were going to kill us if I didn't pay."

"I took so much from you guys." With no other way, Bic allowed himself the luxury of flowing tears. They came easily. "I know I can't change my past mistakes," he said between sobs. "I wish I could, but I can't. But I can protect you and Lucy from the men coming after you. Nathaniel, look at me. It won't make up for what I did, but it's the best I can do..." Bic's voice trailed off in a long sigh of misery.

After a moment, he composed himself, shocked at the release of pain and suffering. It felt like a cleansing of the soul. Then he stood up and wiped his eyes with his ratty shirt. He felt like the orphan he was.

"Where will we go?"

Bic cleared his throat. "Somewhere safe. A hiding place, so I can figure this out."

"You haven't thought about it?"

"No."

"So you *did* come here to kill us."

"I came here to get answers," Bic said sternly. "My friend was a little emotional. His wife got killed because of what you did."

Nathaniel looked at him, his eyes cold and calculating. "Will you let me carry a gun?"

Bic looked at the boy, second guessing his emotional plea. Did the kid think he was weak because he let out some emotion?

"I said, will you let me carry a gun?"

"I..."

Nathaniel took a step toward him. "I'll trust you if you let me carry a gun. That's it. So if I think you're lying at any time, I can shoot you in the head."

A whimper from Lucy caught Bic off guard.

"No," she said. "No, Nathaniel."

"It's okay, Lucy," Nathaniel said, his eyes trained on Bic. "We have an understanding. Right, Bic?"

"If that's what it takes, then yes. Just make sure you don't shoot yourself or your sister."

Nathaniel moved carefully over to where the shotgun lay on the floor.

"Before you pick up that gun, I want to give you a bit of warning. For what I've done, my heart would be fine with you shooting me dead. It would only be right. But my heart and my survival instincts are two different things. Please remember that."

Nathaniel nodded before he bent down, and came up with its business end pointed toward Bic.

Lucy made another sound of distress. Bic stood still, watching the boy's eyes. Slowly, he lowered the barrel.

"You should get some things for the trip," Bic said softly. "Clothes, and anything else you want to take. Keep it real light."

"Lucy," Nathaniel said, his eyes still on Bic, "wanna get us some clothes?"

Lucy nodded, then left the room.

Nathaniel backed up a few paces. "Have a seat, Bic."

Bic nodded and sat on the edge of the sofa next to the charred hole from Nathaniel's previous miss.

Nathaniel, too, backed himself into a chair and sat down, the gun lowered, yet at the ready.

A sound began outside somewhere, grew louder.

A roar of motorcycles.

Bic got up and shot over to the window. "They found us already!" he said, and turned to the boy. "They're coming. I need you and Lucy to find the best hiding place in the house."

The rumble of the bikes grew so loud it sounded like they were at the front door. The boy froze.

"Nathaniel, go get your sister and hide now!"

The boy snapped to and darted up the stairs.

Bic went to the kitchen to retrieve Parelli's gun off the floor.

46

Bic knew having to protect two kids was going to be a huge tactical disadvantage. Hiding in a safe spot was going to be key. The less he had to worry about them, the better their chances. The kids came running down the stairs sounding like a stampede of horses.

"I said to go hide," Bic said as he held the firearm, ready if anyone came through the front door.

"Our uncle's office is the best spot," Nathaniel said.

The girl nodded her head out of habit.

"It's always locked. It's more like a safe room and has no windows," Nathaniel said leading the way to a room off the kitchen. "Apparently my little sister knew where my uncle kept the key and never told me."

Lucy shrugged her shoulders then produced a key.

Nathaniel took the key and tried it on the door. It opened up onto what looked like a large walk-in closet that had been converted into a surveillance hub for the entire house.

"Whoa," Nathaniel said.

"Your uncle likes to keep tabs on you," Bic said.

"I guess so." Nathaniel screwed up his face. He was feeling a little uneasy about this. How much had his uncle seen of his business with the razor?

"Probably was worried after what happened," Bic said. "Wanted to watch after you, keep you safe."

Nathaniel shook his head in frustrated confusion. "Doubtful."

He led his sister into the room, then hesitantly handed Bic the shotgun. "Have some ammo too," he said, unloading a handful of shells from his pocket.

"I'm going to keep you two safe," Bic said as he flipped the shotgun upside down, immediately pushing shells into the loading flap. Doing one after another as quick as he could while adding, "Do not come out of this room until I come get you."

Nathaniel nodded and locked the door.

"Would ya lookee that. They left the door open for us, boys..."

Bic heard the voice of what he presumed to be the leader resounding through the house. With Parelli leaving, he knew he had to be efficient with his limited resources. He had a shotgun with seven shells loaded and two extra in his pocket, plus Parelli's hand cannon, with seven rounds remaining. His hiding spot behind the bullet-blasted sofa was his first advantage. His second was the knowledge that these guys probably weren't trained in urban warfare or any other type of combat training. No ambush makes his presence known like this goof just did. They must not know he's here. They probably think they're just coming for the kids.

He stared at the back of the sofa, focusing on the plain beige fabric, blanking out his mind, listening. He might as well have been back in the jungles of 'Nam listening for Charlie's approach. Charlie wasn't careless. You barely heard them coming at all.

Footsteps fell on carpet, then floor, then carpet again. He knew just where they were.

Bic sprang up. The two men not more than ten feet away had barely any time to react. He blasted the first, pumped the firearm to eject the spent shell, and shot the second. The tight spread of the shot caught the bearded biker in the chest, throwing him back as if he was filled with hay.

Bic pumped again with his aim never leaving the front open door. Anyone trying to enter was going to get blasted. He'd counted eight total when they pulled up in their noise machines. He figured after the first two announced their presence, the others would just come right in for the slaughter, but apparently they had the sense to enter the house from different angles. He'd better get the lay of this house and quick.

Flight, fight, or freeze ran through Nathaniel's mind as he covered Lucy's eyes. "Don't look."

"I wanna see," she whined. Her voice was gaining in strength.

"We shouldn't see this," he said, feeling an intense queasiness in his belly after seeing what Bic had just done. He stared at the console, and watched Bic moving throughout the house. He removed his hands from Lucy's eyes and grabbed the chain of her locket.

"What are you doing?" she protested.

He took the locket off from around her neck and opened it. There was their mother. Nathaniel felt his queasiness mix with a deep longing for everything that was missing in his life. The profound emptiness within him echoed with loss. Their mother was beautiful. Long, silky hair the color of cherrywood. Her eyes were amazing, not for their color or shape, but for the love he felt every time he caught her gaze. And he could almost hear that brown velvet voice of hers.

"Here," he said, fighting a sob in his throat. "Stare at Mom. I want you to really look at her. You can talk to her too. She's in Heaven and can hear you if you talk to her."

She looked at him, her eyes full of sadness.

Nathaniel hugged his sister, fighting hard to keep those tears at bay.

She looked down at the locket, her face full of worry.

Nathaniel turned to the console and began moving knobs. The pictures on the screens moved here and there. He was a quick study. It was pretty easy to figure out which knob did what to which camera.

His eyes fell on the screen showing the rec room. It had a bank of windows looking out of the back side of the house. A smooth glare of light from the Tiffany-style pool table fixture turned to streamers of rainbow light as he adjusted the camera's angle. It finally fell on the window, where a biker was ramming a crowbar through it.

Bic heard the deafening clatter as he stealthily moved to the source of the sound, half wondering if a trap had just been set. He was glad it was on the opposite wing of the house from where he'd stashed the kids.

It was some sort of gaming room. A burgundy-colored pool table sat square in the middle of a playfully decorated space that looked like it was custom-designed to capture all the glory of the 80's. Hawk would've loved this room, he thought, then quickly hoped his friend was okay before he got back to business.

One of the windows along the rear wall was smashed and jarred open. A biker, not realizing a predator was in the hall leading to the room, attempted to climb into the house. Bic waited until the man was halfway in before taking a shot at his big bald head. The man's head exploded. The headless body went limp, stuck half inside and half out of the house.

A shot rang out and a bullet whizzed past his head.

Nathaniel winced. Bic had just shot another one coming through the window. The adrenaline surged to chaotic levels as he found himself rooting for the murderer of his parents. He looked at Lucy, who was staring lovingly at the picture of their mother, cooing softly to it. She seemed to trust Bic. Poor thing was too young to know, too fragile to handle the truth.

He turned back to the screen.

Bic was in big trouble.

Bic had no idea where that shot had come from as he darted into the game room.

He pressed himself back against the wall. Another shot splintered the top molding in the doorway. He poked the barrel back into the hallway and took a blind shot, then poked his head out just in time to see another barrel come around the wall down the hallway leading to the game room. He ducked in and the shot came. More of the molding was blown away, the tiny missiles of wood just missing his face.

"*Let's bum rush this dude!*" he heard a voice say. Another said, "*Shoot his ass right through the drywall.*"

The men charged down the hall, using their superior numbers and firepower to their advantage as they filled the wall and doorway with bullets.

Moving like the soldier he had been, he dove over the pool table, landing crouched behind it for leverage. He locked his arms under the table and flipped it. The enormous mass boomed like a bomb going off when it landed on its side. Balls clattered out and rolled like giant marbles across the floor.

Nathaniel gasped.

"What's the matter?" Lucy said.

He kept his eyes on the rec room camera. "Nothing. Keep talking to Mom. She gets lonely when you don't talk to her."

"Are we gonna die?" she said.

He looked at her. Adult worry on a child's face.

"Everything is fine," he said, trying his best to fake a smile. "Keep talking to Mom."

"Okay," she said.

Nathaniel turned his gaze back to the screens.

From the hall, two guys on each side of the doorway were firing at Bic, using the wall as cover. A third was in the doorway and a fourth had kicked a hole clear through the drywall. He was on one knee shooting through the hole in the wall. Bic was totally pinned down. If he could just warn Bic. Or better yet, he could create a diversion. It would give him a window and give him the upper hand.

That was it. But how? Gunshots? The only gun he knew of was the one Bic was now using. What other diversions? Smoke? Fire?

Fire. That was it.

He could burn the place down, so he had to be careful. Maybe set a small fire in the hallway or something. Bic could escape through the window and he and Lucy could run out the front door. It had to work. He had to try *something*.

He put a hand on Lucy's shoulder. "Stay here."

Her face became panicked. "Where are you going?"

"I'll be right back. Just stay here!"

She shook her head frantically. "No!"

"Yes. I promise. No one's gonna hurt you. And I'm not leaving, I'm just going out for one minute then I'll come get you, okay? I promise."

Lucy clutched her locket tightly, clapping it shut and putting it back on. She pressed it to her heart. The picture of it destroyed him inside.

"I promise," he said again, giving her a hug.

He turned to the door, paused for just a second to steel himself, then opened it with a mission.

Standing there was a massive biker. The parts of his face not covered by his greasy black beard looked like it was set on fire and stomped out with golf shoes.

"Well now, howdy, pardner!" he said with a gap-toothed smile. "Wanna come out and play?"

The gunfight was on.

Shots blasted the front of the pool table as the bikers had total control. Bic knew a pool table could hold up for only so long. He switched to Parelli's handgun. With each continuing shot thumping into the table, he wondered if this one was going to make it through. He needed to do something, but what?

A loud little girl's shrieking scream cut through the gunfire. The call for help abruptly awoke the worst version of Bic's primitive self.

"It's just a matter of time, boy!"

Bic froze. Clarence?

His mind filled with the image of a frying pan smashing his mother's skull, his father's doped-out eyes bloody red and flashing before him. His veins pulsed with rocket fuel. He let out a growl as he thrusted every ounce of his body and power against the pool table, rushing it toward the men like a football sled. Roaring louder as he picked up speed, he reached what felt like sprinting speed as he collided with the wall.

With the force of a seven-hundred-pound wrecking ball, the table blasted through the wall, smashing three of the men to oblivion. Left behind in the wreckage was a mist of dust, broken two-by-fours, and scattered pieces of drywall, just as if an actual bomb had exploded.

Bic turned to the fourth man just in time to see his confused face confronted with the impossibility of what had just taken place.

Another scream from Lucy.

And the devil inside Bic Green awakened with a lust for guts.

With cat-like speed, he closed the distance between him and the fourth biker, springing the gun out of the man's hand as the shot went off. He slammed the man to the floor.

"It's pork chop eatin' time," he said. It was either a squirming biker beneath him, or his father. Rage had blinded Bic Green. Either way, the guy was going to eat dirt.

Bic grabbed a pool ball from the floor and rammed it into the dude's mouth, shattering just about every tooth inside. The guy screamed and gurgled, as Bic wrapped his hands around his neck and squeezed. Bones crunched. The eyes bulged. The face was blue, then purple. The trachea cracked and gave way altogether.

The body went limp as a rag.

Bic released him, grabbed the man's handgun, and sprinted to the other side of the house.

The horror he found in the living room stopped him in his tracks.

47

The biker wore a DOH cut-off leather jacket with no undershirt. Tattoos covered most of his exposed body. One of the man's meaty hands held a fistful of the front of Nathaniel's shirt, the whimpering boy dangling before him. The biker's other hand had a nine-millimeter barrel shoved deep into Nathaniel's mouth. Trapped beneath the man's size 13 boot, covering most of her back, was Lucy—face down and wailing on the hardwood floor.

"Nice of you to join the party!" the biker said. "We were just about to play Tiddly Winks, right kids?"

Using the gun as a lever, he made Nathaniel's head nod. The boy gagged. The biker then put some extra weight on Lucy's body, pushing all the air out of her and eliciting a higher squeak to her wail.

The whines of pain from the kids cut right through Bic's heart. Every single bit of this was a direct result of the kill loop he'd forged when he murdered their parents.

"Let them go," he snarled.

"Sometimes Christmas comes early, you know what I mean?"

Bic noticed one of the man's patches read, 'SGT OF ARMS.' For the bit he studied in the last couple of days, he knew this club officer, of all the members, was the most likely to have prior military training. Definitely not a plus, considering the circumstances.

The biker's eyes grew wide. "You think I can't pull the trigger, you subhuman? Stop me in time. Go ahead, big man. Take the shot."

The beast inside Bic could taste this guy's blood. It wanted nothing more than to say that little phrase right before he butchered him. But there was something else within him, strong enough to know the best move to keep these kids alive was to have patience. He needed to run scenarios until an acceptable out presented itself.

Like an experienced poker player, the biker was calm, waiting patiently for Bic to give him a tell. No doubt he had position on Bic, plus he believed he was sitting with the best possible hand, unbeatable. This was his only weakness right now: *hubris.*

The two main kill switches were the head and the spine. A high A-zone hit, heart or lungs, the boy was dead for sure. With the man facing Bic and Nathaniel's back to him, the spine was not an option. The only option left was the head. The T-box area—the nose and the eyes. He could mash it right into the sucker's brain.

He needed this man shut off in less than one tenth of one second.

Bic could see the tension in the man's finger, it was already snug on the trigger. He knew for sure, if he missed, Nathaniel was going to die.

"Come on," the biker mocked. "Take it, boy. Call me if you think I'm bluffin'. Ten million dollars, boy. That's what I'm walkin' away with."

Bic's mind raced. The head was moving too fast. An instant kill was impossible without a reflexive pulling of that trigger, killing Nathaniel.

With no other recourse, Bic lowered his weapon.

The biker licked his lips. "That's a good doggie."

With this, he took his boot off of Lucy's back. She began to crawl away.

"Not so fast, little girl," he said. "Come, stand up straight, right next to me." Lucy immediately followed orders.

Bic took a step forward, realizing the guy was creating another shield.

"Whoa," said the biker, "hold on there, big fella."

Bic froze, still over ten feet away, his gun pointed at the floor.

The biker gave the gun in the Nathaniel's mouth a little jiggle, clanking the steel against his teeth. "I'm gonna make you a deal, ten-million-dollar man."

"I'm listening."

"I know you been calculatin'. If I shoot the boy, you shoot me dead. Now, how am I gonna collect ten million dollars for killing you if I'm dead and you're alive?"

"Nobody has to die here."

Both men stared at one another. Bic tried to get a read on the biker's face, but it was unreadable. Then the corner of his mouth twitched into his cheek. With a smirk, he said, "On the count of three, you're gonna make a choice. That choice is: who gets shot? Option number one, I blow this kid's head right off his shoulders or, option two, you put one in your own head."

Lucy wailed.

"What about the boy?" said Bic.

"He lives."

"Trust is earned," Bic said, raising the gun back up toward the biker.

"Semper Fi, my brother."

"Let the girl go," Bic said.

"Go on, get." The biker jammed the gun further into Nathaniel's mouth, pulling him closer.

Lucy ran off.

"Make your choice. Now!"

Bic slowly brought his gun to his head. He had been near death many times in his life, but never by his own hand. All the calculating he had done, he now had less than one second to finish. Kill himself for Nathaniel, he had checked the box that he would do that. Now the second part was the question of whether this guy was really going to let the kids live if he did. Bic's final thought as his second ran out was the biker's own words: Semper Fi.

He began to squeeze the trigger just as he realized he would meet his father in hell.

48

The biker's head exploded, sending blood and brain matter against the wall as if they were shot out of a confetti cannon.

What the hell? Bic thought. His trembling hand lowered the gun from his head.

Nathaniel had shown good instincts, quickly pulling the gun out of his mouth before any reflexive action could occur.

Bic charged, just as the boy turned towards him. He tackled him to the floor. Using his momentum, he made sure they ended up against the wall toward the front of the house.

Nathaniel pulled himself out of Bic's clutch. "What the hell are you doing?"

Bic pointed up at the bullet hole in the window. "Sniper's across the street."

Nathaniel jerked his head toward the window and re-cozied up against the wall.

From the position of the hole, Bic could tell that the shot was taken from a high angle with a downward trajectory. That meant only one possibility: the man who took the shot was across the street, either on the second story of the house or attic. Bic had to decide if he should go after the sniper or flee.

"You got shot!" Nathaniel said, his voice panicked.

"It's nothin'," Bic said, looking at his arm. Blood was trickling out of it pretty good. He would have to address that real soon. But now was not the time.

"Lucy," Bic called out, "We are both okay, but I need you to go to the door at the back of the house. *Do not* go in front of any windows. We will meet you there.

Bic quickly closed the curtain. "Lead me to the back door."

Nathaniel led the way. "How about the garage? My uncle has an extra car we can take."

"The sniper would have an easy shot if we tried to leave that way."

"What then?"

"We're going to borrow one of your back neighbors' cars and get out of here."

49

Bic had never driven a Beamer before. But after climbing the backyard fence and making their way through two more yards, they wound up at a house. Nathaniel had chosen it. He seemed to enjoy the idea of taking the Papsideras' car.

The classy ride they'd stolen was the last thing on Bic's mind. The two kids—Nathaniel in the passenger seat and Lucy asleep in the back—those were his main concern at the moment. That and keeping to the speed limit. A black man with a bandaged bullet wound to his arm driving a Beamer through a swanky neighborhood with two white kids would most likely alert a cop or two.

"Why did you do it?"

Nathaniel's plaintive voice cut through the silence.

Bic looked over at the boy, whom he'd assumed up to this point was also sleeping. Nathaniel was staring out the window, his breath making small patches of fog appear and disappear hypnotically on the glass.

"Do what?" Bic said, turning his eyes back to the road as he made a left.

"Kill my parents," the boy said plainly.

Bic took a deep breath. "I was a monster then, Nathaniel. I'm changed now."

"I didn't ask you about now."

Bic took another breath, realizing that he had to summon nerve to speak this frankly with the boy on this particular subject. "I had a code. I had killed a lot of men, but only bad ones who deserved it." Bic sighed again. "Suddenly I found myself taking a job killing a list of innocent people, using the excuse that I needed the money to help someone I loved."

"Why? Was he dying or something?"

"It wasn't a he, it was a she, and her name is Gracie. And no, she wasn't dying. You see, I had been helping and protecting her all her life. She had no idea I was a killer. And I was convinced what I was doing for her justified my actions, but it was all a lie. It was like the only human part of me, the only decent part, was fighting for dominance over the rest of me. But the evil part of me needed to be fed."

"What made you evil? What are you, like, possessed or something?"

"That's one way of looking at it," Bic said without irony. After his succumbing to his father's voodoo curse, he knew better than to question supernatural mysteries. "But there's another explanation. The evil was put into me at a very young age. I was younger than you when it happened."

"When what happened?"

The old rage stirred in him. He had to fight for a moment to control it, feeling his face twitch ever so slightly. "My father killed my mother in front of me. Crushed her skull with a cast iron skillet. He then stuffed a pork chop down my throat to choke me to death."

"What the hell was his problem?" Nathaniel said with cold inquiry.

Bic shook his head. "Some people are evil people. That's all I can say. And it doesn't matter what happens in their lives. They have too much evil inside them to want to do anything about it, I guess. I don't know. He was a bad man. Let's just leave it at that. And he never wanted to be any different."

He looked over at the boy, who was still thoughtfully fogging the window. He seemed to be turning something over in his mind. Bic turned back to the road and soon felt the boy's eyes on him.

"So, your dad was evil. Killed your mom."

"That's right."

"And you grew up to be just like him."

The truth cut through Bic like a rusty blade. "The truth is... I realized, after I killed all those innocent people that I was... a serial killer. No more, no less. I needed to kill."

"And now you're changed."

"For the most part."

Nathaniel leaned forward in order to get a good look at Bic's face. "You think I'm going to grow up to be the same way?"

Bic noticed his palms were sweaty now. "I know what it's like to have a loving parent killed. My mom loved me to no end." Tears began welling in the corner of his eyes. "You had two loving parents. So yeah, I thought that maybe you'd have all the same rage I had inside me eating you up for the rest of your life. That's *not* a life, Nathaniel. It's a rabbit hole to hell."

"You said you changed. How?"

"After I... killed..." The word suddenly seemed foreign. "...all those people, I saw my father's face in every one of them. I could imagine it was him I was killing. When I finally got my father, instead of watching him die, killing the man I had imagined killing with my bare hands a million times, I came to my senses and walked away.

"You let him live?"

Bic looked to the boy, "I didn't say that."

"I don't know if I can ever walk away," Nathaniel said, his breath coming quick now. Bic saw the boy's fists, tight and white-knuckled.

"Listen, Nathaniel," he said, "I don't ever expect you to forgive me for what I've taken from you. I don't deserve it, but you can count on me to protect you and Lucy. I'll do that and still owe you everything for it. You'll owe me nothing for it."

They reached the edge of the neighborhood and made their way to the highway. Once in the clear, Bic gunned the engine.

50

R oman Dog stood before a massive bonfire, watching the flames lick a star-flecked sky of black velvet. The meet-up was happening in a grass field on a farm belonging to a friend of the DOH. Roman's heart was booming. He had just gotten word that eight of the Oakland DOH who were going after the kids were all dead, intercepted by the Black Ghost.

Early that morning, he'd received an additional deposit of ten million. With the deposit came additional instructions regarding two kids. He received an address, pictures of a boy and a girl along with their first names. The intel stated that the Black Ghost was going to use these kids as a bargaining chip, and that they needed to be taken care of, as well, if Roman wanted to get paid. At this point, he wasn't sure what kind of tangled mess he was in. He had planned to take the kids, not have them killed, but make them disappear–in case he needed a bargaining chip of his own later on. But with them being with their main target, Bic Green, it now made sense to take out all three and collect the rest of his money.

Even though nothing had gone right and legions of DOH were dead, Roman Dog never had felt more confident as he surveyed the men who'd turned up to collect the bounty he put out. It wasn't so much the number. He'd seen crowds of bikers ten, twenty times as large as this one. No, it was the *assortment.*

They were a patchwork of types. At least 50 or 60 different species of the human animal. Many had high-grade weaponry–some even had their bikes retrofitted to mount the guns. A colorful faction came armed with homemade weapons the likes of which he'd never seen. The ingenuity was amazing to behold.

He strode through the ranks of the partying men like a proud papa, nodding and smiling at the men as he passed, as if he were bestowing a blessing upon them. In a way he was. He knew after a joint or some liquor the average man got a little braver. These men weren't average, most of them were killers. There was no limit to the amount of damage this crew would be able to afflict.

They were waiting for the go sign. It would come soon enough in the form of a text message. That was another marvel. He remembered the pre-digital days when they relied on poorly synchronized watches and half-assed plans. What he wouldn't have given back then for a taste of the future. And here it was.

He passed by a dingy pickup truck whose bed was loaded to the spilling point with methed-out psychotics.

"Got a light there, cousin?" came a twangy voice followed by a chorus of raucous laughter.

Roman looked up to see one of the psychos holding a Molotov cocktail toward him as if offering it as a gift.

"Ah, ah… my money's on this crew to be the one to collect the twenty million." He gave a flamboyant gesture of salutation to the man and kept walking as the group howled and yelled in excitement. He felt like a pope.

He saw Ugly Jesus resting against his motorcycle, smoking weed and in some sort of deep conversation with Darius. The Sergeant at Arms gave a wave with his stigmata hand. The wound looked fresh and oozy.

"If I didn't know any better, boss," said the perverted messiah, "I would have guessed we got ourselves a rehearsal dinner for the apocalypse."

"Ah, ah… we're gonna rain down hell on anything in our path." Roman looked at his son. "Ah, ah… what is it."

"The kids."

"Ah, ah… I agreed to your idea to keep them as leverage, but now that they're all together, it just makes sense to wipe them all out with one clean sweep." Roman accepted Ugly Jesus's joint and took a hit from it. "Ah, ah… besides, what are you all up in arms about? It got us another ten million up front, didn't it?"

"I'll drink to that," Ugly Jesus said. He finished off his beer, then threw the forehead-crushed can onto the ground.

Roman patted his son on the back. "Ah, ah… we got that additional cash because of you. Good work, son."

Darius grabbed a beer from a half-drunk twelve-pack on the ground and walked off.

Ugly Jesus cracked another beer. "Ever get tired, boss?"

"Ah, ah… all of this mayhem? Never!" the leader answered. "Ah, ah… don't tell me you're going soft like my pouty Christian son over there." He looked at his Sergeant at Arms, who was staring at him with a confused expression.

The dingy biker rubbed his beard. "I meant I always get tired right before a fight. Like real dead tired. Like I could sleep for a week. Then I snap out of it once it's time to go. But, um…" He had a strange smile on his face, like at any moment he was in danger of offending his leader. "Everything okay, boss?"

"Ah, ah… yeah, everything's fine. Why?"

"Oh, nothing. Just wanted to make sure what the kid said isn't getting to you."

They stared at each other for an uncomfortable moment when Roman felt the familiar buzz in his pocket. It might as well've been a four-thousand-volt shock.

He took out his phone, looked at the text, then looked up at his Sergeant at Arms. A smile was all he needed to convey the message.

He turned to the gathering of assassins and raised his hand, accompanying the gesture with a growling scream. "*We head North!*"

A surge of animalistic noise he'd never heard in his life followed. This was bloodlust incarnate, and he was glad for it.

They mounted their vehicles and took off in a hellish roar.

51

Cheeseburgers. Five of them. No, six, Hawk thought as he fought the urge to fall asleep. It was way past dinnertime. He'd never skipped a meal, ever. With no food or water for an entire day and drinking pretty heavily the night before, he was feeling downright delusional at this point.

He closed his eyes. He could practically smell the deliciousness being cooked up somewhere far off in Heaven. His hunger was taking over his whole body now. All intent and purpose was bent toward getting out of this mess and into a plate of cheeseburgers. Yeah, he'd been eating healthy for a long time. He looked great. He felt great. But how long had he been chained up in this place? A dripping, sizzling, ketchup-oozing burger was exactly what his body needed now. Forget health and wellness. He needed a burger. And freedom.

A rumble sound interrupted his thoughts. Wait, was that his stomach, or was it something else? He closed his eyes. It was definitely coming from the outside, and it was close.

The door handle was turning. Hawk's pulse shot up. His breath quickened. He half hoped it would be Millie walking through that door. Coming back to him, saying she had made a mistake and they should run off together.

The door opened and a man clad in black entered. Hawk didn't know the exact time, but it was late. It had been dark for some time.

The man stood there dead silent and staring. So, she'd sent a man to kill him. Perhaps the handsome Latino man was her boyfriend. Lucky bastard.

The man turned and shouted a barrage of commands in Spanish to someone behind him.

Crap, he thought, *cartel.* He needed to keep his cool. Talk his way out of this.

"No," said Hawk, "come on in. The water's fine. I mean, seriously, dude, I can use your help." He wiggled his wrist to jangle the cuff chain against the radiator.

"*Pinche,*" the man said.

"No, no trouble here." Hawk kept his cool. He needed to get this guy talking. "You a friend of the Irishman?"

The man stared for a moment longer, then answered, "We clean, we clean."

AirBnb! That's what this place is, Hawk realized with relief. "Dude, if you can help me outta this, that would be totally awesome."

The man pulled out his phone and started to dial.

"Hey friend, who you calling?"

"Police."

"Come on brother, there's no trouble here. Well, nothing but a little girl trouble, that's all. But who hasn't had that, am I right? She was a hottie too. You woulda liked her. Killer British accent. Looked like Demi Moore with blond hair. *You dig St. Elmo's Fire*, dude?"

"Uh, huh," the man said, his face a mask of uncertainty. "I call the police?"

"Honestly? You can do whatever you want, but I kinda just want to get outta this thing first. Hey, what company are you with?"

"CleanRite," the man said, looking around the room.

"Aw, man, CleanRite! I've been a customer for years. You guys do great work!"

A half-smile grew on the man's face as he stopped mid-dial.

"Ah, my man knows how to treat his customers. I like your style," Hawk said. "Okay, check it out. You got girls out there?"

The man nodded.

"I bet one of them is wearing hair pins in her hair?"

"Hair pin?"

"Yeah... you know... ah man, what's the word for it? *Horkilla?*"

"Whore killer?"

"No, man," Hawk said. "Like a pin for the hair." He pointed to his own scalp, pulling strands of hair back to mimic the effect of pinning."

The man laughed. "*Horquilla,*" he said.

"Yes," Hawk said with a sigh as he pronounced the word correctly. "*Horquilla.*"

"I no think so," the man said.

But Hawk saw that his body language was different. So, this had just turned into a negotiation. He needed out of these cuffs. He reached into his back pocket to retrieve his wallet, using his left hand, which was awkward, but he managed. He pulled out all the cash. "How about you sell me one *horquilla* for eighty-four bucks?"

The man thought for a moment, seemingly unimpressed with the offer.

Hawk sighed. "Okay, I'll throw in my skull ring. Look, totally rad. The chicks dig it big time. So do the men, if that's the way you go. No offense either way. Nothing wrong with that. I mean, I don't, but you do know what I mean?"

The man nodded. "Cool."

"Yes, that's my man!"

The man barked another command in Spanish. A moment later, a pretty woman appeared behind him. At the first glance at Hawk, she started as if she were about to turn and run. The man steadied her with a soft explanation. Her hand went to her head and came down with a pin, which she handed to the man.

"Yes, you're gonna love this ring."

The man gave a command and the woman turned to leave, but not before giving Hawk a suspicious glance that told him everything he needed to know about how he must have looked.

The man approached with the pin.

"Just give it here, my friend," Hawk said with a smile as the exchange was made.

He put the bobby pin into his mouth. The bitter taste of hairspray immediately tingled his tongue. Ignoring it, knowing soon he would be tasting cheeseburger, he bent the pin into an L shape. He then inserted one end into the thin part of the keyhole on his wrist cuff. Jiggling and twisting, he licked his lips and mumbled.

"Come on, baby, open up for Hawk."

Within a minute, there was a satisfying clink as the cuff popped open.

"Radical!" he shouted. "That's how it's done, mofos!"

52

The drive was a couple of hours, but it seemed longer with all the tough questions from Nathaniel. Bic wasn't sure if he'd answered them satisfactorily. He wasn't even sure if he was telling the truth to himself, let alone the kid. What he did know was that he was going to protect these kids and do his best to leave them less messed up than he'd found them. He knew, without a doubt, most if not all of their issues stemmed from him. Bic glanced at Lucy in the rearview mirror. She was wiped out. His heart went out to her.

The navigation led Bic down a private road lined by perfectly symmetrical trees. What the road opened up to took Bic's breath away.

"Is this the right spot?" Bic said.

"Yeah," Nathaniel said, unable to suppress a yawn.

They'd arrived at a vineyard in the heart of the Napa Valley. Flood lights lit the entire place with a ghostly glow. Standing at the center was a huge Victorian-style house, with gingerbread gables and a sloping, ornate roof. It stood on a beautifully landscaped piece of property, with a stone-lined path leading up to an inviting porticoed entrance. The lighting was artsy and perfect.

Bic looked at the boy and could just make out moist eyes reflecting the light. "You okay?"

"I'm fine. We should probably go in."

Bic turned-off the car and turned to rouse Lucy. She woke with a start.

Bic was quick to shush her paternally. "It's okay."

They got out of the car and stretched.

"I know where they keep the keys to the tasting room," Nathaniel said. "In case you wanna sample anything."

"Not a big wine guy," Bic said with a smile. He then frowned. "My friend Tony, on the other hand, he would love this place."

Nathaniel cringed at the mention of the name.

Bic turned around. Through the diminishing rays of the flood lights he could just make out the backdrop of mountains in the distance under the moonlight. He turned around in a complete circle to take stock of his immediate surroundings. There were several buildings—event rooms and rentable lodges, he assumed—which terminated at neat rows of grapes that went on and on as far as he could see.

"You sure no one who's after us knows about this place?"

"I'm sure. My dad set it up that way. With shell corporations and stuff. I promise."

The doors of the main house opened in on a foyer with ancestral portraits on the walls, and exposed wood beams across the ceiling, which must have weighed a ton each. As they made their way into the house proper, Bic gazed into rooms off the main hallway. Each space held its own decorative theme: Rustic chic, contemporary, Swiss chalet, and on it went. Every room had its own array of giant barrels—presumably for show, although Bic wasn't certain they didn't hold their share of aging wine. If so, there was enough here to drown the earth several times over.

Bic now understood what the word 'billion' meant in real world terms. When it's written out, it's just three more zeros than a million. But in reality, those extra zeros meant you could own a commercial winery as extravagant as the mind could imagine. And yet it was *still* just an afterthought for someone worth over eighty billion.

"You kids have rooms in this house?"

"Up on the third floor," Nathaniel said, giving way to another intrusive yawn.

Bic looked back at Lucy, who was barely keeping up, staggering and rubbing at her half-mast eyes.

"You mind getting her to bed?" Bic said.

Nathaniel looked back, then stopped and waited for Lucy to catch up. "Come on, sis. Wanna make forts with our blankets like we used to?"

Lucy nodded sleepily, any plans to build blanket forts, however genuine, falling away into her dreams.

Nathaniel made his way to a staircase off the hallway. On his way, he turned back to Bic. "If you head on back, there's like a lounge area. Two doors down from that is the winter caretaker's bedroom. You can sleep there. I... kinda don't want you to sleep in my parents—"

Bic nodded. "That sounds perfect."

He found the lounge area to be a large, square room with a fireplace at the far end with plush leather couches arranged around it. Throughout the room were red velvet chairs that matched the carpet. The place was filled with soft light. He was instantly comforted.

A guy could get used to this, he thought.

He sunk into one of the leather couches. Damn, it was cozy. Forget the bedroom, this would suit him just fine.

No, he had to remain alert. He'd be damned if he left these kids unprotected.

A text from Caroline snapped him out of his thoughts.

Mack's awake! Stable condition! Smiley faces, crying emojis.

He typed back: *Best news all day. I knew he was a survivor, just like his wife.*

The phone rang. He picked it up immediately.

"Great news," he said.

Caroline's voice was hushed. "I can't talk long, I know who's behind trying to kill you."

"Nathaniel Braddick."

"You figured it out."

"I'm with him and his sister right now, keeping them safe, trying to work things out."

"Well you're going to need to try harder. The FBI has evidence leading to the kid."

"What kind?"

"They know he hired a hitman. Conspiracy to commit murder"

"How? Who?"

"He's just a juvenile, but that doesn't mean they can't try him as an adult. Plus, with him being so high-profile, they might relish the opportunity to make a huge example out of some uber-rich kid. Make him out to be some kind of villain who needs to be brought to justice. Big win for the country type of deal."

"Dammit," Bic muttered.

"They already have a warrant and they're coming."

"They know where he's at?"

"Oh, no. It's Mack, gotta go," she said hurriedly, and hung up.

He felt like squeezing the phone into powder. He almost chucked it into the cold fireplace.

He breathed carefully, attempting to center himself and gather his thoughts. This kid was ruined. His life was going to be a mess. Both his and Lucy's.

It was of no use. His thoughts were his own worst enemy at the moment.

When would it all end? When would he finally face the last of all the effects of his sins? He didn't want to answer those questions. The truth was too painful. Instead, he allowed the comfort of the fine leather to take hold of his body as he closed his eyes, trying to hunt down a tiny slice of calm in the midst of the war zone.

After dozing off for several hours, he suddenly awakened. His nerves jangled. He walked toward the window. He could see the expanse of the vines in their neat rows.

One of the stakes moved.

He squinted through the window at it.

Clarence Green spread his arms. One of them terminated in a bloody stump at the elbow.

"Looks like that gator had himself a snack!" the apparition said, its voice echoing like a hollow cave. "Ah well. It's gonna take more than a gator to do away with me, boy."

The ghost twisted its face into an evil grin.

Another sound came from outside. This time, it was concrete, more permanent than the voice of the ghost. It was coming from the front of the house. Bic turned away for a moment, and when he turned back, the ghost was gone.

He could swear he heard the reverberation of a sick laugh wafting through the grapes.

When he made his way to the front of the house and stepped outside, he gave a sigh of relief.

"This place is totally awesome!" Hawk said.

Bic couldn't help himself. He took the eighties refugee in his arms and nearly bear-hugged the life out of him.

53

Thank you for joining us for the daily news briefing. Today's top story—a series of deadly attacks including one on an FBI transport has authorities stunned. The suspect a wealthy 15-year-old boy billionaire. We'll have more on that top story after the break...

Bic snapped off the TV.

"I was watching that," Nathaniel said.

"Yeah, and you shouldn't."

"It was about me."

Bic took a seat next to the boy. "I know."

Nathaniel shook his head like he was dealing with an idiot. "The FBI is after me."

"You've set in motion a machine that will attack you from all angles. I'm not sure who you hired, but they're going to kill you for nonpayment of funds."

"So, I don't understand. Why did they turn me in to the FBI."

Bic looked away, not wanting to answer.

"What is it, Bic?"

"Once they've killed the richest kid in America, they've killed a criminal who got what he deserved. Think of it like a smear campaign."

"What'll happen if I turn myself in to the FBI?"

Bic rubbed his forehead. "That would be the worst thing you could do." He put his hand on the boys shoulder. "I say we get off this couch and control what we can right now."

Bic rose and Nathaniel grabbed his arm. "Maybe this is best. I can't let Lucy down. She needs me."

Bic stared at the boy for a moment. If he was going to continue fixing his relationship with Nathaniel, he'd have to be honest. "I'm sure the evidence they have against you is overwhelming. They'll probably send you to juvie. But in the worst case, they'll try you as an adult. That means they'll separate you and Lucy. She'll stay with your uncle most likely. As for you, you'll become part of the system for a long time. Now, that might seem like a safe option, but trust me, in the system, it is even *easier* for them to get to you."

As he spoke, Bic could see the face of the scared little boy beneath Nathaniel's thin skin. The memory of his first encounter with Nathaniel, when he locked the boy and his sister away so he could murder their parents, came flooding back.

No, he couldn't go down that road. There was work to be done.

"I have experience in these situations. Best thing to do is deal with problem number one. We'll figure something out about the FBI later."

The boy nodded, fighting back tears. "They'll never find us here."

"Yes, they will, Nathaniel. Believe me."

At this point, Hawk entered the room "What have we got here?"

Bic stepped aside. "Hawk, I want you to meet a friend of mine. Nathaniel, meet Hawk."

Hawk extended a hand. "Pleased to meet you, dude. How's it hangin'?"

Nathaniel got up and extended a wary hand.

"Whoa," Hawk exclaimed, "now *that's* what I call a Kung Fu grip! You crush walnuts with that hand?"

A smirk appeared on the boy's face.

"Nathaniel here's gonna help us out," Bic said, sounding proud.

Smiling, Hawk nodded slowly. "Radical."

54

Staring outward into the endless rows of green grapevines leading into the backdrop of a sunlit mountain, Nathaniel waited.

Hawk wheeled over several huge coils of wire on a hand truck. He was out of breath.

"What is that stuff?"

"Son," Hawk said, "these here are some big ol' coils of 14-gauge trapping wire. Works pretty good for beavers and raccoons. The only problem is…" He set the hand truck down, went over to Nathaniel, and lay a hand on the boy's shoulder. "It ain't beaver or raccoon season. You know what season it is?"

The boy shrugged.

Hawk leaned down. "Biker season!" He gave a hearty laugh and slapped Nathaniel's arm. "Ready to bag us some bikers?"

Nathaniel hesitated. "I think so."

"Good." Hawk lifted a coil off the hand truck. "You're gonna help me tie this between these two trees. Let's say, about neck-high of a guy on a bike."

They started at one tree, then stretched the wire across. Hawk wrapped it around the other tree, wrapping it several times, then hammered what looked like a giant staple over the layers of wire to secure it. He gave one of these staples to Nathaniel and handed him the hammer.

"Do me a favor, dude. Hammer this bracket in for me. I gotta take a squirt."

He disappeared into a row of bushes nearby. Nathaniel shook his head and imitated Hawk's move with the giant staple. There was something satisfying about hammering this thing into the tree. He felt productive. It was a good feeling.

A moment later, Hawk emerged. "Man, you ever take a leak that put life into a whole new perspective? I didn't realize how bad I had to go."

Nathaniel, unable to suppress it any longer, erupted in a fit of adolescent giggling.

"Hey, what's so funny? Leak? Next thing I know you'll be laughing at farts. Or…" He gave a huge belch, sounding out the word, "*buuuurrrrrpppsss.*"

Nathaniel thought he might lose control of his own bladder, he was laughing so hard.

It felt so good, this release of shaking laughter. It felt like something he'd needed to do for a long time.

"Alright," Hawk said, "that's enough about my life. Let's take a walk up to that roof up there and see what the world looks like.

Minutes later, they were on the roof of the main house. It was a large patio usually reserved for outdoor special events. These days, however, it was in service as a repository for empty wine barrels.

Hawk stood with arms folded, nodding and smiling as he surveyed the area.

"Totally awesome," he said. "Yep, this'll do just fine."

"Why do you keep saying that?" Nathaniel said, feeling mischievous.

"Saying what?"

Nathaniel deepened his voice in an attempt at imitation. "*Totally awesome.*"

Hawk unfolded his arms and put his hands on his hips. "See, that's the trouble with you kids. You are completely ignorant of history. What are they teaching you in those schools? Algebra or some other useless endeavor? *Psshhh*, son, you need to brush up on the eighties."

"The eighties?" Nathaniel said skeptically.

"That's right. *The Karate Kid, Fast Times at Ridgemont High, Caddyshack, The Breakfast Club*… ever hear of Phoebe Cates?"

"No."

Hawk gave a whistle. "Now there was a hottie. I had the biggest damn crush on that one. Had a thing for red bikinis ever since. Now, where was I? Ah, yes, the movies. Then there was the music. Hot damn, the music. Duran Duran, Culture Club, Air Supply. And if you wanted something with a little more balls, you had Ratt, Mötley Crüe, and the holiest of all holies…" He put his hand on his heart for emphasis. "Guns N' Roses."

Nathaniel erupted in another fit of laughter.

"Son, right now, I'll have you know, you are committing the worst form of sacrilege known to man."

"You're weird," Nathaniel said as his laughter tapered off.

"I may be weird," Hawk replied, "but at least I know good music when I hear it. When we're through with this stuff, I'm gonna lend you some cassingles."

Nathaniel's eyes went wide. "Huh?"

"Aw, don't even tell me you never heard of cass—you know what? Never mind. Looks like you and me are gonna have to have a long sit-down and discuss your cultural ignorance. I might even introduce you to a Whitesnake video starring a young lady named Tawny that'll melt your retinas."

Nathaniel smiled. "I can't wait."

"But that's for later. Right now, we're gonna build one helluva sniper's nest." Under his breath, but not so much under that the boy couldn't hear him, he added, "Never heard of cassingles? Man, what kind of kids are we raising?"

55

Hearing the sound of Huey blades fading away to nothing after being dropped off for a nighttime operation was the worst part for Bic. Even with your fellow grunts, your best buddy just four feet away, in the silence, you still can't help but feel like you're on an island all by yourself. Bic Green was back in an eerily familiar battle field.

Sticky jungle vines were replaced by neat rows of wine grapes. The enemy was not going to be a silent one. They would come roaring in. That was one thing that gave him confidence. The only drawback would be their sheer number. But he'd been through it before. 'Nam was a hellscape populated by a legion of demons.

He looked around and realized this is where he'd seen the ghost of his father. A chill ran down his spine.

How could he be undone by something so ridiculous? Here was Bic Green, the Black Ghost, master of assassination, terrified by things that go bump in the night. It worried him that he still wasn't right. It worried him that no matter what, he'd never be right.

A loud series of cracks punctuated the night air. Hawk was shutting down the lights.

One by one, they went out. Bic was encased in darkness. He took a breath of the clean, floral-scented air and let it flow through him. It made him think about his mama, her voice, her love, her wonderful energy. He found the calm before the storm. He was at peace.

Bic looked up into the sky. "I'll try my best for these kids, Mama. I won't let you down."

He felt like he could smile, knowing he was making her proud.

That's when he heard it. At first, it was a drone like a beehive. Then it became a steady roll of distant thunder.

Then it became a roar of motorcycles.

56

Ten... fifteen... twenty of them...

Hawk counted them carefully through the scope of his rifle. He readied himself, picturing the motorcycle-riding bullies from *The Karate Kid*. That little chat with Nathaniel had made him want to watch it again.

"Okay, you beach party-ruining bullies, get ready for some sweeping of the leg."

He cheered as the first three zipped right into his wire trap. They were flung off their bikes in spectacular fashion. He could swear he saw one of the bikers heads rolling in a different direction from his body.

The others, having seen the fate of the first three, quickly veered off in other directions. This would be tricky. Then again, he had Bic. He had to remember that.

"Go time, partner," he said into the transmitter on his collar.

"Ready," Bic answered.

"Twenty of them. They just crossed the entry. Three down already."

"Thanks again, Hawk, for always having my back. Your friendship has been one of the most valuable things in my life."

"Don't make me cry, partner, I need to be able to see," Hawk said, catching sight of one of the first to veer off. He was speeding across a massive patch of green lawn.

"You're tiptoein' in the wrong yard," Hawk said.

With this, he took a shot. The body flew off the bike, which rolled and spilled over, sliding off into the darkness.

He saw another coming across the same way and suddenly got into a zone of focus. He could hear the operatic voice of Freddie Mercury belting out the soundtrack of the moment.

As the biker approached his fallen comrade, he apparently recognized the fate could be his own and veered off to the left toward the cover of trees.

Hawk took aim and took the shot, getting the guy in the back.

"Another one bites the dust!"

Two more bikers sped by the house. Hawk took aim. "And another one..." And fired.

He missed.

They were on their way into the vines.

"Here come two your way, Bic."

There was no answer.

57

Two coming his way, Hawk had said. What Hawk didn't know was that there were at least three coming his way already—judging by the sound.

He stayed crouched in the vines, seeing the glow of headlights approaching.

If he could just get one apart...

Yes. They were traveling in a line. Possibly splitting up, but that was okay. He just needed one.

Bic ducked aside, out of the aisle, as the first one approached.

He sprung up, and blasted the guy in the chest with a sledgehammer.

The crunch was sickening as the man's body lifted and the bike went flying off into the grape vines.

Bic hustled over to the sputtering bike, lifted it up, and mounted it. Giving it a few revs for good measure, he took off down the aisle.

A bike intersected his path in front of him.

Bic had to act fast, lest the guy realize that he was in the company of the enemy and not one of his fellow bikers.

Following the biker through the vines, Bic pulled a sawed-off out of the holster on his back.

He fired from behind. The guy lurched forward and the bike toppled. Bic had to act fast to avoid hitting the wreck.

Side-swiping it, he nearly lost balance. He recovered and looked dead ahead.

Another two were coming toward him, firing their semi-automatic weapons, bullets kicking up dirt, making a beeline right toward him.

Bic crashed through a row of grapevines sideways and then down another aisle.

58

I'm scared," Lucy said, her thumb going to her mouth.

"We're going to be alright," Nathaniel said, trying to affect a soothing voice. He was anything but soothed himself.

They were hunkered down in the cellar of the house, with their backs up against one of about a hundred oak barrels stacked randomly in the room. It was dark and cool down here, with dust and the sweet smell of fermentation permeating the air. Not altogether unpleasant.

"How do you know?" Lucy said.

"How do I know we're going to be alright? Cuz the plan is good. Look at all these barrels. They'll never find us in one of these."

"But how are you sure?"

"Because I'm older and smarter than you."

"No, you're not," she said.

"I'm not older than you?"

"You're older, but not smarter."

"Oh yeah?" Nathaniel said. "What's Guns N' Roses?"

"Guns N' what?"

"Guns N' Roses, dummy," he said playfully.

Lucy shrugged. "I don't know."

"It's a band."

"You made that up," the girl protested.

"Nope, it's true. They play hip hop and disco. So, you see? I'm smarter and I know best. And I say we're going to be fine."

Muffled pops of gunfire made him jump for a moment.

"I hate that sound," he said, barely loud enough for her to hear.

"What about Bic?" Lucy asked after a moment.

"What about him?"

"Is he going to be okay?"

"Of course," Nathaniel said.

"And Hawk?"

Nathaniel smiled. "He'll definitely be okay."

"And you?"

"You know, I think I liked it better when you just squeaked. I forgot about all the questions you ask." He smiled. "Just kidding. I love that you're talking." His smile contorted to seriousness. "Anyways, I think it's time now."

Lucy nodded vigorously. "Time to play hide-n-seek."

The wine barrel was just big enough for the two of them. They climbed in. Nathaniel looked one last time at the sea of barrels, and theirs amongst them, then squatted down and pulled the lid over them. And there they sat in darkness.

"No more talking," Nathaniel whispered. "Go to sleep."

He felt Lucy's head against him. It made him want to sob like a baby.

If something happened to her, it was all his fault.

59

Hawk's voice squawked in his ear. "I just picked off two more..."

Bic didn't bother to answer, as he had a couple of problems of his own. The two bikers on his tail followed his every move as he weaved in and out of vines and aisles.

Everywhere he turned seemed to be a path he'd already traveled down. If it weren't for the pristine nature of the vines, unassaulted by motorcycles, he would think he was riding in circles. He definitely had retraced a couple of routes in order to evade the others.

A thought occurred to him, and it was this: his one saving grace was that they were just as much in the dark about the layout of the territory as he was. If he could just retain his sense of direction...

He slowed, just enough for at least one of them to get him in view, then veered left, tearing up the vines as he did.

He kept to an internal clock, allowing his keen sense of time to guide him as far as when he should turn. He was tracing a huge figure eight on a relatively small plot of land.

He gunned the bike hard, nearly losing control.

As he rounded the eight and was coming back up to complete it, he smiled.

The two came into view at the X intersection of lines, just as he envisioned they would.

His gun was ready. He fired, hitting one in the neck, and the other in the shoulder.

He slowed the bike, wondering if he should ditch it altogether. He could definitely retain silent cover that way.

He shut the engine and his ears pricked up. First, it was at the sound of the dead men's sputtering bikes, then the drone of the remaining bikers and the sporadic popping of Hawk's gunfire. And then, silence.

Bic stepped out of the cover of the vines into the open. All the moving headlights were gone. Just a couple from spilled bikes, shining up from the ground.

"Is that it?" Bic asked into his mic.

Before Hawk could answer, a roar erupted as a motorcycle darted out of the dark like a leopard.

Bic had no time to dive out of the way of the 500-pound machine. Instead, he dove directly at the bike, getting his body perpendicular to the ground, clearing the handle bars and tackling the moving man.

All of Bic's weight drove the man into the ground. Bic had already anticipated the man would try to escape by trying to crawl away. As he did, Bic wasted no time locking his legs around the man's waist. He gave a good twist to the man's chin in a life-ending snap.

Bic stood. The returning silence gave him hope it was all over. But, before he could catch his breath, another sound, deeper, more menacing, pierced his ears.

The headlights of the bikes swarmed onto the property as a second, larger wave of attackers charged.

60

S wanky place, Roman Dog thought. *Can't wait to lay waste to it.*

He sped past the dead bodies of fellow Dogs of Hell. Poor, pathetic bastards. A fallen club member was always a tragedy, but not when you balanced it against the sheer stupidity of their demise. One of them had lost his head.

He himself was not stupid. He'd outfitted his bike with a multitude of lights that would alert him to any such traps. He'd seen the wire and been able to alert the rest with a hand signal. All these poor bastards had to do was ride around the trees that held the wire. Dummies.

This brush with the first line of defense only invigorated him. It was a little needle poke in his side, infuriating his anger at the elementary nature of it. He was sick and tired of seeing the DOH fall to this man. It was time to take out the fly swatter and squash this bug.

Behind him, the convoy roared with both the engine and the throat.

Up ahead, the swanky, plush, perfectly manicured land of the uber-rich sprawled out, waiting. He was itching all over to see it destroyed. That was another thing that invigorated him, as it was the very thing he lived for: the club motto—*Make Everything Worse. Period.*

The pickup truck, its bed overflowing with cousins, pulled up next to Roman.

Staring at the main house, Roman gave the command. "Ah, ah… burn it down."

The men hooted and hollered as the driver gunned it.

The group split in two, with each faction taking either left or right around the booby-trapped path.

He was glad to see them spreading out like a wave.

Like a virus.

The healthy host was just ahead. He gunned his motorcycle and sped toward it.

61

"Okay, Bic," Hawk said, bracing himself, "we got ourselves one dilly of a pickle. Uh, too many to count..." He slapped at his side and cursed to himself. "Looks like... I don't know... thirty? Forty?"

He began picking them off—not so much at random, as he realized he needed to isolate each kill shot as much as possible so as not to alert the others of his location, or at least to delay alerting them. He had the kids hidden in the basement of this fortress.

"Bic, you there?"

"I'm here..."

Hawk closed his eyes and breathed a sigh of relief.

"You had me worried for a minute there, dude."

"I'm on foot."

"Okay," Hawk returned, "might be your best bet. Just out of curiosity, any thoughts of a Plan B?"

"Let's keep you low-key and get them coming after me. We want to keep them as far away from the kids as possible."

"Okay, have them come after you instead of me. I like it. Sounds solid."

Bic laughed.

Hawk moistened his lips, realizing his mouth had gone bone dry. "Alright, listen, Bic, I will—whoa, holy... What in the name of Vanna White is that?"

The sky lit up. And a bright red shooting star was making its way toward him.

Hawk ducked and covered as the fireball hit home a few yards behind him.

He looked back. A flaming stick had landed and slid across the roof, leaving a puddle of fire behind it.

"Dammit," Hawk said, then got on his radio. "Bic, we got a problem... hold on! Incoming!"

He ducked and covered once again to avoid the second fireball.

He got back on the radio. "Those medieval sons of bitches are shooting flaming arrows at me. And they're coated with napalm!"

Two more fireballs arced over his head.

Hawk took aim and fired at the pickup truck bed, hitting one of the guys in the chest. The bullet ricocheted off the guy like he was Superman. The men in the back of the truck were obviously wearing some type of body armor. As the truck circled by, he got a better look. The crazy mofos were fully decked out wearing literal suits of armor-like medieval knights.

They were a primitive fire-bombing squad from hell. Some tossing Molotov cocktails through windows while others were shooting flaming arrows into the sky, creating a steady stream of fireballs raining down on the house.

Hawk changed strategy. He steadied himself, waiting patiently for the next turn. The men came into sight. As one of the men was about to throw the Molotov, Hawk took the shot. The bullet hit the glass bottle, rendering the rear of the truck completely engulfed in flames. Men scattered from the pickup like flies, as the gasoline supply in the bed of the truck exploded with the sound of total warfare.

"Tubular," Hawk said. But his self-congratulation was short-lived when he turned to see the damage that had already been done.

The entire roof was ablaze.

62

Roman Dog had to laugh. The cousins or brothers or sons of cousins and brothers, whatever those misfits crammed into the back of the pickup truck were, had certainly come prepared. He'd stopped to admire their handiwork. Flaming arrows launched from high-powered crossbows. It was the perfect mix of ancient and modern warfare that, had he not seen it with his own eyes, he'd have thought it came from some genius of the battlefield, and not these toothless, backwoods, banjo-playing weirdos.

One of them stumbled over with a flask in his hand.

"Ah, ah... your crew took a heavy hit."

"We're alright, only lost two. The rest are inside the house right now finishin' the job."

"Ah, ah... good to hear."

The man took a swig and followed it with a swipe of his arm across his mouth. "Perdy sight," he said, glancing up at the burning roof. He opened his mouth in a broken smile. "Kinda like the Fourth of Joo-Lie."

"Ah, ah... yes, the smell of burning wood. Nothing like it."

The battered flask came forth. "Saved some for ya. Let's celebrate our ten million buck-o-roos."

"Ah, ah... job's not done yet," Roman said.

"Come on, cousin. Don't be a sour persimmons."

Speak English, Roman thought.

"Ah, ah... I said there's still work to do."

"Hell, my boys inside will find 'em. Come on. It's old family recipe." The man shoved the flask toward him.

"Ah, ah... I'm sure it's dee-licious."

"It'll take you up to the moon and keep you there for a while."

Roman ignored the man, preferring instead to focus on the task at hand. Someone, possibly Parelli, was sniping from the roof. As for Bic Green, he was in the wine fields trying to draw the men to him. The kids had to be inside the house, hidden somewhere. And by the looks of it, they were about to be either smoked out or barbecued.

"It'll put hair on your momma's backside," said the hillbilly.

Without warning, Roman grabbed the flask and smashed it into the man's head, knocking him to the ground. He then shot the man in the face with his MP5, and murmured, "Oops."

It felt good to let off a little steam. He needed to stay patient in order to avoid any mistakes. The volume of men was his advantage, and he needed to let that play out.

Just as the thought crossed his mind, it did just that. Bic Green was sprinting toward the house.

Roman's instinct was to jump on his bike and chase the man into the house, but instead he waited. *Patience*, he thought. *Patience...*

63

Bic spoke into his shoulder, frantic and nearly breathless. "Can you make it outta there?"

"I might get a little tan on my ass," Hawk said, "but I should be okay."

"I'm coming in."

"Hey, dude, not for nothin', but do you think that's at all wise? I mean, there's a lot of those guys and they're gonna pretty much surround us and burn us to the ground if we're not careful."

"They already are," Bic said, noticing a figure out of the corner of his eye.

"Come again?" Hawk said.

He didn't have time to answer. The figure had hopped off his bike, a swinging chain in his hand. The chain caught Bic in the face, just below his left eye.

He saw it swing around again. He was ready.

Chains are clumsy weapons. All you have to do is follow the arc. It was a lesson he'd learned throughout the years.

The chain was coming around the guy's right shoulder. So Bic dove down and to the left, completing a somersault just in time for the chain to whip around the biker's own left leg. Bic reached out and grabbed it, giving it a hard yank out of the guy's hand.

The biker spun around and Bic sprung up, landing a punch under his attacker's chin that snapped his head back. He recovered quickly. But not quick enough.

Bic got the chain around his neck. From there, it was the awkward dance move to the other side of the body, taking the chain with him, pulling tighter, tighter.

He felt hot blood on his hands. The links were cutting into the guy's neck. The biker burbled and gagged, his hands useless in their attempt to free him from Bic's death grip.

The body went limp and Bic allowed it to drop.

Another biker roared up.

Bic blinked and shook his head. He couldn't be hallucinating.

A biker with a red mohawk and war paint on his face had a gleaming sword in his hand, which he swung around like a knight of old.

Bic used the speeding bike to his advantage, jumping and rolling forward instead of back or to the side. The blade missed him, but the bike sideswiped his right arm as it passed. He felt his own blood running down his arm. His rage was fueled to new heights. It was a fresh hate, a recent vintage cultivated over the past hour.

As the bike skidded and turned, Bic grabbed the chain from around the dead man's neck. As the spiked hair knight swung his steel, Bic met the swipe of the blade with a countering arc of the chain. It coiled around the blade like a boa. All Bic needed to do was to give it a good yank. Both the steel and swordsmen fell.

The biker reached for the blade. Bic leapt up and landed on the hand, crushing it to powder with the entirety of his weight. The biker screamed like his life was ending. In a way, it was.

Bic lifted the sword and plunged it into the man's chest, staking him like a vampire. He held it there for a moment, watching the man twitch, blood spewing from his mouth.

The body stopped, and Bic withdrew the sword.

He then ran into the house, which was quickly becoming engulfed in chaotic flames.

64

A mere couple of steps into the grand entryway, there was fire. And it was everywhere. A man dressed in armor charged. Bic readied his sword. But before the man had any chance of earning his knighthood, a bullet entered the back of his head and exited the front. Bic looked up to see Hawk with his sniper rifle hanging over the second-floor railing.

"Another canned corpse," Hawk yelled, then came rushing down the stairs.

"Man, Bic," Hawk said, his eyes wide. "You okay, dude?"

"I'm okay."

Hawk squinted. "Is that...? That's not..."

Bic turned to the ornate mirror on the wall nearby and saw what had distracted Hawk. His face was splotched with a dark-colored mess from the chain hit.

"It's grape juice," Bic said plainly. "Must have spattered up from the vines."

Hawk made his 'not buying it' face. "What are you thinking?"

"Did you get a look from up top how many more are out there?" Bic said, wiping the sticky juice from his face on his shirt, which was none too clean itself.

Hawk shook his head. "I lost count. I'm gonna say there are maybe... twenty-five?"

"They've got a lot of firepower."

"No kidding," Hawk said, gesturing to the growing flames.

They heard the roar of engines and hollers from outside, and they were getting louder.

They were already mobilized outside. Options were limited.

"Bic," Hawk said, "We need to come up with something quick

before this place goes up like a hillbilly belch in a campfire."

Bic dropped the sword and began reloading his weapons one by one. He had a sawed-off and a pistol. He wished he had something larger. Hawk was resourceful, but he was no Anthony Parelli.

"I'm going out front. Make them think we're fighting our way through. I can draw them in."

Hawk's face was a mask of worry. "Is that wise, Bic?"

"I'll make enough of a stand, get all of their attention. You should be able to get the kids from the cellar and bring them out the back."

"That's a suicide mission. We're not there yet, Bic. Sorry, dude, but there's gotta be another way."

Bic smiled calmly. "I'm not going to let them shoot my old friend."

Hawk breathed a sigh. Bic could see he was quickly running through his options and ticking off each one with a large NO.

Hawk nodded. "Love you, man," he said, with a look of resigned defeat on his face, and went off to the cellar to retrieve the children.

Bic stared at the grand front door. Flames crawled the walls. How he was going to get out the door without being gunned down in seconds?

It was the literal burning question.

65

"Should we see what's happening?" Lucy asked.

The inside of the barrel lit up with the light of Nathaniel's phone. It was nice to see his sister's face. They'd only been inside the barrel for thirty-eight minutes, but it felt like hours. He made sure she saw him smile at her.

"Hey," he said, "what type of ice cream are we going to celebrate with when this is over?"

"Chocolate. With tons of colorful sprinkles," Lucy answered.

"Mm, no. Strawberry with gummy worms."

"*Ecch*. I hate strawberry."

"You'll like it when I mush it in your face."

This elicited a giggle from the girl, which warmed his heart.

"I'll mush it right back in yours," she said, "and then I'll put whipped cream and a cherry on your nose and make you into a sundae."

She could barely finish the sentence, trailing off in a fit of giggles that they both needed.

A loud, clanking sound came from outside the barrel.

"Cousin," a man said with a twangy drawl, "look at all this Jesus juice."

"Let's just burn it," another replied.

"I say we drag us a coupla barrels outside and drink it. Already got a big old bonfire goin'."

Lucy squeaked. Nathaniel tried to cover her mouth.

"We got company down here, cousin," the man said.

Lucy's eyes were the size of saucers. Nathaniel could only hope she didn't make another sound, but it didn't matter when he heard the three knocks at the top of their barrel.

"Knock, knock," the man said.

There was silence for a moment, then another man replied, "Who's there?"

"Not you, you, back hill idiot."

The knock came again, then the man said, "If no one answers, I'm gonna put a sword right through this barrel."

The knock came again, followed by two distinct noises which sounded like the ringing of a tin can at a carnival.

The sword came into the barrel from the top, just missing the children.

Lucy screamed.

The sword retreated slightly, then pried off the top of the barrel. The children's eyes squinted from the light that poured in.

"Hey, kiddos! It's me, Uncle Hawk!"

Lucy jumped from the barrel into Hawk's arms.

"Whoa," Hawk said. "Come on, we're getting outta here."

"Is it over?" Nathaniel asked.

"Unfortunately, no," Hawk said, uneasiness in his voice.

"What do you mean?"

"No time for questions," Hawk said. "Listen, we got a little fire to deal with, courtesy of our knights in shining armor, but don't be scared."

Nathaniel looked to the two armored men lying on the floor. It was then he realized the tin can noises he heard were the sounds of bullets popping through their armor. Truth be told though, he'd rather deal with those two scary men than fire. He was deathly afraid of fire.

"You okay, kid?" Hawk said, putting a hand on the boy's shoulder. "You're trembling like you've just seen Freddie Kruger."

Nathaniel didn't look at Hawk as he rapidly took in breaths. His eyes were in the next room, staring in a trance at the licking flames waiting to burn him. "Anything but fire," he said, his voice quaking.

"Listen," Hawk said, "just pretend it's like one of those games you guys play. Like on Atari or something. What do they call it? Escape the House?"

"Escape Rooms?" Nathaniel said.

"Yeah, that's it," Hawk said. "Pretend you gotta like escape the room. Only it's on fire."

"You have no idea what you're talking about," Nathaniel said, "and video games don't have real fire!" There was a strange sort of powerlessness eating away at the boy's reserve. Cutting he could control. *Measured* doses of pain were his purview. Those flames, though, they were chaos.

Hawk breathed out a sigh of concern. "Listen, kid, just follow me and I promise both of you will be fine, okay?"

Hawk took a step. Nathaniel tried to follow, but he couldn't. His feet were locked in concrete. Suddenly he felt the chaos enter his soul like a swarm of burrowing red ants.

Lucy tried to pull Nathaniel by the hand, but she couldn't budge him. She pleaded as she pulled at her brother, "Hawk, do something!"

"It's safer to stay put," Nathaniel said as Hawk approached.

"Listen, partner, not to scare you or anything, but it's like a Michael Jackson Pepsi commercial up there. Every damn thing is on fire. And pretty soon every damn thing is going to collapse into this basement with you in it. You understand?"

"No, it's safer here," Nathaniel said. "Please."

"I'll give you points for saying please, but…" Hawk finished the sentence by hefting the kicking and screaming boy over his shoulder and bringing both children into the next room.

Which was full of flames.

66

"Is he okay?" Bic asked when he saw Hawk entering the grand foyer with Nathaniel over his shoulder.

"Other than a serious case of pyrophobia, we're good," Hawk said, setting the boy back on his feet. The boy steadied, Hawk nevertheless kept his hand firmly around Nathaniel's arm.

Lucy quickly clutched her brother's hand tightly.

Bic approached the kids and bent down on one knee.

"Your arm is bleeding," Lucy said, her voice on the edge of tears.

Bic smiled. "I fell off my bike. I know it looks bad, but I've had worse."

"What's that stuff all over your face?" Nathaniel asked.

"Would you believe it's grape juice? I fell into some vines."

Both children looked at him with extreme skepticism in their eyes.

Bic smiled again. "I guess you kids are too smart for a lie like that. Listen. I'm gonna run out that door. There are a lot of bad guys out there waiting for me. I'm gonna get them to come after me while Hawk here is going to sneak you out the back."

"Will there be anyone back there waiting for us?" Lucy asked, her voice tiny and weak.

Bic was about to lie, then remembered a moment ago. Plus, it felt good to be honest with these kids. It all felt new.

"There might be. But I want you to be brave, okay? And I trust Hawk with my life. He'll be able to handle a couple of guys if I draw the majority of them to me. Just make sure to listen to him. And make sure you run real fast. I know you can."

The girl nodded.

Bic turned to Nathaniel. "And you're gonna take care of her like the brave man you are, right?

239

"Mm, hm," Nathaniel said, nodding.

Tears flooded the boy's eyes. Bic could sense he was trying to be extra brave in front of him.

"Good."

Without realizing that he was doing it until it was actually happening, Bic spread out his arms to receive both children in an embrace. He felt hot tears in his eyes and fought against the choking lump in his throat.

He pulled away from the kids.

"I'll see you around."

"Goodbye, Bic," Lucy said, on the verge of tears herself.

He felt her care and love. It felt right, like the feeling that radiated off Gracie. But at the same time, not knowing the outcome, it destroyed him inside.

He stood up.

"Watch for my diversion," he said to Hawk, "then get these kids out of here."

"Done and done, brother," Hawk said as the men embraced.

67

Bic ran into a room on fire and came out kicking a flaming wine barrel on its side in front of him.

He had to work quickly, as the flames were spreading faster and faster. The heat was nearly unbearable. He knew Hawk and the kids could feel it even all the way in the back.

He got the barrel in place, then readied his weapons.

After one moment of centering, he kicked open the door and sent the barrel out.

A barrage of gunfire began to tear it to pieces.

Looking to his left, he spotted an antique tractor, rusty and bearing a sign saying, "Tastings Right This Way" with an arrow pointing upward. He sprinted for it.

He felt the wave of bullets behind him. He took a dive through the air and landed behind the tractor, but not before taking a bullet in the leg.

It stung like crazy and brought fresh tears to his eyes and fresh anger to his heart.

Various hollering voices closed in. He saw flickering shadows moving toward him.

He just hoped Hawk and the kids made it.

"There he goes!" Hawk said, barely hearing the kick of the front door through the roar of flames. "And we're off!"

And without even a forethought, he scooped Nathaniel up like a sack of flour and took off with Lucy at his side. The little girl could run. That was cool.

They got a few paces out into the open when the darkness lit up with gunfire.

"Lookout!" Hawk cried. "Lucy! Zig zag back to the house!"

Lucy did as she was told. The dirt around their feet exploded with bullets as they ran back to the flaming house.

Bullets popped and ricocheted off the tractor. Rusty bits of the thing blew off, the shrapnel missing his head by inches.

His mind raced. There had to be a way out.

Things got very quiet all of a sudden.

There came a voice out of the smoke. "Ah, ah... Hey, Mr. Green, it's time to meet your maker."

A chorus of laughter followed, and a barrage of gunfire followed that.

He looked around. Everywhere was open territory. He'd be naked.

Of course, he could take out as many as he could. A little blood for blood for good measure, his last gesture on earth.

Bic stood and took two quick shots, hitting two men. The only problem was that, in doing so, he'd gotten a good look at the twenty or so men left, most of whom were sporting automatic weapons. A couple began to flank him. He was seconds from being flushed out.

He couldn't believe he was thinking like this. But this is what it had all come down to. It was now or never. His leg screaming with pain, he got his pistol at the ready and made a final peace with the decision to end his life this way.

Bic suddenly remembered his mother's voice.

He missed her so much. He would never see her again. He was bound for somewhere different. He readied himself one last time, trying to find peace, knowing his mom would be proud of his trying to save these kids.

A fresh new sound cut through the roar of flames, bikes, and gunfire.

Whop, whop, whop, whop...

And there came a light from above.

.50 caliber fire erupted from the whirly bird.

So this was how it ended.

68

"Remember me, you biker rats," Parelli screamed while hanging out of the chopper. He then gave the order to Publio, his old 'Nam buddy, into his headset as they circled the winery. "Light 'em up!"

A spew of .50 caliber fire picked off bikers one by one, and chewed up everything else in its path.

The chopper hovered, receiving paltry bits of gunfire from the crowd below.

"Go easy on the tractor," Parelli said, spotting Bic through his night vision binoculars. "Bic's there."

"Come get you some, *perritos!*" Publio shouted, as pure destruction rained from his weapon onto the men below.

Parelli looked at the other men. Sergeant O'Donnell, Corporal Riggs, Gino, Crocker, and Anderson were surveying the carnage. Parelli held up a hand and caught their attention.

"You boys ready?"

Each man gave a wave of approval, readied their weapons, and got into position.

"Oorah!" Parelli shouted, his voice full of bravado. The men replied back with the same.

And on this command, the men descended from the sky on ropes of glory.

Bic couldn't believe his eyes. For a moment, he'd covered his head, bracing for the impact of bullets. But after seeing the Dogs' bodies exploding in bursts of blood, he realized the fire was not intended for him.

He wouldn't dare stand up though. There was a lot of spray, and friendly fire was a real thing he had personally witnessed back in his battle days. He kept down, glancing around every so often to gauge the progress.

More than once he wondered who it could be up there. He entertained the thought that maybe Caroline and Mack had come through for him. Maybe that was the FBI up there.

He couldn't believe his eyes. Ropes were falling from the chopper, A moment later, men descended. This had to be the FBI.

Yes, he'd deal with them somehow. His thoughts of a last stand turned to hope. Hope for these kids, hope that he still had time on this earth to right more of his wrongs. But that hope was short-lived, however, as a noise from his right brought his attention to the house.

The part of the flaming house's roof had just caved in. And he heard a high-pitched scream come from inside.

ic ran through the flaming entranceway and into the house. Hawk was on his knees before a large mass on the ground. Moving in closer, he realized to his horror that Nathaniel's leg was trapped beneath a massive hardwood beam. The boy was crying in pain. Hawk was trying desperately to lift it.

Bic went to Hawk's side and tried lifting it with him to no avail.

"I bet it's a coupla thousand pounds!" Hawk cried, as more of the building's structure cracked around him.

"I don't want to burn!" Nathaniel screamed. "Bic! I don't want to burn!"

Bic quickly surveyed his surroundings. The structure had minutes to remain standing. Minutes at best. Seconds at worst.

"Get the girl out," he shouted.

"Not leaving—"

"Do it," Bic shouted with a tone that would not tolerate resistance.

Hawk grabbed the sobbing Lucy and hefted her up. "See you on the other side, brother."

As Hawk took off with Lucy, Bic crouched down to the boy. "You're gonna be alright."

The boy suddenly stopped crying, and there was a look of adult resignation on his face. "We're not getting out of here, are we?" he said calmly between wincing breaths.

"It doesn't look good, but I won't leave you."

"Can you...?" the boy stopped, his eyes pleading.

He didn't have to finish the sentence. Bic knew exactly what he was going to say.

"No," Bic said, putting his head on Nathaniel's chest as sadness overwhelmed him. Tears dripped onto the boy's body. "I won't kill you. That's not the way out."

"I forgive you, Bic," Nathaniel said through his own tears.

"I don't deserve that," Bic said, lifting his head. "I just don't."

The boy looked him in the eyes, more serious than the death he was asking for. "You do, if you do this one last thing for me. You'll earn my forgiveness."

"I can't," Bic said. The heat was almost unbearable. He could feel his skin cooking.

"I don't want to be burned alive, Bic. Promise me you won't let that happen!"

Bic stared at the boy. He owed him so much. He didn't mean to say it, but the words stumbled off his lips. "I promise."

Bic's purpose came to one central focus. It was to save this boy's life. And as he channeled his love for this boy, this child, his mother, and all things just, his limbs suddenly felt massive. The power in his body was electric, and he wedged his huge arms under the beam of wood.

With his throat opened up in a howl, he lifted with everything he had.

It budged just enough to crush Nathaniel's leg a little more. The boy wailed.

Veins were exploding in Bic's neck, but he wasn't going to be denied, until his leg with the bullet in it gave out, and he fell to his knees.

"You promised," Nathaniel screamed. "Now do it!" The flames licked down the beam toward him. "You owe me, you son-of-a-bitch! You killed my parents in cold blood. I found them in pools of blood with bullets in their heads. Their eyes were open, you fucking scum! Pay your damn debts!"

Bic popped up to his feet. The boy continued to scream.

It's an act of love, he told himself as he pulled his pistol from his belt. The boy would be burned alive in a matter of seconds. It was the right thing to do. Yes, God help me. It's right. Tears streamed from his face.

"Thank you, Bic, I forgive you!" the boy said, nodding with an anxious smile as tears pealed from his eyes steadily.

A shot was fired.

70

All Nathaniel could see were opaque stars flashing within a sky of smoke. But the gun in front of him was not the one taking the shots.

Bic turned toward the sound and returned fire. His pistol was out of bullets after three shots.

He turned back to Nathaniel. "I won't let you burn, I promise." And with that, he disappeared into the smoke.

Nathaniel screamed for Bic not to leave him.

The quick outburst of air, left him lightheaded and weak and with the realization that Bic did abandon him.

He took a deep breath. He reflected on his bouts of self-harm. How the pain relieved him, gave him life when there was none to feel. He closed his eyes and felt the excruciating agony in his leg. And he pictured his mother and father as he remembered them. Their life together. The love Mom and Dad flooded him with. Bic's expression as he brought them into the movie theater so he could slaughter their parents in cold blood. The emotional agony settled on him, around him, and he reveled in it. And then he moved his attention to his screaming leg. And thus, the two forms of pain were united as one.

He opened his eyes.

Bic Green was still gone.

"Ah, ah… where you at, you dumb pile of horse crap. I got a bullet with ah, ah… B-I-C written on it."

Outside, bursts of gunfire pierced the night air as the last of Roman Dog's men faced off against the saviors from the sky.

Bic used the aural and visual confusion to his advantage as he stooped down to the level of Roman's feet.

He waited as the DOH leader continued to squint through the smoke.

Roman stepped close, and Bic deployed a sweeping leg kick. Usually Bic would knock anyone flat on their back with this move, but his shot leg was weakened, and the biker was merely knocked off balance.

Bic's stealth advantage quickly became a disadvantage as Roman swung his gun at him. Bic stopped the weapon before it made it to his face. With all Bic's attention on the weapon, Roman landed a blow right below Bic's right eye with his free hand.

It stung like a mother. Roman was either wearing brass knuckles or rings the size of Texas.

Another blow cut him in the left cheek. And another on the side of the head. A ringing in Bic's ear blotted out sound and added to his confusion. Blood flooded his eye. The smoke burned at the fresh wounds. Bic knew what he needed, *who* he needed, but his thought was cut short.

"Ah, ah… Time for me to earn that tattoo," Roman spat as he pulled back his free arm for a death blow.

Nathaniel had heard the sounds of the scuffle. He'd seen vague, silhouetted forms violently dancing in the smoke. And then the shot rang out and a body dropped. Three more shots hit the body on the ground.

White eyes pierced the smoke. Nathaniel's fear of fire momentarily subsided as something that seemed even more fearsome emerged from the haze.

A Black Ghost.

Bic had heard the sharp snap behind his eyes activating the part of the brain where he had buried the black ghost. The snap seemed very real and occurred the moment he'd let the half century of rage back in his heart. He never thought he'd make a deal with the devil, but he knew the old adage: Never say never.

Clarence Green was sitting on top of the beam, grinning at him.

"You sure done mucked up this time." The apparition glanced down at the boy. "Or should I say *well done?*"

He threw his head back in a vicious cackle.

Bic Green continued to let the old man's laugh feed the rage inside him. It was the old stuff. The rare vintage from years past. It had lain dormant for some time. Now, once again, face to face with his evil father, it roused to life. He felt it course through him, burning hotter than the flames that surrounded. All pain subsided. All feelings disappeared. It was pure, biting rage.

Bic noticed the look of pure horror on the boy's face as he lunged at him and locked his huge arms under the beam of wood.

Bic roared as he tried to lift the immovable object with the rest of the house falling in around him.

"You're gonna burn, boy," Clarence Green roared through the sound of the fire. "We're all gonna burn. You, me, this little white piglet here. All of us." His eyes glowed a hellish red as he waved a gator-chewed stump at Bic. "Your momma included. You should see how I treat that bitch in hell, boy. It's a sight to see!"

He threw his head back in a sickening laugh.

The rage surged in Bic Green's body.

Yes, he would see the old man in hell. And he'd take care of him there. He had enough rage in him to transcend mere mortal existence. It pulsed within him, fortifying his nerves to withstand anything. Even flames.

Even a huge beam.

It budged an inch. The boy cried out, which added more fuel to Bic's fiery anger.

Bic looked dead into his cackling father's eyes and screamed, "IT'S PORKCHOP EATIN' TIME, MOTHERFUCKER," and somehow lifted the beam up higher, then higher.

"*Move,*" he heard himself growl to the boy in an inhuman voice.

Nathaniel, his face contorted in searing agony, pulled himself on his palms, inching his body away from the beam.

"*Faster,*" Bic said in that animal voice. "*I can't hold it!*"

The boy inched back little by little.

Bic gave a loud scream. It was a scream for his whole life, plus the lives of everyone he'd ever known. It was for Mack and Caroline. For

Parelli. For Hawk. For every single life he'd ever extinguished off this rotten earth.

And it was for Gracie. The one, true angel in the world.

He gave the beam one last lift and then let it drop.

It missed Nathaniel by half a foot.

The house collapsed around them.

He grabbed the boy, anger surging in his body like vomit. He lifted him up and over his shoulder and ran through the flames as fast as he could.

He felt them lick his lacerated face.

"I don't want to burn!" the boy screamed in his ear.

A burning piece of ceiling detached from the already crumbling frame and swung down. Bic swatted it away, feeling as if his own arm was made of the same stuff. It broke and splintered away from him in a display of sparks and fiery dust.

The boy screamed again, piercing his ear.

With a howl, he hopped a pile of burning debris and made it out of the building just as the rest of the house fell in on itself in a cataclysmic collapse.

He froze with the boy on his shoulder.

Anthony Parelli was pointing an M-27 at him.

It discharged, lighting up the night and sending a shock wave through Bic's chest.

71

D idn't mean to scare you," Parelli said.
Bic's breath returned to him as he realized the full scope of what just happened. Parelli walked past him to inspect the true target of the gunfire.

The body lay in a heap, the head completely destroyed.

"Good shot," Bic said.

"That there is Darius Dog, Roman's son." Parelli turned back to Bic. "Man, your face got hammered pretty good." Parelli stepped in for a closer inspection. "Yeah, that's gonna require a little ol' Band-aid."

Bic nodded towards Darius. "His daddy's dead inside."

"Then it's done," Parelli said. "But you owe me one for not letting me kill that scumbag myself."

"I'll see what I can do."

Parelli walked back toward his men, who were congratulating themselves on a job well done, as the place was littered with a good forty or fifty bodies.

"Close your eyes," Bic said to Nathaniel. "You've seen enough for a lifetime."

He walked Nathaniel over to the tractor and put him down as if he was made of fine china.

"Rest here. We're gonna get you some help."

"That was the guy from back at our house, wasn't it?"

Bic nodded.

"So, you and him are friends again?"

Bic thought for a moment. "Maybe. I guess you could say it's complicated. How are you?"

"It hurts real bad."

"Okay. You're a real champ, you know that?"

Lucy ran to her big brother's side, collapsing to the ground next to him and giving him a huge hug.

The moment dissipated as Nathaniel's face transformed. He seemed to be a kid again, with an expression full of worry. "What's gonna happen to us, Bic?"

Bic didn't know how to answer. "You're gonna heal, that's the most important thing. After that, I don't know. And I'd be lying if I told you I did." He held out his bruised and bloodied fist. "But we'll figure this thing out, okay." The kid stared at Bic's fist, then into Bic's eyes. Then he bumped the fist with his own.

"You okay, kid?"

It was Parelli, who'd come up behind Bic.

"It hurts, but I'm okay."

Bic stood up. "The kid's tough."

Parelli smiled a half-smile. "You ain't kidding."

"I'm sorry about your wife," Nathaniel said.

Parelli's face went deadly serious. "Listen, kid. What happened… was not your fault."

Nathaniel lowered his head.

Bic looked at the kids, then over at Parelli. Gratitude overwhelmed him then, and he gave Parelli a massive hug. "You guys came just in time."

"You didn't think I was going to let you kill all the bikers by yourself, did you? Come on, Bic."

Bic smirked at his friend. "Not a chance."

"That's what I thought. Now, I'd like to celebrate, but we're on kind of a time crunch here."

"FBI?" Bic asked.

"A whole damn SWAT team. They'll be bringing the heat any second now."

As if on cue, a stream of headlights pierced the dark sky.

"Chopper just found a place to land over in the clearing about a hundred yards away," Parelli said, taking Bic by the arm. "Hawk's already there. Let's go. The Feds will take the kids to the hospital. They'll be fine."

Bic went over to Nathaniel and bent down. "Hang tight, little man."

Lucy hopped up from her brother and hugged Bic around the leg.

He bent to one knee, eye to eye with her deep blues. "Take care of your brother, okay, Wonder Woman?"

She hugged him again, and it hurt all over. Bic didn't care. It was a pain he could deal with.

Parelli pulled Bic up. "Hey, man, I'm sorry. We need to go."

The men walked away just as a swarm of black SUVs came rushing into the entrance of the compound. Bic saw his 'Nam buddies and teared up all over again. They'd all come to help. They were waving for him to get a move on.

He turned to Parelli. "Go. I can't leave the kids."

"Bic, come on. This ain't the time to play Big Brother."

"Go on, my friend. It's done. I'm going to finish what I started."

Slowly, it dawned on Parelli, and resolution washed over his face. He nodded. "Take care of yourself, Bic."

"You too."

Parelli took off at a sprint to catch up with his crew.

Bic walked back to the children.

"You came back," Nathaniel said, his eyes wide in astonishment.

"Here's the plan," Bic said. "Do not say a word about anything." He pointed to Lucy. "You, Wonder Woman, just for now, go back to not talking. Squeaky mouse girl, you hear?"

She nodded.

"Nathaniel, anything they accuse you of, just deny it and say you have no idea what they're talking about. Okay? Yeah, it's lying. Make it up to God or society or whatever some other day. Right now, you both got lives ahead of you and they're more precious than you can possibly realize. Understand?"

Nathaniel nodded.

Bic sighed. "Good. You do that and I'll take care of the rest."

Bic put his hands on his head and walked out to meet the onrushing FBI.

72

Hawk sat at the counter of the bar and nursed the rest of his beer. He had just devoured a cheeseburger and was contemplating another one. Even though it had only been a couple of days since he'd left Bic and the kids, he felt like he'd gained ten pounds, most of it in beef and cheese. Tomorrow, he told himself, yes, tomorrow he'd go back to eating clean. He just needed another day to sulk about not getting to say goodbye to Bic. He kept running scenarios in his head. Bargaining. Isn't that what those self-help jerkoffs called it? He could have convinced Bic to let him take the kids and run, or whatever, something crazy like that. For goodness sake, he could have done... *something*.

The tune on the jukebox ran out and no one replaced it. That was a damn shame. He went over and perused its contents. Culture Club, Def Leppard, REM, hell, yeah. It was a good mix. They even had some Madonna. The Material Girl could get his juices going any day, even if he didn't particularly care for her music. He scanned the other titles. It was all on the light side. He wanted to see some Ratt, Mötley Crüe, or Winger. That would have made his day.

He punched up Def Leppard, closed his eyes for a moment to groove on the tune, then returned to his beer.

Just as he was finishing, the tune ended and a new one came on. "True" by Spandau Ballet. Not exactly his jam, but he pursed his lips and nodded along to it, lost in the memories of better days.

"It's a shame there's no German techno. I could really go for that."

The British accent made him nearly lose control of his bladder right then and there.

She looked fantastic. Cherry red hair, a black leather jacket over a black shirt, and a black skirt over black leggings with Doc Martins at the end of her gorgeous legs.

Hawk was speechless. He didn't know whether to be terrified or swooning with affection for the girl.

She leaned on the bar. The bartender came over as if on an invisible leash.

"This chap will have another round and I'll have whatever he's having."

"Two pints of Guinness."

She raised an eyebrow at him. "Your tastes are improving."

"Goes good with a burger."

Millie smiled at him. "You have questions."

"About a thousand."

She bit her bottom lip and turned her head downwards. "Before you get to any of them, I have something for you. First is an apology."

"Yeah," Hawk said, "that works for me. Drug me up and leave me for dead in some crappy Airbnb and all is forgiven."

"Um, excuse me, not for dead. I knew the cleaning crew would be in. As a matter of fact, I knew *exactly* when they'd be in. I timed everything to go along with that one variable. You don't do what I do for as long as I've done it and not learn how to plan accordingly."

He started to speak and she held up her hand.

"Hang on," she said. "Hawk, I really, *really* like you. And I really loved that night we spent together. I don't expect forgiveness, really. But I wanted you to know that. Maybe it'll go some way towards your healing." She reached out, put her hand lightly over his heart.

Hawk felt a deep sadness weighing him down.

"What is it?" she said.

"You betrayed me. I liked—*like*—you too. I just don't understand."

"It's my business, Hawk. That's all. That's the only thing keeping us apart. Here, take this."

She reached into her bag, pulled out a thumb drive, and handed it to him. With that, she began to assemble herself and rose from the stool.

"What's this?" Hawk said.

"Let's just say it contains some answers your friend Parelli is looking for. By the way, I know what it's like to be on a quest for revenge, especially when it's for a spouse. I went along with it when I found out that was his motive. I just didn't realize I was on a path to kill a couple of children." She gave a wry smile. "I'm an assassin, Hawk, not a psychopath."

"So, I'm confused. Parelli hired you?"

"No. It was actually the kids' uncle, a real sneaky bugger that one."

Hawk felt his jaw drop. Then a thought came to him. "So, your husband... he was killed?"

She nodded. "Mm, hm."

The bartender placed two beers on the bar before them. Millie reached into her wallet and took out a hundred. She placed the bill on the bar and slid her beer over next to his.

"I'll see you around, Hawk."

"If you're ever in town and need a dance partner..."

She smiled. "You think I'd pass that up?"

She gave him a wink that nearly melted him off his stool.

As quick as she came, she was gone.

He sighed deeply and started on the first of the two drinks.

73

They led Bic Green out of the courtroom. Shuffling his shackled feet like some clown, he winced from the explosion of news reporters with mics and cameras that came upon him as they exited.

"Bic Green… Black Ghost… Mr. Green… Ghost…"

He ignored them all, keeping his head down.

"Mr. Green, what do you have to say about framing a fifteen-year-old boy… Mr. Green, what happened to your eyes… Mr. Green, is it true you're wanted for at least fifty other murders…? Are you the notorious Black Ghost…?"

He heard the booming voice of the DA behind him.

"Ladies and gentlemen," the man said, "justice has been served. Bic Green is finally property of the State. Yes, it's true, he tried to frame poor, innocent Nathaniel Braddick, a fifteen-year-old boy, for murder. But the State is too smart for that and Bic Green will finally get what's coming to him…"

"Is it true the death penalty is still on the table?"

"We will appeal the court's decision of life without parole, yes."

The sound of reporters and the din of the crowd jeering him and calling for his head receded behind him.

His head down, he nearly missed the two figures at his right.

He looked up to see Mack in a wheelchair, with Caroline standing behind him.

"Ah, vee meet again, Herr Green," Mack said.

Caroline rolled her eyes. "As you can see, he's feeling more like himself every day."

"But the doc says I may never play the violin again."

"I don't know what to tell you guys," Bic said, sadness weighing on his soul.

"We know what you did in there, Bic," Mack said, throwing his chin toward the court. "I think you can say you redeemed yourself."

"What's more," Caroline added, "you're off to complete the act of making it right."

"Thank you."

"I hope you don't mind," Mack said, "we're not gonna be driving you this time."

Bic couldn't help but give a small smile. "It's alright."

"If we're ever in Colorado, we'll visit you at ADX."

"Yeah, that'd be nice."

A man came forward, with other men surrounding. Bic didn't know these men, but they had FBI written all over them.

"AD Bender, what are you doing here?" Mack said.

This man was all business. "Caroline, Mack, you need to come with us."

Caroline scoffed. "Not a chance. Tomorrow is our last day and we are officially retired. If you think we're going to work, it's not happening."

Bender removed his sunglasses. "Caroline, come with us, now. Your lives depend on it."

Bic watched as the men surrounded Mack and Caroline and escorted them off. Then Bic himself was loaded into the back of the transport vehicle.

74

The sun felt good on Seth Braddick's face as he typed away at his laptop. He was taking stock of his finances, and that felt good, too.

Eighty million in his pocket after giving those dopey bikers twenty of it. Nice chunk of change. And while it was true that it wasn't exactly his brother's empire—that would come in time, it was enough to live comfortably on while he forged the next part of his plan. He was going to gain control over his brother's social media empire if he had to spend the rest of his life doing it.

He chuckled to himself now as he thought of it. He had outsmarted everyone, hiring multiple assassins all anonymously through the dark web, controlling everyone like wooden puppets with strings attached. It felt... divine. The only thing he hadn't figured on was this silly unwillingness to kill kids. Of course, the DOH were more than happy to do it, but the Irishman, a supposedly cold-blooded killer, had an issue with it. And then the biggest surprise of all was the Black Ghost himself not taking out the kids when he, Seth Braddick, masterfully had them all converge at his house. Oh, well, he learned some lessons and he couldn't wait to do it again. It probably wouldn't be as exciting as this little adventure had been, but it would still be fun.

The door behind him slid open and Nathaniel came out and took a seat next to him.

"Hey, big guy," Seth said, "what's shakin'?"

"Nothing."

"Where's Lucy?"

"At her speech session."

"Oh, good," Seth said. "At least something good came from this terrible situation. You've been through a lot. You know, I always knew you were a good boy, Nathaniel. You'll grow into a fine man." He gave a chuckle. "And you know, I knew Bic Green was bad, but to frame a child! What a scumbag. I hope they decide to fry him."

"I remembered something about my parents this morning," Nathaniel said.

"Oh? What's that?"

"A fight they had. Mom spilled her coffee she was so mad."

"Parents fight, Nathaniel. Did you think it was your fault? Cuz I can tell you right now it wasn't."

"No, I didn't think that. I knew it wasn't my fault. It was yours."

"Mine?"

"You double-crossed Dad, and Mom said she couldn't trust you as far as she could throw you."

Seth stared at the boy. "You poor child. You've been through so much, haven't you? I hate myself for not being there for you to help you make sense out of your life. It's not like that at all. I wrote the code for that company. You know that."

"Whatever," Nathaniel said, leaning back in his chair. "At least it's not your company."

"Is that right?"

"Yeah, it's mine and Lucy's. And you'll never get your grubby hands on it."

Fuming, Seth rose from his chair. "Now, you listen to me, you ungrateful little snot. If it wasn't for me, you would have nothing. Your father could barely type his name let alone write the code that became the backbone for the largest social engine in the world. You need to give me the respect I deserve and stop being such a spoiled little son of a—"

A hand landed on his shoulder and spun him around.

And Anthony Parelli laid him out cold with one punch.

75

Seth Braddick awoke in darkness, a strange smell all around him. He couldn't place it, but it was coming from everywhere as if it was seeping from the walls. He tried to move but his arms were zip-tied to a chair.

After a minute of consciousness, it dawned on Seth just what had happened. He didn't get a good look at the man who'd knocked him out. If he did, the guy had hit him hard enough to make him forget. One thing that he knew for sure was that he was in trouble. How much remained to be discovered. He had been very careful to cover all his tracks. He began to reassure himself that whatever this was, he would most likely be able to buy his way out of it. His mind raced at the possibilities. The only likely suspect was his little brat nephew.

The lights in the room flickered on and Seth quickly took in his surroundings.

He was in an import-export warehouse, sitting in front of a folding table in a metal chair. He immediately noticed a couple of things. On the table were a basket of dinner rolls and three bananas. Then about ten feet from him was something the size of a large rectangle, probably five feet high and fifteen feet wide, and covered with a tarp. The most menacing part of the whole setup was the ten-foot-tall fence built around him, basically enclosing him in a large cage with whatever was under the tarp.

Hard-soled shoes clacked against the concrete floor in the distance. Seth looked down at his watch, and then realized why he was so groggy. The date on his Rolex told him two days had passed.

Before the man came into focus, each step came with that daunting reverberation. Dressed in a tan fine Italian leather suit, Anthony Parelli appeared from behind some stacked crates of cheese, then entered into the caged area. Seth quickly realized this was a worst-case scenario. Through his research over the years, he had come to find that Parelli was Bic Green's handler and his direct link to the resources of the outside world. He knew that without Parelli, Bic would be essentially cut off from any outside assistance. Seth's plan backfired when the mercenaries he hired not only failed to kill him but managed to kill his wife and make things personal.

"Listen," Seth said, "I don't know what you're thinking, but whatever my nephew told you, it's not true. He's a lying, privileged little snot."

Parelli fixed his white dress shirt sleeves by pulling them out. By doing so, he exposed them from under his suit coat and bared a gaudy looking cufflink, one studded with lines of red rubies.

"Barbara gave me these," he said sentimentally. "My favorite color is red. No one knew that but her."

"There must be some mistake. I don't know who or what you're talking about."

"I like my pasta just a touch al dente. I enjoy that texture. She always did it just right."

"I'm sorry about your wife," Seth said. "I'm not sure what even happened, but I swear on my life I had nothing to do with it."

Parelli smirked, staring at the man with his dark eyes, the eyes of a killer. "Who said anything about a wife?"

"I just assumed... I mean, clearly, the way you are speaking about this lady, she had to be your wife."

"I put a lot of thought into a lot of things in my storied life, but what to do with the man who was responsible for having my Barbara killed? There's nothing bigger or more important I've had to do than come up with something special for you."

"Listen, I'm sure this is some type of misunderstanding."

"My first idea was to take you to a train yard, tie you to the tracks, and then sit there and listen to you scream for your life as you wondered if the train coming was on the track I tied you too. But that was too... mmmm... old school silent movie? Besides, a quick death wouldn't feel satisfying at all, so I switched my plan to burning you alive. But you see, I don't like the smell of burning flesh. It makes me queasy, and I won't eat good for a week. A piece of scum like you deserves something... *elegant*. Something with a bit of flair, a little style and wit. You know what I mean?

"So I started to think on another level, really take it up a notch. I got this good friend, who by the way is in jail because of you, and he knew how to make people pay.

"And I thought, you, I thought, you're so greedy that you were willing to kill your own flesh and blood to steal your brother's company. And not just flesh and blood, but two innocent children. It got me thinking of a story I heard a while back about jealousy.

"You see, this couple brought their chimp a birthday cake for its 39th birthday at a sanctuary where he was stayin'. What they didn't realize was, this made a couple of the other chimps so jealous that they somehow got out of their cage and attacked the man.

"Now the thing about chimps is they're vicious. They take away things they know you need—your fingers to gather, your nose to smell, your eyes to see, your dick to mate—anything on your body that might be useful, they're going to bite or tear it right off your body. What is jealousy, anyway, but a lust for territory. You, pal, you were jealous of your brother. You infringed on his territory. And then you infringed on *mine*."

Seth screwed up his face as it became clear what was under that tarp. Seth was not a brave man, he knew that about himself. When in real danger, he retreated to something close to infancy.

"You don't know this," Parelli continued, "but you've been drugged out of your mind for a couple of days now." Parelli walked over and pulled the tarp off. There were three separate cages, each with one chimpanzee. "And each day, three times a day, we've kept two of the chimps in their cage while you sat here at this table and gave the other one bananas and dinner rolls. The rolls are a special treat. These guys love them. It's a huge deal to them, you know? I can only imagine how pissed these other two are right now."

"Please," Seth said, "I can give you a lot of money."

Parelli put a hand to his chin. "Do you think there is any amount of money in this world to make right what happened to Barbara?"

Parelli went to the cage and hit the release button. The chimp came out and hopped onto the table, immediately devouring the dinner rolls.

The two other chimps came to life with a chaotic series of different calls and screams as they shook their cages. These noises didn't really seem to bother the chimp on the table as he finished the last of the dinner rolls and made his way to the bananas.

The more frenzied the noises, the bigger Parelli smiled.

A box cutter appeared in Parelli's hand. With his other meaty hand he clamped down on Seth's wrist. His grip felt like a vise lock as he cut his right hand free. Seth immediately tried to grab at Parelli but was struck with a hard, open-handed slap to put him back in his seat.

Stunned, Seth watched Parelli exit the cage and lock the gate behind him. Parelli then pulled a cigar out of his inner pocket and lit it. Seth, with his new-found freedom, made a dash to climb the fence with his left arm still tied to the chair.

"Better hurry," Parelli said as he pushed a button on a remote to open the other chimps' cages.

Seth's hopes increased as he got halfway up the fence. But that optimism dissipated as one of the chimps launched onto his back and bit off his ear as he peeled him off the fence.

On the ground, Seth Braddick was conscious. He knew that his left arm was freed from the chair. But besides that, he didn't really know what was happening, except that there was a barrage of biting, tearing, and ripping happening all over his body.

The cage rattled as Seth's body smashed up against it. His body flew around the cage like a rag doll. After a couple of violent tosses, things on his body were broken and missing. Everything now numb, Seth figured the worst of the pain was over.

As quick as the violence had started, it stopped.

Seth lay on the floor motionless, each breath a heavy wheeze. The chimps, now calm strolled around the cage disinterested as if nothing had happened.

Seth made the mistake of a quick glance that caught one of their attention.

The Chimp climbed on top of him, making deep eye contact with Seth. Fragments of light prismed in the chimps light brown eyes almost making them seem spiritual. Maybe the animal was regretting what it had done.

After seconds that seemed like minutes, the chimp screamed as both of his hands lunged down and snatched Seth's eyes right out of their sockets.

THE END

Acknowledgments

To my wife, Jennifer, you are the best partner anyone could ask for. No matter what mountain life has us climb, with you by my side everything is possible. Thank you for continuing to make the Black Ghost series prosper by handling everything else besides the writing.

To Sofia, Freddie VV and Charlie for giving the gift only children are able to give. ☺

To the person who has always made me smile, right from the very first one. Thanks, Mom.

To my Sister, Nina, thanks for the website design and cool graphics.

Erik Gevers, you are such an integral part of the Black Ghost. Jennifer and I cannot imagine doing this without you being part of the process.

Dane Low, I thought you hit your limit with the last cover, but they just keep getting better.

Thank you, Linda Harris, for being there each and every time to give your insights from your beta read. You are truly amazing.

To my friend, Chad Richards, thanks for your inspiration on Revenge Spiral.

To the man who still wears cool driving gloves, Peter J. Wacks. Thanks for all of the conversations, it is always a great part of the writing process.

Thank you to all of our family and friends for continuing to support us on this journey, it is truly appreciated.

"A reader lives a thousand lives before he dies..."
George R.R. Martin

AND THEN THERE WERE FOUR. I cannot thank you enough for staying with me now through the fourth book in the Black Ghost Series. The support and love for the characters has been amazing, especially of Bic Green. You, the fans, have gotten that character and hopefully are still enjoying his arc as much as I am in telling it. The next book will take a step back into how Bic Green, as a young teenage boy, became the Black Ghost. I feel that it's time to tell that story before moving forward.

Once again, the readers continue to make the Black Ghost, book 1, a top ten book on Amazon in several categories in the US.

The Canadian readers continue to show up BIG making all books in the Black Ghost series show up in the top ten in a couple of categories. You continue to inspire me to get better with each book. It has been thrilling to see all three in the top 10 at the same time.

Any feedback or questions feel free to email me at freddie@freddievillacci.com. It would be an honor to hear from you.

Visit my website, FREDDIEVILLACCI.COM, for more material, free songs and the trailer to FACELESS, the movie I wrote that was released in February 2021.

I am forever thankful you lived another life through reading the fourth book, REVENGE SPIRAL, in the BLACK GHOST THRILLER SERIES. I hope you had a blast!

With gratitude,

Freddie Villacci Jr.

*Also, **please** review the book on Amazon, if you liked it* ☺*, that would be greatly appreciated!*

About the Author

Freddie Villacci Jr. is an American author, screenwriter, and songwriter. Born and raised in Wood Dale, Illinois, a suburb of Chicago, Freddie went on to earn a degree in marketing while playing baseball at Berry College in Rome, Georgia.

At the young age of nineteen, Freddie began investing in the stock market and later pursued a successful career in the insurance and financial services industry, where he gained valuable experience and knowledge that would later shape his writing.

In 2020, Freddie published his first novel, Black Ghost, which draws on his professional background to provide depth and authenticity to the plot. Additionally, Freddie writes screenplays and songs. His independent film, Faceless, was released in 2021.

Freddie thrives in the sunshine and cherishes his time outdoors. Whether he's playing baseball with his sons or embarking on family adventures, he relishes every moment. His daughter's newfound love for lacrosse has become his latest source of pride, and he enthusiastically supports her every step of the way. Freddie and his wife, Jennifer, have a passion for supporting charities that help children.

Connect with Freddie and discover more about his works and endeavors at www.freddievillacci.com

www.ingramcontent.com/pod-product-compliance
Lightning Source LLC
Chambersburg PA
CBHW052033240626
47153CB00006B/2068